SOMETHING IS ROTTEN

Recent Titles by J M Gregson from Severn House

Detective Inspector Peach Mysteries

DUSTY DEATH
TO KILL A WIFE
THE LANCASHIRE LEOPARD
A LITTLE LEARNING
MISSING, PRESUMED DEAD
MURDER AT THE LODGE
REMAINS TO BE SEEN
A TURBULENT PRIEST
THE WAGES OF SIN
WHO SAW HIM DIE?
WITCH'S SABBATH

Lambert and Hook Mysteries

AN ACADEMIC DEATH
CLOSE CALL
DEATH ON THE ELEVENTH HOLE
GIRL GONE MISSING
JUST DESSERTS
MORTAL TASTE
SOMETHING IS ROTTEN
TOO MUCH OF WATER
AN UNSUITABLE DEATH

SOMETHING IS ROTTEN

J.M. Gregson

This first world edition published in Great Britain 2007 by
SEVERN HOUSE PUBLISHERS LTD of
9–15 High Street, Sutton, Surrey SM1 1DF.
This first world edition published in the USA 2007 by
SEVERN HOUSE PUBLISHERS INC of
595 Madison Avenue, New York, N.Y. 10022.

British Library Cataloguing in Publication Data

Gregson, J. M.
    Something is rotten
    1. Lambert, John (Fictitious character) - Fiction 2. Hook,
    Bert (Fictitious character) - Fiction 3. Police - England -
    Gloucestershire - Fiction 4. Detective and mystery stories
    I. Title
    823.9'14[F]

ISBN-13: 978-0-7278-6533-5   (cased)

All Severn House titles are printed on acid-free paper.

Typeset by Palimpsest Book Production Ltd.,
Grangemouth, Stirlingshire, Scotland.
Printed and bound in Great Britain by
MPG Books Ltd., Bodmin, Cornwall.

To Anita Newton, the best theatrical director I ever knew.

One

'Of course, the person we really need is your husband. His considerable presence would make our cast complete.'

Detective Sergeant Bert Hook decided in retrospect that it was at that moment that he should have nipped the idea firmly and fiercely in the bud. Everything which followed could probably have been avoided, if he had only spoken up decisively at that point.

He was never quite sure why he didn't. It is very flattering, of course, to hear that your participation is important; that a whole enterprise might collapse without you. But Bert Hook was more armoured against flattery than most men. He immediately suspected it and wanted to know what was behind it when he heard it, and he was usually right to be sceptical. Few people offered you flattery without an ulterior motive.

He didn't want to be accused of being an eavesdropper. His wife Eleanor and this mystery voice were closeted together in the room beside the front door at the front of the Hooks' semi-detached nineteen-sixties house. It was technically the dining room but, as well as chairs and a table, it had two comfortable armchairs: most important of all, it was the room in the house which was least used and almost always kept tidy and thus suitable for the reception of visitors. With two boys of eleven and thirteen in the house, and a husband who Eleanor Hook always maintained was an overgrown schoolboy, you couldn't rely on order anywhere else.

Bert couldn't catch his wife's voice as clearly as he had heard the cut-glass tones of her visitor, but he thought Eleanor muttered something diffidently about him never having been on stage.

'Oh, his appearance is just what we need for the part, and he'll manage the lines all right with a little coaching!' said that confident, dominating voice. The woman offered this as not just her opinion, but as a fact that could not be contested. Bert had heard voices like that many times before. Indeed, from the age of twelve to sixteen, it had seemed to him that such voices had controlled his present and future life, with their firmly stated assessments of what he should study at school and what he should do and not do to earn himself an honest living afterwards.

Bert Hook was a Barnardo's boy, and he was quite convinced that the policies of the home where he had grown to adolescence had been dominated by the voices of worthy middle-class women of impeccable virtue and formidable decibel levels. He could not remember the voices of the men anything like so clearly. As a police officer, Bert had spent over thirty years dealing with a vast variety of dangerous villains. The men and women who worked with him believed that nothing could shake staid and reliable old DS Hook, who had seen it all and come out on top far more often than not.

Perhaps it was only Bert who knew how he still quailed inwardly when he heard a voice like the one now booming so imperiously in the adjoining room.

He couldn't listen any longer without becoming an eavesdropper. DS Hook braced himself, drew himself up to his full height and marched determinedly into his dining room. He asked with bold and artificial bonhomie, 'Do I hear my name being taken in vain?'

He noted Eleanor looked startled but relieved. She said, 'This is Mrs Dalrymple. You haven't met her before. She organizes us all in the charity shop. Makes sure we operate efficiently and profitably.'

Mrs Dalrymple laughed, a high, baying sound which sent a thrush away like a bullet from the eaves outside the window and chilled Bert Hook's heart with a recollected horror. 'Call me Maggie, for God's sake! Everyone else does, nowadays. And your wife is far too kind to me, Mr Hook. You can only insist on so much efficiency when all your workers are part-time and unpaid.' The laugh with which she accompanied this disclaimer was reduced to a modest cackle. She resumed the conversation more earnestly and with a breathy intimacy which was even more unnerving. 'How are your histrionics, Detective Sergeant Hook?'

'Non-existent. The last time I appeared on stage was as a

boy soprano in *Oliver*. I was one of Fagin's urchins. Leaping about the stage in rags and trying to pick a pocket or two.'

Maggie Dalrymple smirked happily at the thought of the stolid policeman as a diminutive street thief. 'How delicious! And no doubt of happy recollection to you, now that you operate on the other side of the law! But you see, you are not without theatrical experience, after all. No doubt once you tread the boards again, the feel for an audience will come back to you. The roar of the crowd, the smell of the grease-paint, you know!' She gestured with a vague right arm towards the ceiling of the low-roomed modern house and looked a little desperately towards Eleanor Hook for support.

'We didn't have greasepaint in *Oliver*,' said Hook, feeling daring even making this small correction to his formidable visitor. 'I thought it had gone out altogether, these days.'

'I was speaking figuratively,' said Mrs Dalrymple loftily, wondering if the phrase was quite correct. 'But, of course, you're quite right. And your knowledge shows how in touch you are with the modern theatre. You may not have had many opportunities of late, but I suspect that there is a small, secret part of you which has for years been longing to get on stage.' She beamed delightedly at each of the two blank faces in turn. 'We all have that yearning, you know. Well, most of us anyway. And I expect that Detective Sergeant Hook in his secret moments thinks that he is a bit of a Richard Burton manqué!'

Eleanor Hook did not dare to catch her husband's eye in the light of this suggestion. She said, in belated support of him, 'Bert is usually kept very busy at work. You wouldn't be able to rely on him for rehearsals. When emergencies come up and he's working on a serious crime I often don't know when I'll see him next.'

'Oh, Gloucestershire and Herefordshire are sleepy counties for serious mischief. And this is a quiet time of year for crime.' Maggie Dalrymple spoke with the confidence which often comes from the wholly British combination of social standing and profound ignorance.

Bert Hook was still contemplating the brazenness of this pronouncement when he slipped into the error of inquiry. 'What was it that you were thinking of putting on, anyway, Mrs Dalrymple?'

'Not me, my dear man, the Mettlesham Players. I am but a cog in the wheel.'

Some cog, thought Bert. He said unwillingly, 'I've heard of them. They have quite a local reputation.'

Mrs Dalrymple preened herself: it was an awesome sight, especially within the confines of a modern semi. 'We have our modest successes.' Her tone indicated that they were anything but modest.

Bert repeated his question patiently, 'And what is the production you are contemplating at the moment, Maggie?' He forced out the name, his eyes closing for a moment with his daring, as he rejected many years of subjection to formidable ladies like this in his boyhood. No doubt she wanted him to play some caricature of a policeman, a thicko uniformed fool who would flex his knees and say, 'What's going on 'ere then?'

'It's *Hamlet*, Mr Hook.' Maggie Dalrymple tried not to look pleased with herself and failed comprehensively. 'We shall bring a little culture to the masses in rural Gloucestershire.' That sounded like a phrase she had used many times before. She misinterpreted the looks of surprise on the faces of her listeners. 'It's Shakespeare, you know.'

'Yes.' Bert was still trying to digest the ambition of this project with an amateur group: people who had probably never spoken verse aloud before.

Eleanor Hook said loyally, 'Bert knows quite a lot about Shakespeare. He's almost completed an Open University degree. He specialized in English Literature.'

Mrs Dalrymple looked for a moment totally shocked by this intrusion of the labouring classes upon the Bard. Then she continued, determined to turn the information to her advantage. 'That's all to the good, then, isn't it? Mr Hook may not need as much coaching as I anticipated. I'm sure he'll be absolutely marvellous, once he's got the hang of it.'

Bert tried to take the personal implications out of this. 'If you don't mind my saying so, *Hamlet* seems a rather ambitious choice, for both the players and their prospective audience.'

Maggie Dalrymple looked for a moment as if she certainly *did* mind his saying so. Then she controlled her reaction, reminding herself of why she had come here and thinking of the greater good of the Mettlesham Players. She took a deep breath and said, 'That is a perceptive comment, Mr Hook –

or Bert, if I may be so bold. I see that you and I will be on a common wavelength when it comes to the literary and dramatic challenges of the piece. And in the ordinary way of things I should agree with you. But it just so happens that we have a quite outstanding candidate for the main role. We have a young man who is about to go off to drama school at the age of twenty-four and who I predict will be one of the foremost actors of the next generation. The chance to play the gloomy Dane is a great opportunity for him and a splendid windfall for us.'

Bert failed to ask who this stellar presence might be, partly because his fearsome visitor obviously expected him to want a name. He said stubbornly, 'It's a very long piece for a village hall.'

Mrs Dalrymple trilled a merry laugh. Her amusement was more spine-chilling than her earlier cackles. 'And for the concentration of village yokels and lumpen milkmaids, you mean.'

Bert hadn't meant anything of the sort. He'd been thinking of the combined effect of amateur acting and rudimentary seating upon the buttocks of an audience who had been dragooned into attendance. He said desperately, 'I wasn't really intending—'

'Oh, we've already got the mechanics of the production under control. Mettlesham has an excellent village hall, with a surprisingly large stage. And my husband has been good enough to pay for the hire of the hall for as many nights as we shall need, over the months of rehearsal. His firm's gesture towards the sponsorship of the arts, he calls it.' She smiled happily at this evidence of marital harmony, whilst Bert's sympathy for a man he had never met rose sharply. 'We're hoping to attract a discriminating audience from a wide area, but it needn't be too long for the locals. If we cut out Fortinbras and one or two other characters and shorten a couple of the soliloquies, we reckon we can get through it in not much over two hours.'

Bert wanted to say that perhaps you shouldn't be thinking in terms of 'getting through' the most subtle and intellectual play in the English language, but he knew that would sound priggish. Moreover, he was suddenly aware that the more interest he showed, the more he would be tacitly agreeing to an involvement in this ridiculous enterprise. He said resolutely,

'Well, I shall look forward to the production with interest, but I'm afraid it would be impossible for me to be involved. I'm sorry to disappoint you.'

'It's a very important part. I'm not sure whether we shall be able to go ahead without you.' Maggie produced a look of reflective disappointment, which did not deceive Bert at all.

He smiled modestly. 'I can't think that a man who last appeared as a ragamuffin in *Oliver* can be vital to a production of *Hamlet*.'

Mrs Dalrymple was for a moment overcome by the irrefutable logic of this. Then she said in a deep, actressy voice which sounded like a parody of herself, 'Balance is important in Shakespeare. The best productions can come unstuck if they lack a confident ensemble, Mr Hook.' She estimated this insight for a moment, then nodded with quiet satisfaction at the profundity of it.

Curiosity, although part of the make-up of any successful CID officer, is always a perilous companion elsewhere. It now led DS Hook into a cardinal error. Before he realized that he was expressing a dangerous interest, he asked, 'What part was it you had in mind for me?'

He caught a glimpse of Eleanor's startled face as he realized the mistake he had made.

Maggie Dalrymple said magisterially. 'It's Polonius, Mr Hook. With your knowledge of the play, you will realize what an important role that is. Indeed, how flattering it is that I am here to secure your participation in our great enterprise.' She gave Bert a dazzling, coquettish smile, which froze his marrow more than any of her previous expressions.

Polonius! The doddering old fool who meddles his way to his doom! Bert had been hoping for Claudius, that devious, smiling, efficient villain who dominates the action of the play. He'd met a few Claudiuses in his years of serious crime and had always nursed a secret and totally unrealistic yearning to play the slippery king. Even the ghost of Hamlet's father, booming magisterially through the mist on the battlements, would have been quite acceptable. But Polonius! Bert Hook wanted to laugh at himself and his own absurd pretensions. But he could manage only a sickly smile.

Mrs Dalrymple studied him with interest. 'You'd need a lot of make-up, of course. But although he's usually played as a tedious old bore, he has a young daughter and might well in fact be about your age. And our director sees him more as a man of wisdom than a figure of farce.' She beamed first at Bert and then at his wife, embracing the household in her bonhomie. 'But all that will become clear to you in due course at rehearsals. I mustn't get ahead of myself!'

Bert Hook felt himself thrust back thirty years to his last days in the Barnardo's home, when he had been steamrollered by ladies like this. Panic rose within him and he felt the blood throbbing in his temples. 'I'll need to check it out at work. I'm not quite a free agent, you know.'

'Of course I understand. The nation's interests must come first. The rising tide of crime must be resisted with every breakwater we can thrust into its path!' Mrs Dalrymple paused for a moment, savouring her metaphor. Then she dropped her voice into her contralto temptress tones. 'But even the most conscientious officer is allowed a private life. Indeed, I would say that dedicated officers like you need a very different range of interests away from work, if they are to keep their sharpness as detectives. Wouldn't you agree, Bert?'

This second use of his Christian name was the final deadly blow. Bert Hook said in blind panic, 'I'll check it out and let you know, Mrs Dalrymple.'

'Maggie, please! I'm sure that we shall get to know each other very well over the next few months, Bert!'

And with that final devastating statement, the galleon of modern drama which was Mrs Dalrymple sailed out of the house under full sail.

Two

B ert Hook's encounter with Mrs Dalrymple had been conducted on the evening of Monday the sixth of November.

As he drove through the Herefordshire countryside towards Oldford Police Station on the Tuesday morning, Bert was even more determined to make himself unavailable for the production of *Hamlet*. His recent studies of Shakespeare had given him far too much respect for the writer for him to risk involving himself in what seemed almost certain to be a disaster.

It was one of those autumn mornings which seemed designed to clear the mind and assist good decision making. This seemed to Hook as pleasant a place as almost anywhere on earth – a touch of hyperbole, perhaps, but Bert was Herefordshire born and bred, and entitled to a little bias. The forest trees were still in full leaf, but the leaves were turning now towards the many shades of amber and orange which would allow them their full glory. The day was still, with a soft, low, morning sun lighting up the colours at the same time as it threw long shadows across the lanes. Winter frosts and snows might not be far away, but for the moment nature was at her softest and most benign.

Bert had seen his boys on to the school bus at eight o'clock, and he had plenty of time to savour his journey. This relaxed introduction to the day hardened his resolve about histrionics: he would get John Lambert to forbid him to participate in Mrs Dalrymple's absurdly ambitious scheme. It might be the cowardly way out, but it was foolproof. If his participation was vetoed by Lambert, then surely even the formidable Mrs Dalrymple could not argue with the edict of a Chief Superintendent. If she did, John Lambert would handle her firmly; the chief didn't have all he baggage of being reared in a Barnardo's home to contend ith.

On this particular morning, Lambert had arranged for a ting with Detective Sergeant Bert Hook and Detective

Inspector Chris Rushton. Bert had worked with the Chief Superintendent for twelve years now, so that each usually knew the other's thoughts without them being put into words. DI Rushton, in contrast, felt himself to be a generation behind Lambert and almost as far behind Hook. John Lambert had been given a Home Office extension to his service in recognition of his record as a thief-taker and solver of serious crimes. He had a reputation which extended far beyond his local celebrity.

Rushton was a career CID man, his eye always upon promotion, and he regarded Bert Hook with deep suspicion because Bert had a few years earlier refused the possibility of promotion to inspector for no better reason than that he was perfectly happy as a detective sergeant.

Chris Rushton was not only serious but often rather humourless, which meant that the two older men were wont to indulge themselves with teasing their younger colleague whenever the routine of detective work became boring. Rushton was never quite sure when the duo who had worked together for so long were pulling his leg and when they were serious.

It was the temptation to have some fun at Rushton's expense which now proved fatal for Bert Hook. When they had dealt with the fairly routine business of the day, Bert said casually, 'I had a visitor last night. A lady who is the driving force behind a local amateur dramatic group. They're going to put on a production of *Hamlet*: a rather truncated version, I gather. But I think they could have a part available for you, Chris, if you play your cards right. These societies are always short of handsome young men.'

Chris Rushton looked at him with a suspicion born of long and embarrassing experience. 'Acting? Me? You must be kidding.'

Hook continued as if the younger man had never spoken. 'You'd meet lots of young totty, you know, during a production. And after a triumph on stage they'd be putty in your lively young hands.'

Rushton's love life was a perennial source of interest to the older pair, who were both happily married. He had been divorced three years earlier, an experience more common in the police service than in almost any other occupation. He was six feet tall, without any grey in his short-cut black hair, and conventionally handsome. But a natural diffidence and a fear of rebuff held him back from forming new relationships with the opposite sex. He said stiffly, 'I'm not interested in what you call "totty", Bert. Casual liaisons are not in my line.'

'But an appearance on stage would be good for you. It would bring out your hidden depths.' Hook looked to Lambert for support.

John Lambert nodded his agreement. 'If there's a vacancy for a juvenile lead, you'd be ideal, Chris. Hamlet might be a bit much for a first attempt, but I can see you winning the ladies' hearts as Laertes or Horatio.'

'Horatio?' Chris Rushton remembered some tale from primary school about a hero on a bridge, but too vaguely for him to venture more.

'Friend of the prince. But Laertes might be more in your line – a much more flamboyant part. Wouldn't you agree, Bert?'

'Indeed I would. He gets to leap into a grave and clasp his dead sister's body to his bosom at one point – very much your kind of thing, Chris.'

Rushton was sure now that they were having him on. He said very firmly, 'I'm not going on to any stage. And certainly not in Shakespeare. Not at any price. And that's final.'

Hook sighed. 'It's a great pity that you should spurn these opportunities I work so hard to secure for you.'

It was then that John Lambert said, 'How did this occasion arise, Bert? You say that this lady visited you in connection with a proposed production. But she couldn't even have known about this budding actor in our midst at the time, surely?'

Bert shot a sharp glance at his chief's lined but studiously innocent face. 'It was a Mrs Dalrymple. You may have heard of her: she's a JP. She's also the motivating force behind the Mettlesham Players.'

'And why was she visiting you, Bert?'

Hook shifted uncomfortably on his chair and looked at the wall behind Lambert. 'She was asking me if I'd care to take part in the production, actually. I told her that that was impossible, of course.'

'Really? She is obviously a very determined lady, this Mrs Dalrymple. And a perceptive one, to spot such dramatic potential in a copper. What part had she in mind for you, Bert?'

'Well, we never really got as far as discussing parts. Not seriously. Anyone taking part would have to audition, of course, and even then I suppose they'd want to look at all the possibilities for—'

'What part, Bert?'

'Polonius, actually.' Bert transferred his attention from the wall to the carpet in front of Lambert's desk.

'Ah!' Lambert's long-drawn-out monosyllable carried a wealth of suggestion.

Hook reflected that it was no advantage to work with a Chief Superintendent who knew his Shakespeare. Most senior officers wouldn't have known much about Polonius and his implications. Bert said doggedly, 'As I said, I told her that it was impossible. So it's not an issue.'

'Oh, I think you were a little hasty there, Bert. I'm sure that the Chief Constable would regard it as good PR for you to be involved in a local Shakespeare production. Especially as Polonius.'

'Who's Polonius?' said Rushton, catching on belatedly to the idea that he might turn the tables on Hook here.

'Key part in the play,' said Lambert. 'The whole production could come unstuck without a good Polonius. He's a most entertaining old bore, if that's not a contradiction in terms.'

'Typecasting, then,' said Rushton. This was a new experience for him: it was immensely pleasing to be contributing to the repartee instead of being the butt of it himself.

'He gets to die dramatically, too,' said Lambert, warming to his task. 'Hamlet stabs him through the arras.'

Rushton winced extravagantly. 'Sounds very painful, that.'

'And then Hamlet says, "Thou wretched, rash, intruding fool, farewell". It's one of the most ruthless epitaphs in literature, to my mind.'

Rushton savoured the words of the quotation for a moment. Then he said, 'It sounds as this would be the ideal part for you, Bert. I can see why this lady came looking for you.'

Hook favoured the pair of them with a molten look. 'I told Mrs Dalrymple that it was quite impossible. That my duties here would not allow it.'

Lambert beamed at him. 'Oh, I think we could accommodate your participation, Bert. With a little imagination and goodwill within the CID section, we could ensure that you'd be able to attend all the necessary rehearsals. Wouldn't you agree, Chris?'

'Certainly, sir. I'm sure I can adjust the duty rotas to take account of DS Hook's outside commitments. I expect everyone concerned will be only too anxious to help, once they understand that Bert is making his contribution to local culture. Providing, that is, that you are favourable to the idea yourself, sir. Our system demands that Bert works very closely with you, and if you feel that you might be unable to release him for this . . .'

Lambert pretended to give the matter grave consideration before he reached a decision. 'I think I must make the sacrifice, Chris. We have a duty to make our contribution to the wider world outside the police service; you'll recall the Chief Constable telling the press only last week that we don't exist in a vacuum. And we owe Bert some consideration for his years of faithful service. He's a modest man, but I can see that he's set his heart on this. I think we should give him his head.'

Hook said desperately, 'But I don't want to—'

'That's settled then,' said Lambert with satisfaction.

'If you let us know the dates of the eventual production, I'm sure I'll be able to sell lots of tickets around the station,' said Rushton brightly. 'We might even be able to fill a coach, with the enthusiasm I anticipate for this. Will you be wearing tights, Bert?'

'I'll fail the audition!' muttered Hook. He sounded at that moment very determined that he would.

'Nonsense!' said John Lambert loyally. 'You're a natural for the part, Bert. I can see you being quite a memorable Polonius. I'm sure this will be a production which all of us will enjoy. I find it always adds something when you have a personal interest in the performance.'

'I'll put it in the station newsletter in due course,' said Rushton happily. 'And I can probably get you some wider publicity in all the nicks within forty miles of here. I'll get back to my computer and give some thought to that immediately, if there's nothing else, sir.'

'By all means,' said Lambert expansively. 'Fortunately, this seems to be a quiet time for serious crime in Gloucestershire and Herefordshire.'

It chilled Bert Hook's soul to hear the colleague he revered above all others echoing the sentiments which that awful Mrs Dalrymple had uttered from the depths of her ignorance. He left the room without catching Lambert's eye, conscious of how comprehensively the chief had cooperated with Chris Rushton into turning the tables upon him.

'Judas!' Bert snarled as he went.

An hour later, DS Hook had forgotten all about his possible involvement in *Hamlet*.

Bert had always maintained that the best way to put the problems of your private life into perspective was to immerse yourself in your work. He had done that successfully throughout his career, even during the week when his younger son had almost died of meningitis. He could surely do it now in the face of this much less serious and faintly comic intrusion into his settled domestic world.

The interrogation of a suspect in a minor crime was just what he needed. It was also something he was very good at. That is why Lambert suggested that Hook might be brought into what seemed a routine case of shoplifting. Even Chris Rushton admitted that Bert Hook, with his unthreatening, village-bobby exterior, usually seemed to get more out of young tearaways than officers who were supposedly closer to them in age and outlook.

Becky Clegg was hardly a young tearaway. But she was a twenty-one-year-old with a history of petty offences. The young, fresh-faced uniformed constable who had arrested her when called to the scene had made no progress at all; Ms Clegg had treated his interrogation with something approaching contempt. He was relieved to sit beside Bert Hook for this second session of questioning, though he secretly thought that the old lad was wasting his time with this tough, streetwise young woman.

'Do you want a brief?' Hook asked the girl.

'No need. I ain't done nothing. I'll be out of this place in half an hour. Without any help from some poncy lawyer.'

Bert Hook nodded thoughtfully. 'Could be a mistake, that. But I like a woman with her own opinions. Even when they're mistaken ones.'

He looked for a moment as if he was out of touch with

this, as if he had forgotten the procedures for such trivial things through his long involvement with Chief Superintendent Lambert and more serious crimes. Then he set the cassette recorder working and announced the time of commencement of the interview and the names of those present. He set a bright silver ladies' watch on the square table of the interview room and said nothing for several seconds, allowing the discomfort to grow in the smooth but slightly pinched features of the girl on the other side of the table.

Eventually Hook said with deliberate banality, 'Nice watch, this.'

'Fancy bit of bling.' Becky Clegg tried to produce the phrase with contempt and dismiss the watch from her consideration. But she found it difficult to take her eyes from the bright little object: the only alternative vision seemed to be that of the earnest, unmoving, avuncular face beyond it.

'Expensive bling, Ms Clegg. The most expensive watch in the shop, in fact.'

Becky shrugged her shoulders extravagantly. But she found that what had been an easy, automatic gesture with the young man who had arrested her was now a deliberate, self-conscious effort. 'I wouldn't know about that, would I?'

'Oh, I think you would, Becky. I think you know a lot more than you'd like us to think you do.'

'Say what you have to say, pig, and send me on my way. You can waste your time all you want, but don't waste mine.' It should have been instinctive, the kind of scorn she had thrown earlier at the young man in uniform. It had been effective then. Now, when she threw the words at this thick-set man in plain clothes, who might have been the father she had not seen for years, they seemed no more than a ritual defiance, a few phrases of aggression which were necessary to her but had not the slightest effect on the man in the grey suit.

Hook scarcely seemed to register what she said; he was certainly totally unruffled by it – he knew it would be diffi- cult for the girl to maintain her aggression while she wasn't getting a response. He looked again at the watch and said, 'I expect your fingerprints are all over the evidence.'

She almost sneered at him that she wasn't that stupid, that she'd had her white gloves on at the time. She only just avoided what would have been a ridiculous beginner's mistake. She was shaken for a moment; perhaps this old fool warranted a little more attention than she had first thought. She said, 'You'll find that the young piglet who made the mistake of arresting me has put his dabs all over that thing!'

Hook looked at her carefully made-up young face, at the lightly flowered dress beneath it, where most girls of her age would have had a shirt and jeans. 'Dress carefully for these forays into the retail world, do you, Becky?'

She dressed very carefully, according to the shops she was visiting. The preparation was part of the pleasure, when you lived by your wits and lifted stuff for a living. She didn't like the way that this man seemed to understand that. She said sullenly, 'I dress to please myself, nobody else.'

'Oh, I'm sure you do, Becky. And to suit the kind of adventures you plan to undertake on any particular day.' He nodded slowly, as if digesting that thought, then said suddenly, 'How'd you come by the watch, Becky?'

The question had come at her like a bullet, after all his relaxed observations. She had known it must come, that it was at the centre of this, but the manner of its arrival was still a shock to her. 'It was in my bag.'

'Exactly. You wouldn't be here now if it hadn't been. You were stopped outside the door of the shop, with the item in your bag.'

'Yeah. Strange, innit?' Her language changed to a different argot when she dropped into her automatic defiance of the police.

'Not strange at all, Becky, to my mind.' He looked very calm – almost as if he was trying to help her.

That increased her irritation. 'Someone must have dropped it into my bag.'

'Must they?'

'Yeah. Only possible explanation, innit?'

'No, Becky. Overwhelmingly the most probable explanation is that you put it there yourself, when you thought no one was watching you.'

'So prove it, pig! Or stop wasting our time and let me out of the sty.'

'Becky, the store detective saw you lifting it.'

'Them bastards always say it's us kids! The sods pick on us, and stupid pricks like you go along with it!' She found it

difficult to get any real indignation into her words. The per-
secution suddenly seemed as preposterous to her as it obviously was to Hook.

'You're not a kid any more, Becky. You're twenty-one years
old and a responsible adult or so they tell us. And I don't
think the magistrate will see it your way. Not with your record.'

'Be his word against mine then, won't it? The word of a
poncy store detective, who has to pinch people to justify his
job.'

'And we both know whom the magistrate will believe, don't
we, Becky? Just as we know whom the jury will believe, when
you go on to greater crimes and end up in the Crown Court.'

She said, 'It's once a villain always a villain, isn't it, with
you lot? Anyone with a record doesn't have a chance.' But
suddenly she didn't have the energy for this ritual of confronta-
tion, this meaningless flinging of phrases into the faces of
people on the other side of the law. Her carapace of contempt
for these pigs was cracking about her, almost as if it had been
a physical thing. She had been proud of her hardness, of her
brash defiance of the law. Now she was suddenly close to
tears.

Hook watched her, his own face an inscrutable professional
mask, showing neither anger nor concern. After a few long
seconds, he reached across, announced that the interview was
suspended and switched off the cassette recorder. Then he said
with a world-weary harshness, 'You're as guilty as hell, Becky
Clegg. It's a straightforward case for the boys of the Crown
Prosecution Service. We'll get a conviction without any trouble,
if we want it. With your record of thefts and violence, you
might even get a custodial sentence, if we press for it.'

It all made sense. Becky stared wearily at the desk. 'So get
on with it then. I'm pissed off with all this.'

'So am I, Becky. Thoroughly pissed off with it. This is a
tedious business for us. Lots of paperwork to secure a routine
conviction. To mark one step further in the progress of a young
offender into a serious criminal.'

Becky felt a sudden shaft of hope coursing into her veins.
No fool like an old fool, that woman in the hostel had told her
– though she had been speaking about relieving an old fool of
his money, in a very different context than this. She said, 'So
let me off with a caution, then. I won't do it again, honest.'

Her whining disclaimer came out all wrong – it sounded like the hollow assurance that she knew it was, like a caricature of remorse, when she was trying to produce something which sounded more genuine. Hook scarcely seemed to hear it, so preoccupied did he appear with his own thoughts. 'You were in a council home for four years, weren't you, Becky?'

'Yeah.' She was cautious, wondering where this was going. She'd have thrown in the stuff about abuse, as she had years ago with the social worker, but something told her that lies wouldn't wash with this man. She said quietly, 'You don't know what it's like, being in a home.'

He was watching her as earnestly as he had throughout their exchanges. And now, when she least expected it, he smiled. 'Oh, I do, Becky Clegg. I have a much clearer idea of life in a home than you might think I have.'

'There's a clever pig, then.'

'And you've been around since then. Lived in a squat, amongst other things.'

'I'm not there now. I'm in a hostel. That's until I get a pad with a friend.'

'Good friend, is she?'

At least he hadn't assumed it was a boyfriend, as everyone else seemed to. 'I think so, yes.'

'Because if you pick the wrong person to set up house with now, Becky Clegg, you could end up in the clink. With nowhere to go when you got out.'

She wondered how this old man who was part of the enemy could pinpoint her secret fears so precisely. She said roughly, 'So, why should you care, pig?'

She still couldn't prise a hostile reaction from him, a bit of temper on which she might feed. He said calmly, 'Because we already have little enough time to spend on serious criminals, without being distracted from the big boys by small-time riff-raff like you.'

Becky Clegg felt very small. She found herself fighting an absurd impulse to please this big even-tempered man. She heard herself saying, apropos of nothing at all, 'I don't do drugs. Never have done.'

'I'm glad to hear it. Maybe there's hope for you.' Hook believed her: he had assessed the brightness of her eyes and the alertness of her mien as soon as he came into the room, before he decided that this cocksure, abrasive, vulnerable creature was still malleable and worth his efforts.

'I'm getting it right.'

'By stealing expensive watches?'

'I shouldn't have got myself caught.'

'No, Becky, you shouldn't have got yourself involved at all.'

'I needed the money.' She was going through the formalities of protest now. She had admitted to his accusation, at some moment which she would never be able to pin down.

'Rubbish!' Hook blazed into sudden genuine annoyance; it was the first time during the interview that he had lost his calm. The young man in uniform beside him, as well as the girl on the other side of the table, twitched with shock. 'You're not starving. You've got a roof over your head, even if it's a hostel roof. Don't parade that rubbish about need. You don't know what need is, girl!'

Hook's Herefordshire burr came out more strongly as his emotion rose. It touched some chord within Becky's subconscious, so that his outrage with her became more powerful than the logic of his words. She said abjectly, 'What is it you want me to do?'

'It's what you want to do that's important. Unless you want to get back on the right track, and want it more strongly than you've ever wanted anything, it won't work. You'll be back in here or some other nick, talking to someone who isn't such a fool as me, and he'll throw the book at you. And when I hear about it, I'll cheer him on!'

Becky Clegg fought back the tears. 'I want to go straight. To keep out of trouble. I've got a job interview tomorrow.' She could have said she had been stealing to get clothes for the interview; she had fully intended to offer that excuse in court, if it had come to it. Mitigating circumstances, they called it, and people on benches were more likely to be swayed by a contrite, pretty girl with her eyes cast down before them than by an inarticulate young man with tattoos. But she wouldn't try things like that on this man.

'Then for God's sake go for it. And if you don't get this job, go for the next one.'

'I will. I'm getting other things going, too. With other people, outside the hostel. The kind of people you'd approve of.' She tried to curl her lip on this sentence, but, for some reason she could not fathom, she wanted to convince this burly older man that she was trying to change her life.

Bert Hook realized belatedly that he was breathing almost as unevenly as the young woman in front of him. He studied this girl, who so wanted to convince him, for a few more seconds, wondering how much of a fool he was and what weaknesses he was displaying to the young copper beside him. Then he said, 'Give her a caution and send her on her way, Constable Jeffries.' He turned back to the young woman opposite him as she finally burst into tears and waited until she was quiet before he said, 'And as for you, madam, if I find you making a fool of me as well as yourself, you'll regret it. Just remember, I don't ever want to see you again, Ms Clegg!'

As he left the interview room without a backward glance, Bert Hook did not realize quite how quickly he would meet Becky Clegg again.

Three

Chief Superintendent Lambert was restless. He had despatched his figures to the Regional Crime Division for the quarterly compilation of the Serious Crime Statistics before lunch and was on top of his paperwork. For once, he didn't have to give a written explanation to account for his overtime budget in the Oldford CID section. Serious crime in his area was thin upon the ground at present.

And that, shamefully, was the reason for his inability to settle, for his roaming around the station in search of interest, for his almost fretful concentration upon the details of the unremarkable crimes that were being reported. After thirty years in the police service, twenty-three of them in CID, John Lambert knew himself better than most of us do. The absence of a juicy murder, or a complicated fraud, or a serious gang robbery left him a little at a loss. Fretting. Frankly, a little bored, if he was honest. By mid-afternoon, he was even turning his thoughts towards the retirement which he knew could not be delayed for ever.

There was relief around the station at Oldford when he went home earlier than usual. The old boy might be universally respected as a detective – even those who thought his methods were outdated had to give grudging recognition to the results he achieved – but he made everyone nervous when he began to involve himself in the more minor avenues of crime.

Christine Lambert knew her husband even better than he knew himself. She was a schoolteacher, now only working part-time after a heart bypass a couple of years earlier. But she was still used to dealing with difficult children.

She sent John into the garden when he came home unexpectedly early, because she knew that was the best method of alleviating the minor tensions which came to him with inactivity. 'I can see you're wondering what to do with yourself.

If you're in your planning mood, decide on the plants you want to move during the winter and the places where they should be replanted. If you're feeling more energetic, you can dig over some of the vegetable patch before the frosts come.'

The popular press might choose to build John up as a superman during his occasional high-profile cases, but he was a conventional man in many respects. The concern of senior British coppers for their roses has become almost a cliché, but only because it is so often borne out by the facts. Lambert was no exception. As he wandered over the lawn alongside his rose beds, he was delighted to see them still carrying so much flower after the long summer heat, and congratulated himself on the disease-free growth and sturdy habit of his most recent purchase.

He spent a vigorous twenty minutes in his vegetable patch in the early autumn dusk, turning the soil a spit deep with his spade, settling into a steady rhythm and enjoying the physical exertion of work with a purpose.

Christine watched him from the window, glad that the tall, lean man was still capable of such effort, thinking of the men who had turned this earth in much the same way for centuries before him. In the end, she could scarcely see him in the gloom, and only the occasional shadowy movement showed her that he was still there, working steadily towards the end of the patch he had designated for his efforts.

When he came in healthily tired, she sat him in his familiar armchair and brought him a beer. 'The labourer is worthy of his hire.'

John said, 'I'm all right for up to half an hour; I couldn't dig for much longer nowadays! The spring cabbages are looking good.' He found himself rejoicing in the simple, innocent banality of a man in control of his garden.

Then he began to speak in a desultory, relaxed fashion about things at work, and she asked him the odd question to keep him talking. It was trivial stuff, but she was delighted to hear it, because at one time she had been excluded completely from his work. The young, intense CID officer had shut her out of his concerns; she had never known when she would see him, and when he had come home he had been silent about what he had been concerned with for so many hours. He had never been a womanizer, and she hadn't worried about that, but he had shut her out so completely from his thoughts and his successes that their marriage, which young officers now saw as so secure, had almost drifted on to the rocks.

It was as they were eating their evening meal that Lambert said, 'You'll never guess what's happened to Bert Hook.'

'He's been offered a part in *Hamlet*.' Christine cut up her quiche calmly, as if the precision of her knife was the most important thing in her life at that moment. But when she glanced up and saw the astonishment on John's face, she couldn't repress a giggle, and he saw for a moment the pretty young girl he had pursued so keenly when they were both twenty. 'I saw Eleanor in the supermarket at lunch time. She was full of this overbearing woman who'd been round and almost dragooned Bert into the production.'

Her husband smiled. 'Bert isn't good with women like that: middle-class ladies with a high decibel level and a cutting edge.'

'Eleanor said he was relying on you to keep him out of it.'

'Whereas Chris Rushton and I pitched him straight into it.'

'You didn't!'

'We gave him every reason why he should participate. Well, almost every reason. The only one we left out is the innocent but ecstatic pleasure it would give to us and to everyone else at the station.'

'You can't be so cruel!' But she knew he could, even as she said it. Men were merciless when it came to their fun.

'Be very good for Bert, we thought. It will bring out his hidden depths. He'll be a splendid Polonius.'

'Polonius! That's a big part, and an important one.'

'I think Bert realizes that. If he doesn't we'll make him well aware of it in the weeks to come.' John Lambert took an appreciative sip of the glass of red wine he allowed himself because it was good for his heart.

Two hours later the phone chirped insistently. John Lambert was dozing comfortably in front of the television under the combined effects of fresh air, exercise, good food and alcohol. 'That will be Caroline,' said Christine confidently as she went to answer it.

Christine was at the phone in the hall for a quarter of an hour and more so her husband decided that it must indeed be their elder daughter. He always wondered what women found to talk about on the phone; he used it himself merely as an instrument for conveying or receiving information, as clearly and as succinctly as possible.

A glance at his wife's face as she came back into the room told him immediately that something was wrong. 'Is it one of the children?' he asked.

'No. It wasn't Caroline at all. It was Jacky.' For a reason she could not herself explain, she always gave their elder daughter her full name, whereas Jacqueline was always shortened to Jacky.

'But something's up, isn't it? What's wrong?'

Christine sat down carefully, staring unseeingly ahead of her, feeling for the familiar chair behind her with her hands as if she was in a strange place. She said in a low voice, 'Jacky said she's getting divorced.'

To Bert Hook's inexperienced eye, the Mettlesham Village Hall didn't look like the sort of place where you would put on *Hamlet*.

It had a smallish stage with rather rickety and uneven flooring and tiny dressing rooms on each side of it. It was a wooden building with 'No Smoking' notices prominently displayed on every vertical surface. With skilful packing and minimum concern for human comfort, Hook computed that it might hold a maximum of four hundred people.

The shabby setting strengthened his conviction that this enterprise would be aborted long before the end of its gestation. All might yet be well, he thought. Then Maggie Dalrymple arrived and his heart sank swiftly into the trainers he had donned as his gesture to the drama.

That formidable lady looked trimmer and more attractive in jeans and trainers than in the full skirts of her councillor and JP mode. 'Good evening, Polonius,' she said impishly. Bert decided that impish might be more terrifying than serious where this woman was concerned.

Fortunately, the man sitting with his head over the text looked up at that point and said defensively, 'Nothing is settled, as yet. No roles have been cast, apart perhaps from the principle one.'

He was a man in his mid-fifties, Hook's practised eye told him, with plentiful, neatly waved grey hair and small observant blue eyes. He came forward and offered his hand. 'You

must be the Detective Sergeant Hook of whom I've heard
great things. Terry Logan, putative director of this dubious
enterprise.'

Bert liked that word 'dubious'. It suggested to him that
salvation might still be available, despite John Lambert, despite
Chris Rushton. Despite even the redoubtable Mrs Dalrymple.

He began to frame a disclaimer which dwelt on his lack of
theatrical experience, but his plans were interrupted by the
arrival of a striking young man with fair hair and lithe, easy
movements, who seemed from the moment he entered the
shabby hall to be effortlessly the centre of attention. He was
smooth-skinned without looking effeminate, and had a nose
which was a fraction too long for classical perfection. But he
had very large eyes, of a blue which was lighter and much
more dazzling than those of Terry Logan. He seemed to know
almost everyone in the hall. For he nodded to them affably
before he came over to smile into the face of Bert Hook.
'Polonius, by the mass! It must be he.' He shook Bert's hand
firmly and informed him that his name was Michael Carey.

It was not until Carey transferred his attention elsewhere
that Bert Hook realized that another man had entered the room
whilst this twenty-four-year-old sun had thrown the hall into
temporary eclipse. He was a slight, observant, balding man
of around fifty, with brown, humorous eyes, which seemed to
miss nothing and to be sardonically amused by what they saw.
The kind of man you'd want as a witness to a crime, Bert
decided: a man who would give you a confident and detailed
account of whatever he had seen. His name was Ian Proudfoot;
rather unexpectedly, it emerged in the next half hour, the plan
was to cast him as the villain king, Claudius. The part which
Bert in his fantasies had secretly desired for himself.

Terry Logan said, 'We're only here for a read-through tonight.
Although Maggie tells me that she hopes someone may arrive
later, we presently have no Ophelia and no Laertes. No matter:
I'll read in whatever bits are necessary. I just want us to get the
feel of the thing and decide whether we really wish to proceed
with what by any standards is a highly ambitious project. We'll
begin with the first court scene, where we don't need an Ophelia
and I can read in Laertes' lines. Remember that we've already
learned in that nervous opening scene on the battlements that
"something is rotten in the state of Denmark". That feeling runs

through this brilliantly clothed court scene, where only Hamlet remains obstinately in the black of mourning.'

Bert Hook kept his head firmly down over his copy of the text, waiting with trepidation for the first lines of Polonius. But even in the midst of his preoccupation with his own problems, he could not escape one startling revelation. Mrs Dalrymple was right about their Hamlet: Michael Carey was good, very good.

Ian Proudfoot had a grasp of Claudius, masterly and avuncular by turns, and Bert was suddenly glad that his own pretensions were not being exposed in the part.

Maggie Dalrymple was unexpectedly competent as the Queen, at once vapid and over-confident that her son Hamlet could be won round to the new regime. Typecasting, Bert thought bitchily to himself; but he knew he was probably allowing his natural resentment of the woman and her overbearing ways to sway him.

As the scene proceeded, what became ever clearer was that they had a potential star in the name part. Even with his head bowed in concentration, Bert could not escape the excellence of Michael Carey. The young man caught every nuance of Hamlet's bitter jibes against the man who had stolen his father's throne, of his transference of his hatred of his mother to the whole of womankind, of the combination of melancholy and frustration and danger in this complex hero.

All too soon the King was asking, 'What says Polonius?' and Bert was into his first intricate lines. And, such is the perversity of human nature, he found that when the moment came he wanted to impress. Having been determined before the evening began that he would display wooden incompetence and be rid of this trying assignment, he now strove to show that he could handle it.

Perhaps it was just that he hadn't the bottle to make a public fool of himself, but there was something more than that, he thought. Since he had heard the brilliance of Michael Carey and the brisk and unexpected assurance of the others, he wanted to be involved in this. Bert Hook might have been identified by these people as a natural for that tedious old wiseacre Polonius, but it was a part that needed playing, that could draw that heady mixture of laughter and sympathy from an audience. Bert Hook was excited.

He got through his few lines with reasonable competence, breathing a silent sigh of relief when they were over, feeling his heart pounding in the quiet room as he had not known it pound for years. Not since he had come out as a tail-end batsman for Herefordshire in his last season in Minor Counties cricket, to face a young fast bowler who would later play for England.

Such reflections were rudely interrupted when the director briskly gave instructions at the end of the scene. 'Right. Now I'd like us to move forward and look at Act Two, Scene Two, please.' Bert turned the pages wonderingly and found that it was the scene in which Hamlet's apparent madness was discussed and Polonius had more lines than anyone. Blind panic overtook him for a moment; his brain swam and he missed Terry Logan's brief introduction to the reading of the scene.

Then they were away and he was into the deliberately convoluted lines of his character, struggling hard to make sense of them, even as he realized with horror that he was being auditioned. The others were sure of their parts, but he was being vetted by being made to read this, his character's most important scene, where he would have to interact with Claudius and Gertrude and then with the nimble-witted Hamlet. The others seemed to be relaxing and enjoying this, but he knew he was on trial.

Through the tension of his absorption, Bert sensed that it wasn't going too badly. He managed to stress the right phrases, and he even caught the occasional snigger from his companions as he produced some roundabout phrase as if it were a witty epigram. Maggie Dalrymple enjoyed telling him imperiously to produce 'more matter, with less art,' and the others laughed out loud at the effect, so he must have done his part all right.

When the scene was over, the three experienced people who had been reading with him somehow let him know that he had done well, without being so patronizing as to put the idea directly into words. Bert Hook was absurdly pleased with himself when Terry Logan began to discuss rehearsal schedules, and he realized first that what had seemed an absurdly ambitious project was actually getting off the ground and secondly that he seemed to have secured the part of Polonius.

It was only when the evening was coming to an end and he was studying which of the rehearsals he would need to attend that he realized that he had never delivered the one important speech of the evening, the one he had prepared for himself before he came here. The one in which he set out clearly and unequivocally the reasons why he could not possibly be involved in this ridiculous *Hamlet* venture.

It was whilst he was still wondering how his perspectives could have changed so completely that there was a sudden disturbance in the dimness away from the lights at the back of the hall. 'I'm sorry to be so late. They kept us way after the time they said. There were five of us, you see, and—'

'No matter, my dear,' Maggie Dalrymple interrupted her magisterially. 'You're here now, and that's all that matters. I'm afraid you're too late to join in anything tonight, but do come and meet the core members of our happy band.'

She ushered forward to the lighter end of the hall a slim young woman with short dark hair, wearing a flowered dress which was unusual for one of her age and which seemed to Hook vaguely familiar. Maggie Dalrymple announced, 'This is the young lady who I thought might be our Ophelia. She couldn't be here earlier because she's been attending a job interview.'

As the girl came into the full, rather harsh light at the front of the hall, Bert Hook saw with a shock that it was Becky Clegg.

Four

DS Bert Hook was determined to keep his counsel at Oldford Police Station the next morning, despite the pointed questioning he knew he would face about his attendance at the Mettlesham Players' rehearsal the previous night.

The station sergeant, who was almost as old as Bert and much more set in his ways, studied the plain-clothes man closely over his glasses as DS Hook came past his desk and moved towards the CID section. His scrutiny was so noticeable that Bert stopped before the big swing doors and turned back to him. 'All right, Stan. What's the joke?'

'Oh, no joke, Bert. No joke at all. Just a natural curiosity, I suppose – we're not allowed to make jokes about it any more.'

Bert sighed. 'I've no idea what you're talking about.'

Sergeant Stan Smith looked carefully around the deserted reception area of the station over which he presided, as if it were important that no one should hear what he had to say. 'I was watching your walk, if you must know, Bert,' he said in a hoarse dramatic whisper.

'My walk?'

Smith looked duly embarrassed.

'Don't be stupid, Stan!' Bert said, trying to sound menacing, but he could not conceal a touch of amusement, so that his words did not carry the threat he had hoped for.

Bert glared at him in the way he had been used to glare at batsmen after whistling a ball past their chins, then stalked away as if he was striding back to his mark for the next express delivery. But he found that for the next few minutes he was self-conscious about his progress, holding himself very erect and taking slightly longer strides than usual. He was glad to slump at his desk and put his elbows on its surface, whilst he immersed himself in the reports of the previous night's break-ins. Amongst them, he found a note signed by two of his DCs, wishing him luck in his new career and encouraging him to 'break a leg'.

Within five minutes, DI Rushton made an occasion to leave his computer and came to consult Bert about an appearance in court for the detective sergeant in a case which still did not have a date. Then he looked at him curiously and said diffidently, 'Go all right last night, did it, Bert? The rehearsal, I mean.'

The whole of the station now seemed to know about his reluctant venture into amateur dramatics. That didn't surprise him; he had ample evidence that the police grapevine carries gossip faster than any branch of the Women's Institute. He said haughtily, 'It was only a read-through with the director and a couple of other people. Rehearsals don't begin until next week.'

'But you got the part?'

'It seems they still want me to play Polonius, if that's what you mean.' Bert couldn't tell him that he had awoken this morning with a pleasant sense of achievement.

'Congratulations! I'm sure you'll be marvellous, darling.' Chris Rushton was enjoying the unusual pleasure of teasing the man who had so often set him up as the butt of humour.

Bert said heavily, 'Is this going to go on for the next three months?'

'Oh, I expect so. We'll all be anxious to collect the latest news on our new star. This place is full of culture vultures, you know. Is the actual performance as far away as that?'

'Further. We'll be doing largely reading and casting in the next few weeks. Intensive rehearsals will only get under way after Christmas.' Bert noted with dismay that he was now speaking of 'we', then saw with even more dismay that Chris Rushton had noted it too.

'Will you be wearing make-up for rehearsals?'

'Of course not!'

'Pity. I thought you might have enjoyed that aspect of it.'

Bert Hook decided not to pursue an avenue he suspected he had already explored with the station sergeant. Instead, he decided belatedly to carry the fight to the enemy and said darkly, 'I think the part of Laertes is still up for grabs, but you'll need to get in quickly.'

'Not interested, Bert. Sorry.'

'The Ophelia they've got lined up is very pretty. Of course, in the play they're brother and sister, but I'm sure if you played your cards right after rehearsals you'd be in with a chance. I could—'

'I've got myself a girlfriend, thank you, Bert.' In his anxiety to stop this talk of his involvement in theatricals, the words were out before Chris Rushton could stop himself.

'Ah! Anyone we know?'

Rushton sighed resignedly. 'It is, actually. You interviewed her when her flatmate was killed last year. Anne Jackson.'

'I remember her. Very pretty. A student.'

'She didn't go to university straight from school. There were a couple of years in between. And she's completed her degree now. She's currently on a teacher training course.'

'Ten years younger than you, though.'

'Almost that, I suppose,' said Detective Inspector Rushton stiffly. He was intensely aware that there were exactly nine years and eleven months between him and Anne Jackson.

'Shows that you can still pull, though. A student, eh? I expect you'll be getting yourself a scarf and drinking in the union bar with the other lads.'

'I certainly shall not!'

Bert noted that once he was thrown on to the defensive, Chris Rushton dropped back into his normal rather prissy mode. That was quite heartening. When Chief Superintendent Lambert came in, he managed to lure him into partnership in a dual lecture to the hapless Rushton about the dangers of pot for the young and the immature.

By nine-thirty, things were reassuringly back to normal.

Eight miles away from Bert Hook, on a council estate in Gloucester, two very different police officers were having very different problems.

They were both twenty-one, one male and one female, sitting self-consciously in their smart new uniforms with their hats placed on the table beside them in the stifling room. A twenty-year-old in a t-shirt was lounging back in the shabby armchair whilst they sat rather awkwardly on the upright chairs beside the table. His name was Jack Dawes; the inevitable nickname of Jackdaw had been fastened upon him at school.

It had proved wholly appropriate. He was like a lean, alert bird, taking every opportunity to thieve and live by his wits.

Today he was making fools of his raw young police adversaries and all three of them knew it.

'It's a serious charge, armed robbery,' said PC James Standing. He was trying to sound threatening, but the fact that he was saying this for the second time rather diminished the threat.

'I agree with that,' said Jack Dawes from his armchair. 'Once you get the bloke who did it, I shouldn't like to be in his shoes.'

PC Emma Jones said determinedly, 'We've got him. He's right here in front of us.'

Jack Dawes smiled at her, enjoying seeing the dismay that his insolence brought to the young woman's too-revealing face. 'They're saying stupid things, again, Mum. I'm getting tired of it.'

His mother's face glowed with pride at the wit of this clever son. Sally Dawes was a peroxide blonde of forty-one, running a little to fat and so hastily made up for these visitors that her face had a touch of the clown about it above the grubby neck and the breasts which were thrust artificially forward behind the sagging neckline of her blouse. 'I should think we could have them in trouble for saying things like that, son. Maybe sue them for wrongful arrest. Get some compensation out of them. We'd like that, wouldn't we, Jack?'

'He isn't under arrest, Mrs Dawes,' said James Standing. He realized that he'd reacted too hastily and added belatedly, 'Not yet, anyway.'

'Not yet, not nohow, not never!' said Jack Dawes smugly. He was a slim-faced, streetwise young man of 'twenty going on thirty' as his doting mother told anyone prepared to listen to her. 'I told you, I was nowhere near that shop. You'd best be on your way and try to find the buggers who did it. Though if you ask me, the Paki bastard had it coming to him.'

'We're not asking you. And there's no need for racist remarks,' Emma Jones reminded him ill-advisedly.

' "No need for racist remarks," ' Jack mimicked her words in a ridiculous, high-pitched voice, as if he could undermine her sentiments by the freakishness of his delivery. 'Oh, but there is, PC Jones. There's every bloody need, if we're not to be overrun with Muslim trash. But we're going to clean up the country in the next few years. Our National Front men will be elected here in the next local elections, same as they have been in the north. We'll take over the local councils. Then even you pigs will have to listen to the voice of the people, won't you? We'll be your masters, then, PC Jones.'

Jack Dawes lay even further back in his chair and crossed his legs at the ankles, to show them how relaxed he was. He wasn't sure how much of that stuff about the National Front he believed, but he liked to show the fuzz that he wasn't just a hoodlum, that he had intelligence and a grasp of politics.

James Standing shot a look of warning at his colleague. They didn't want to be diverted into a racist argument which they could never win. He said, 'Mr Joussef is a Christian, actually. He is also a man who is in his late fifties, working very hard to make an honest living. Something you might try out yourself, if you want to keep out of prison.'

Jack Dawes allowed a grin to creep across his narrow, crafty face. He was not bad-looking when he smiled, and he was well aware of that fact. He had also registered the titles of these struggling enemies, and he liked to keep reminding them how junior they were. 'Oh, I'm trying very hard to make this honest living you talk about, PC Standing. And I'd like you to make a note of that, too, WPC Jones – you never know your luck, I might be ringing and asking you for a date, now that we've been introduced.'

Emma Jones hoped that the revulsion on her face was the only reaction she needed to give to that. She said hastily, 'You threatened him with a knife to make him empty his till last night. That's armed robbery, Mr Dawes.'

Jack wondered whether to mock her serious, slightly nervous delivery again. But he didn't want them dwelling on that knife. And he knew that you mustn't get too cocky with the fuzz, that being too truculent when you knew you were guilty could lead to complications. He'd seen some of his less intelligent companions get into big trouble by being too cocky. He fell back on the well-worn defence he had prepared before these two came into his house. 'I was nowhere near the place at the time. I know that doesn't stop you flatfoots from locking poor lads like me away, but you'll find it difficult to frame me for this one. I got an alibi, you see, ducky.'

Emma tried not to wince away from the word and the insolent, aggressive face behind it. She'd heard much worse, in her short time as a police officer, but the fact that they were losing this one was getting to her. 'You were there, Mr Dawes. We know that. Denying it isn't going to help your case, in the end.'

Jack gave a little nod to his mother, who said plaintively, 'My boy was here with me at the time. He's a good lad, my Jack. I don't know why it is that whenever you lot want—'

'And what time would that be, Mrs Dawes? What time precisely?' James Standing did his best to give the impression that she had made a mistake and he was now producing his trump card.

Panic flashed for a moment across the coarse, revealing features of Sally Dawes. Then her son said easily, 'All night, wasn't it, Mum? I didn't go out at all last night, if you remember.'

'That's right. He's a good boy, my Jack. Good to his mother, not like some of them. We had pie and chips and ice cream, and then we enjoyed a bit of telly together, didn't we, son? Quite cosy, we was.'

Jack felt her overplaying her hand. Before they could ask him about the content of the programmes, he said, 'I wasn't really watching, though, most of the time. I was reading a book.' He grinned brazenly at each of the two police faces in turn. 'I like to try to improve myself, see? You should try it some time, if you ever want to make sergeant.'

PC Standing said stubbornly, 'We have witnesses, Mr Dawes.'

'Witnesses to some other poor bugger, not me. I wasn't there, you see. My mam's just told you. Or is pigs' hearing as bad as their eyesight nowadays?'

'The shopkeeper will identify you in an identity parade. Mr Joussef has had enough of your bullying and—'

'No he won't! Not if . . .' Jack stopped suddenly, dropping his eyes to the carpet.

'Not if he knows what's good for him, you were going to say, weren't you, Mr Dawes?' said James Standing, seizing on his first success, wondering how he could capitalize on the man's mistake. 'You're saying he's frightened of more physical violence if he identifies you. Threatening a witness can lead to very serious charges indeed.'

He had made a mistake in spelling things out like that. It enabled the sharp-witted young man in the armchair to marshal his thoughts and recover from the gaffe he had made.

'Now did I ever say anything like that?' Jack Dawes asked. 'I may think the old sod is trash, but did I offer any threat to him? Did I ever even mention physical violence?'

He turned his face of hurt innocence towards his mother.

Mrs Dawes said loyally, 'Course you didn't, son.' She turned to the two young officers. 'You want to be careful what you say to my boy, rozzers. You haven't got him in a cell where you can beat the shit out of him, you know. There are witnesses here to what you're saying and the nasty accusations you're making, so you just be careful!' It was a long speech for her, and she smoothed the dress which was a little too short down over her plump thighs with a satisfied air at the end of it.

Emma Jones decided that it was time to cut their losses and get out of this overheated, hostile room. She stood up. 'We shall be continuing our inquiries. When your chickens come home to roost, Mr Dawes, you'll wish you'd been a little more cooperative with us this morning. If there is any further attempt to intimidate Mr Joussef, we shall know where it has come from.' She picked up her hat and made for the door. PC Standing followed her dolefully, trying unsuccessfully to conceal the fact that this was a retreat.

Jack Dawes rose without haste, then bathed all three of the people in the room with his victory smile. 'Chickens, eh, love? Well, there's only two people here who are chicken, if you ask me. And that's the two who came here making false accusations. Goodbye to you, officers of the law. Have a nice day!'

Thirty-five miles away in the ancient English wool-town of Burford, Chief Superintendent John Lambert was approaching a very different house from the one occupied by Mrs Dawes and her son.

The thatched cottage had dormer windows cut into its roof and a path to its oak front door which ran between the perennial plantings of a traditional cottage garden. The front of the house was still in shade, and the heavy autumn dew clung becomingly to the foliage. So healthy was the neatly tended growth that scarcely an inch of soil could be seen. The last of the Michaelmas daisies were still in luxuriant blue and purple bloom and there was a scent of roses, though it was only as Lambert approached the door that he caught sight of the crimson blooms of the climber beneath the low eaves of the house.

There was no sign of life in this pleasant place, yet the old door swung silently open before he could knock. The slim, dark-haired woman on the threshold said, 'Dad! You're the last person I expected to see. There was no need. There's nothing you can do.'

'It wasn't a problem for me to come here, Jacky. We've no serial killers or major bank robbers operating in Oldford at the moment.' It had been an instinctive, spontaneous reaction on his part to rush to comfort her in her distress; he hadn't even told Christine, because he hadn't planned it.

Father and daughter smiled weakly at each other. She turned and led him back through the hall into the low-ceilinged living room. They sat down opposite each other; he on the edge of a sofa and she on a chair opposite him, as if to relax would be a denial of the situation, a kind of treachery to the emotions neither of them was able to deal with.

Lambert looked round at the neat, cool room and then at his daughter, tentatively, almost shyly, as if they were strangers feeling their way into a tricky situation and a new relationship. Jacqueline said abruptly, 'I'll get us coffee. It won't take a minute,' and fled from him into the kitchen.

The room with its old oak furniture was as tidy as if this were a show house. Too tidy, too wanting in human dishevelment. It lacked a half-read newspaper, a crumpled cushion, a letter waiting attention. It lacked a man; to be precise, it lacked all the tiresome trivia of a husband.

Lambert had never liked Jason, his son-in-law, and he knew that that wasn't going to make things easier now. He wasn't good at picking his way in conversation; CID interrogations demanded skills, but the skills of a more direct approach. Jacky brought coffee and biscuits into the room on a tray, set it on the low table, and sat down on the sofa beside him. He could see in her careful movement the intense concentration of the ten-year-old who had once brought him breakfast in his bed on his birthday.

They postponed all contact whilst she conducted the ceremony of the coffee, offering him milk and sugar and then a

biscuit as carefully as if she was enacting some ancient reli-
gious rite. He said stupidly, 'You seem to be coping.'

She smiled wryly. 'I was always good at coping, Dad.'

Suddenly, she burst into tears and hurled herself against his
chest. Her howling was the more bleak and terrible in the
quietness of that old room, which had seen so many other
lives and so many other human crises. He held her, awkwardly
at first, then more firmly and tenderly as both of them relaxed.
Her collapse had shattered the tensions between them.

'It's bad, isn't it, love?' He thought about the traumas of
his own marriage at around the time of her birth. He remembered with a distressing vividness the day when Christine had
walked out on him and he had thought it was over, the day
he could never recall to this child of his who was now a grown
woman with her own trauma.

Jacky couldn't speak. She nodded hard against her father's
chest, wanting to feel the smell of him; the warm, intimate,
comforting smell she remembered from her childhood, smelling
instead only the scents of the washing machine on the clean
shirt, the front of which was now sodden with her tears. She
hid her face there for long minutes, shutting out the world which
had gone so putrid.

Eventually she prised herself away, made herself look up
gratefully into the familiar long, lined, concerned face, and
said, 'You could have done without this, couldn't you, Dad?'

For the first time, they smiled at each other. 'We could all
have done without it, love. Life doesn't always give you a
choice, though, does it?'

'It didn't this time! At least, bloody Jason didn't.' Anger
was a relief: she wished she had the energy for more of it,
but the long hours without sleep hadn't left her much of that.

Lambert knew he had to be careful, even at this moment
when he wanted to be most spontaneous. He cursed his son-
in-law for that as well as everything else. 'Is it final, do you
think?'

She wept again, when she had thought that she had no more
tears left. She snatched at a moment when her breathing settled
to say, 'It's final, Dad. He's got another woman.'

John Lambert knew that that wasn't always final, knew also
that this wasn't the moment to voice that thought. 'Perhaps
you should come and stay with us for a few days. Your mum

would like that, but it's up to you. Whatever you think would be best, love.'

She nodded determinedly and he could see her again in the childhood which seemed so close to him and so distant to her. He could see in her determined face the slim girl with plaits, sitting recounting her first day at secondary school.

'I think I'd like that. I'll need to sort a few things out first. At least having your own business makes things easier when this happens.' She felt a sob rising again, and fought it back with determination. Jacky supplied temporary office staff of every type, from cleaners to computer operators to personal assistants. Her usual effortless efficiency seemed at this moment to belong to someone else entirely.

She clenched her teeth and set her jaw firmly. She could do this. Bloody Jason wasn't going to make her into a whining wimp. She'd show him and the rest of the world. 'I'll make a few phone calls and get things moving. There's a factory office in Oxford beset by an outbreak of flu. I'll sort that and be over at your place tonight.' She'd almost said 'home'. That wouldn't be the emancipated and independent woman at all, would it?

Lambert knew when to accept a small victory and get out. He patted her on the shoulder when he got to the door and said, 'You've got a lot of support, you know. We'll sort it.'

Jacky managed a smile. 'See you later, then, Dad. And thanks for coming.' She watched him walk down the path, stooping a little, and then turn to wave shyly at her from the gate. She'd never expected this visit, would have told him not to come, if he'd phoned first.

Now she felt immeasurably grateful to him.

Jack Dawes shut the door truculently on the two young police officers and made a triumphant V-sign at the back of it.

He went back into the living room and set his DVD player to work, but he could not concentrate. After the heady excitement of frustrating those two young pigs, he felt curiously deflated. Anticlimax, they called it. He remembered that from school, recalled putting his hand up and giving it as the answer to some woman who had been surprised that he knew it. He'd enjoyed some of the books they'd read, and, even now, he surprised himself sometimes by his ability to remember odd bits of the poetry he had so despised at the time.

The teachers had wanted him to stay on, had told his mother that it could be the making of him, but he'd been determined to leave and get himself among the money. There was the odd moment when he regretted that decision, but he thrust those moments firmly away. Still, he'd been good in the plays. Everyone had said that. There were times when he quite missed the excitement and the applause and the praise which had been heaped upon him then. Childish things, he told himself: he had real and greater excitements in his life now.

His mother brought him a cup of coffee, sat down opposite him, and said, 'I'm on late shift at the supermarket. You'll have to get yourself something tonight.'

'No problem. I can always go to the chippy.'

'You go there too much. You should get some proper food into you.' She sat down opposite him, as she did not usually do. Jack felt a sudden shaft of tenderness for the pretty, ageing, rather vacuous face. His mother looked very tired. She sipped her coffee for a moment, dunked her ginger biscuit into it, seemingly without any consciousness of what she was doing. Then she said, 'You won't get away with it for ever, you know.'

'I'm all right, Mum. Don't you worry about me. I know what I'm doing.' But he wondered as he uttered the automatic phrases just how true they were.

'And that Mr Joussef is an old man. There's no need for you to go roughing him up. It's not right.' She couldn't remember when she had last tried to moralize to him: not since he was very small, she thought.

Jack stirred uneasily in his armchair. This was far too near to his own secret thoughts for comfort. 'He wasn't really roughed up much. Anyway, as you told the fuzz, I wasn't even there.' He tried to make a joke of it with a wink and a conspiratorial laugh, but she refused to be diverted.

'You're going the right way to get into serious trouble, Jack. You need to get yourself in with a better crowd.' She took a deep breath. 'You need to do something respectable.' She wasn't sure quite what she meant, but she'd worked on the phrase in the steamy kitchen before she came in to him.

'It takes time to get a job, Mum.'

'It does when you've been in and out of trouble like you have.' That was very daring for her, but she felt bolder because he hadn't immediately put her down when she'd scolded him.

'You were a clever boy at school, Jack Dawes, cleverer than you'd ever admit. You could have stayed on and got yourself a good job.'

He smiled at the earnest, vulgar, loving face. 'I didn't do much work at school. I was good in the plays, though, wasn't I?'

'You were the best, son. The best. I can still see you all padded out as that pompous frog.'

'Mr Toad. Of Toad Hall. I was only thirteen, then.' He smiled reminiscently at the thought of the laughs they'd had together in the cast, at the laughs they had brought tumbling down the school hall from the audience.

'You should do that acting again. Get yourself in with a better crowd.'

There might just be something in that, Jack Dawes thought after she'd gone.

Five

'You look tired.' Angela Proudfoot told her husband. She made it sound almost like an accusation.

'I've had a busy day, that's all.'

'You should delegate more work to your staff. You always used to say that delegation was the secret of management.' She was a flat-faced, querulous woman who had devoted herself to her family and felt at a loss now that the last of them had just gone off to university.

Ian Proudfoot was very conscious of being for the first time in years the centre of his wife's attention. It was proving a very mixed blessing. 'Being a branch manager isn't at all what it was when I began in the bank,' he said patiently. 'You don't lock yourself away in your office and concentrate upon the important clients. There are constant directives from head office and you have much less room for manoeuvre and much less independence than managers used to have.' Ian sounded resentful and he was: if he'd known all those years ago that the job he'd set his sights on would be like this, he'd have chosen a different career.

'Well, you look tired. I'm telling you because no one else will. You're getting older. You can't pretend you're Peter Pan for ever.'

With his dark, thinning hair, his prominent nose and his furrowed brow, Ian Proudfoot looked a pretty unlikely Peter Pan. He knew what was coming next, but he couldn't see any way of averting a familiar conversation. He said wearily, 'I'm only fifty.'

'Nearly fifty-one.' Angela was almost two years older than him and the mention of age was always a sensitive point with her. 'The age when you should be sitting quietly by your own fireside on winter evenings. Watching the telly and giving your wife a bit of company.'

'I'm not keen on television. Not the programmes you enjoy,' he said mildly.

'Doesn't mean you have to go off with that lot.' Angela gave her full venom to the last two words.

He ignored the implied slur on the company he kept. 'You know I've always enjoyed amateur dramatics. And a man needs a hobby. I heard you telling Mrs Frobisher that the other day.'

'Not one that takes him out getting colds and disease in winter, when he should be sitting cosily in his own house. I was talking about do-it-yourself and things like that.' She knew that she wasn't going to win this argument, but she was driven on into the familiar rituals of marital dissension. The little spat must be played out to its conclusion and the points tallied for future occasions.

'This project is more interesting than most.' Although he knew in his heart that he would fail, he tried to take the vinegar from her face and replace it with a little of his own enthusiasm. 'I've always wanted to have a go at Shakespeare, and I've never had the chance before.'

'Shakespeare!' She tried to infuse all of her contempt into the two long syllables, and made a fair fist of it.

'Our greatest writer, Angela, and by common consent the world's greatest. Not many people ever get the chance to speak his lines. It's a rare privilege, if you look at it that way.'

'It's all right for schoolboys and schoolgirls.' Angela was conscious that two of her children had enjoyed great success in school productions. 'Unless you're good enough to be a professional, that's where it should end.'

Perhaps he could have been a professional if he hadn't followed his father into the bank. That was one of the fantasies Ian Proudfoot liked to indulge in during the quiet hours of the night when his wife snored gently beside him. He'd had some good reviews, down the years, in a wide range of roles. He knew he had talent. How much talent, he would never know, for it had never been tested in the hard school of the professional stage, where even good actors were often 'resting' for long periods. Perhaps he wouldn't have had the fortitude to survive in that difficult world, but he wished now that he'd given it a try.

He allowed a little of his excitement to show as he said, 'We've got some good people. If we can bring this off, it will be the biggest thing the Mettlesham Players have ever achieved.'

'*Hamlet.*' Angela Proudfoot sniffed derisively through her small nose. 'You people don't live in the real world.'

'But Shakespeare did. He knows more about the human heart and the human mind than anyone who ever lived, and he can put it into words as no one else can.' Ian Proudfoot realized that his zeal would only make his sceptical wife more scathing. He sought for something which might gain her support. 'It's a very good part. One of the very best.' He knew that she liked to boast among her friends about his successes, however much she derided them to him.

'What part?'

'Claudius. The King of Denmark. He's usurped the throne, and all through the play he's trying to—'

'What happens to him at the end?'

'He gets killed. He's a villain, you see, a "smiling, damned villain", as Hamlet calls him, and he gets run through with a poisoned rapier.' It sounded silly when he said it like that. He wanted to tell her about the mighty intellectual exchanges of the play, about the political skills displayed by Claudius, but that would only put her off. She wouldn't like him being a villain. He said lamely, 'More or less everyone gets killed at the end of *Hamlet.*'

Angela sniffed again, then shook her head sadly at this new evidence of immaturity in her husband. She tried another tack. 'I thought you didn't like that Terry Logan.'

'He's a good director. Personal differences don't come into it.' Ian set his face into a mask of inscrutability.

'Even differences as deep as the ones between you and him?' Angela sensed a weakness here.

'There are a lot of other people involved in a Shakespeare production as well as Logan. There won't be any embarrassing personal exchanges. I expect we shall hardly speak to each other, except to discuss how certain scenes should be played.' Ian Proudfoot had been over this in his own mind, and was determined that it should be thus. He said stubbornly, 'I told you, Logan's a good director, and that's all that matters.'

'Good director my backside!' Angela relished this rare lapse into the vulgarity which she only permitted herself with this recalcitrant husband. 'You go off and play your childish games, if you must, but if you ask me, this sounds a particularly daft one. I don't think it will ever get on stage!'

Angela Proudfoot did not have a good record of success with her predictions. No one could possibly have foreseen how sensationally this one would be proved right.

Detective Inspector Chris Rushton was beginning to feel relaxed and easy with his new girlfriend. It was not before time. They had been dating each other for three months.

It was just as well that Anne Jackson liked his diffidence. It was one of the qualities which had attracted her to the tall, dark-haired man when they had come across each other in the unpromising context of a murder investigation. He didn't seem to realize how handsome he was or how many women would have been quite happy to mother him back into confidence after the trials and stresses of his divorce. Chris didn't seem to realize how attractive that old-fashioned virtue of modesty was in a modern man.

'Kirsty's coming to see me again on Sunday,' he said suddenly, as if it was a confession he needed to have out in the open quickly. 'I'll quite understand if you don't want to be involved, but it will mean that—'

'I'll be delighted to be there,' Anne said quickly. She'd got on quite well with Chris's five-year-old daughter on the only previous time she'd seen her. She was glad now that she was the eldest of three: it meant that she wasn't completely hopeless with young children. And she liked watching Chris with his daughter: these were the hours when he forgot all about the impression he was creating and was completely natural with his child. He was an unaffected, effortless father; had Anne Jackson read a little more romantic fiction and a little less Hardy, she would have been indulging a secret vision of this handsome man with the very dark brown hair as the future father of her own brood.

'You don't have to, if you'd rather not, you know. I'm quite happy to have her on my own.'

She put her hand on top of his and said, 'Kirsty is a delightful kid and I'd be delighted to see her again. Besides, we're in the midst of child psychology in my teacher training course.' She didn't tell him that it was another step towards the intimacy with him that she increasingly desired, perhaps because she didn't want to acknowledge that even to herself.

He smiled, happily relaxed. 'Old Bert Hook's going to be in a play.'

'Bert?' She pictured the man with the village-bobby exterior who had been unexpectedly kind and thoughtful to her after her flatmate had disappeared. 'He doesn't really seem the type for amateur dramatics.'

Chris smiled, enjoying the luxury of gossip with a woman outside the job, a pleasure he had not had for many years now. 'Hidden depths, Bert. He's about to complete an Open University degree, as well. He knows a lot about literature, does Bert Hook.'

Anne stored the information away. Perhaps if they ever met socially, she'd be able to talk to Bert about Hardy. 'What's the play?'

'It's Shakespeare. *Hamlet*, I believe. Bert even tried to persuade me to be in it with him.' Chris threw in the information casually, as if it could increase his attraction, show that he was something more than the staid play-it-by-the-book policeman that he felt himself to be in reality.

'You should have done it. You'd have enjoyed it. It would have brought you out of yourself.'

'No, it wouldn't. It would have been agony. Besides, I have other fish to fry; other ways of revealing my hidden depths.' For Chris, it was a daring speech. He should have looked deep into Anne's eyes upon it, but instead he deliberately looked away from her, as if he feared her laughter. After a moment, when laughter did not come, he squeezed her hand, almost as an afterthought.

She got him out of the pub quickly after that. It was six o'clock on a mild evening, and they walked for a little while in amicable silence beside the Wye. She put his hand around her waist and leant against him as they strolled, looking up at the stars in the clear, moonless autumn sky. 'I'd like to meet your Superintendent Lambert and Sergeant Hook again some time, if the opportunity arises. I thought they handled Clare's death with a lot of understanding and sympathy.'

He walked another few yards, enjoying the feeling of her against him, wanting it to go on for a long time. Then he said, apropos of nothing, 'They're teaching me to play golf. Getting a few laughs out of it.'

'I play golf,' she said diffidently.

'You never said.'

'It hasn't arisen, has it? I didn't know you played until now. Difficult game, when you're starting, isn't it?'

'You can say that again! Near impossible, I found it. And didn't those two enjoy my struggles!' He had turned up in immaculate new golf gear and been reduced to a tattered scarecrow an hour later, much to the amusement of his colleagues.

The germ of an idea entered Chris Rushton's mind. He walked another few yards, squeezing her lightly against him, feeling the warm curve of her breast against the top of his hand. 'Any good at golf, are you, young Annie?'

'Good enough to teach you, old Chris! And if you play your cards right, I'll be much kinder than your male colleagues. You make progress and you never know what rewards you might get!'

He giggled, turned her towards him, and kissed her tenderly in the dark. They walked quite a distance before he reiterated his question. 'You really any good, though?'

'I've played since I was a girl. Caddied for my Dad before that. I'm not bad, I suppose.'

'I've thought of a way you might be able to meet John Lambert and Bert Hook again, if you'd really like to.' Chris Rushton smiled a secret smile in the darkness.

Maggie Dalrymple was getting more excited by the day about *Hamlet*.

It really looked as if the project was going to get off the ground now. She'd pretended from the start that there were no doubts about that, trying to carry everyone else along in the current of her enthusiasm, but she'd known in her heart how ambitious it was. Maggie wasn't by any means stupid. Sometimes it suited her to play up the Lady Bracknell which everyone thought was her natural métier, but she was not out of touch with reality.

Maggie knew that it was a highly, possibly even an absurdly, demanding undertaking for an amateur group to put on Shakespeare's most complex tragedy; that the odds must be against the thing ever getting off the ground. But she enjoyed working against the odds, bringing off coups which most people thought were impossible, and it looked as if she might succeed with this one.

It was early days yet, to be sure, but they had a young man who would be a startlingly good Hamlet, which was an essential. They had a director who was both able and realistic, who would know just how much was possible with an amateur cast and draw it from them. Whatever her past history with the man, Terry Logan knew what he was doing in the theatre.

That girl Becky Clegg could be quite good as Ophelia, if she put her heart into it – Maggie's fertile imagination could already see her cavorting barefoot in the mad scenes. And the boy who'd come along today and offered his services might be a find as Laertes: he certainly looked the part, and he claimed he'd had success in school plays. Terry had apparently directed both of them when they'd been at school and he seemed to rate them.

She was secretly delighted that she seemed to have no rivals for the role of Gertrude. She knew from experience that Ian Proudfoot was going to be a splendid Claudius, and she was going to enjoy being his louche and lascivious queen. Gertrude was a bit vacuous as well, of course, but Maggie was sure she could convey that as well: that was what acting was all about.

She looked at her husband across the dining table. 'You'll never guess who we've got for Polonius.'

He looked at her as he raised the very full glass of red wine she had poured for him. Then he said sourly, 'No, I won't. You're right there.' He looked at her for a moment over the thick black rims of his glasses and went back to his steak. When your wife laid on your favourite meal for you, there was usually a catch.

Andrew Dalrymple liked both his life and his wife to run smoothly on the lines he mapped out for them. The former he could usually engineer; the latter was a more complex problem. Andrew had the florid face which sometimes comes in their fifties to men who achieve business success and the good living which goes with it. He had enjoyed building his plastics firm up from small beginnings over the years, but that hadn't left him much time for exercise or hobbies. He had been an active sportsman in his youth, had almost made it into the Olympic fencing team in 1980, but those days were long gone.

Andrew was running a little to fat now, though not extravagantly so. The doctors had told him to lose weight after his latest BUPA check, but he hadn't taken much notice of them so far. He had his hands full with matters at work and at home, he told himself.

Money was not a problem, within limits. His wife, Andrew Dalrymple had discovered over the years, often was. Maggie did not accept limits, or at least not the ones her husband wished to place upon her.

Maggie now said determinedly, 'Polonius is a key part. Apart from anything else, you need a few cheap laughs when you're working with the audiences we get.' She nodded sagely, pleased to give her husband this evidence that she had her feet on the ground.

Andrew sighed, realizing that he wasn't going to be able to avoid the topic of *Hamlet*. He paused to savour a larger mouthful of his claret as consolation, then said resignedly, 'So whom have you unearthed for this gem of a role?'

'A CID man. Detective Sergeant, as a matter of fact. We'll have to age him a little with make-up, but he almost looks the part already. And he's not just a PC Plod: he understands the play.' She was unable to conceal her own surprise and satisfaction in this startling discovery. 'And he's called Bert. I like the idea of a man called Bert playing Polonius.'

Andrew Dalrymple had never had the same sense of humour as his wife; that was one of the things which had divided them over the years. He said heavily, 'At least Terry Logan isn't involved.'

Maggie stared hard at the delicate lace edging of the very white tablecloth she had got out for this occasion and tried to sound matter-of-fact. 'He is, actually. I'm sure that I told you that before.'

Andrew kept his voice from rising, just as he had noticed she had done. 'I didn't know that. You certainly haven't mentioned him this week. You haven't said which role he's playing.'

'I'm sure I did mention Terry, you know. I'm sure we discussed it when you agreed to hire the hall for us. But he won't be on stage. He's directing.'

'You said you weren't ever again going to do anything in which he was involved.' He mouthed the words very carefully, as if clear diction could conceal his anger and his hurt.

'Andrew, Terry is a good director. The only one who could possibly do Shakespeare. There's no alternative, if we're going to put on *Hamlet*.'

'You promised.' Andrew's full lips set with the obstinacy of a pouting schoolboy. He stared at his steak before he raised a forkful of it to his mouth. This time he could find no solace in his claret.

'I know I did. I . . . I understand why you have these objections. But there's really no need to worry.' She sought desperately for some further reassurance for him and said foolishly, 'There'll be a big cast in *Hamlet*, even when we've cut it down a bit. Lots of people around.'

Andrew said no more, not wishing to endure the pain of a further argument. His steak had turned to ashes in his mouth. He downed three glasses of the claret over the next ten minutes, without tasting any of them. When Maggie came back into the room, he pushed aside the treacle sponge pudding she had made to remind him of his days at boarding school. How uncomplicated the pains and the pleasures of those far-off days seemed to him.

She had expected disappointment from him when she announced that she was going out, but her departure was in the event a relief to both of them.

'I shan't be very long,' she said. 'It isn't a rehearsal; it's just four of us discussing how the play might best be cut down to size for the resources we have.'

She could see him digesting the idea that Terry Logan must surely be involved in this, but he said nothing. She called artificially cheerful goodbyes to him from the hall, but he remained obstinately sullen.

'Suit yourself!' she muttered angrily to herself as she went out to her car. But a little of her felt guilty about the hurt she was leaving behind her in that vulnerable, slightly ridiculous figure which was her husband.

Andrew Dalrymple sat for a long time at the table after she had left. Then he plodded slowly upstairs, his legs moving as if they were drawn upwards against his inclination, by some invisible force. He'd known all along that Logan was going to be part of this. He moved into the large main bedroom of the house, hesitated for a moment, then moved into his wife's dressing room at the far end of it.

Even though he was alone in the house, he found himself looking shiftily over his shoulder for a moment, towards the distant open door of the bedroom, before he slid open each of the drawers in a unit in quick succession. The bottom one was locked, but he found the key for it beneath the unopened packets of tights in the drawer above it.

There was a kind of treachery in this – and he knew it. But he had no control over his slow, deliberate, almost reluctant actions.

The things were there, as he had known they would be. The remembrance of things past; the souvenirs she had promised to throw away, to dismiss from her life and from his. He handled them slowly, with a kind of horrid reverence, as if it was necessary for him to prolong his pain if he was to harden his resolution.

He spent a long time looking at a photograph, one of those casual instants in time which the camera preserves for ever. Then he shut the drawer and locked it, as deliberately as he had done everything else in that private place.

Six

It was six days later, on a muggy November Monday afternoon, that Bert Hook got the unexpected phone call.

He had spent the morning in court. His evidence was straightforward and not contested. Although the prisoner had an experienced barrister to defend him, provided by the bigger, faceless criminal organization behind the accused, DS Hook was not given the fierce cross-examination he had half expected. The young man in the dock pleaded guilty, which made the case simpler. He then made a great show of repentance, nodding his acceptance and contrition as the judge addressed him before sentence. With bowed head and shoulders slumped in shame, he made such a good impression that, in spite of previous convictions, he got away with a two year sentence for dealing in drugs.

With the time he had spent in custody and remission for good conduct, he would be back on the streets in nine months. And almost certainly dealing again, thought Detective Sergeant Hook cynically: he had interviewed this man after his arrest and he knew just how genuine were the remorse and the determination to mend his ways which he had displayed so readily to the court.

Bert was completing the file on the case when his phone rang. He rapped out his name automatically into the mouthpiece. The educated voice on the other end of the line said, 'This is Terry Logan. Do you have a minute?'

The name did not immediately register. 'If you have a crime to report, sir,' Bert said, 'you should get in touch with—'

'It's Terry Logan, your director, actually, Bert. The Mettlesham Players. Remember?' The voice had used his first name rather self-consciously. 'And I'm afraid this is personal, not business. Connected with our venture into Shakespeare. Can you spare me a minute?'

'Sorry. The name didn't register at first. How can I help you, Mr Logan?'

'By meeting me, for an hour or so, if you can spare the time. We need to discuss things, before we go any further with our great enterprise. I think we're all agreed that *Hamlet* is a challenging – some would say a foolhardy – production for amateurs, so I'm trying to have discussions on a one-to-one basis with each of the principals involved before we finally commit ourselves to it. Check that everyone knows exactly what he's taking on. I'd like to see you. Tonight, at my house, if you can manage it.'

'Yes, I can do that.' Bert looked around him, checking if anyone was listening to his arrangements: he'd had quite enough twitting already about his histrionic potential. 'Eight o'clock be all right?'

'That would suit me admirably. I shall look forward to it, Bert. And you really must call me Terry: we don't have any barriers in the theatre world, after all. You'll no doubt wish to call me much worse than that before this thing is over!'

Bert managed a small, self-conscious laugh, flattered to be addressed as a principal, but wondering once again quite what he had taken on. 'Terry it shall be, then.' It was difficult to be affable and at the same time restrained; he had to keep his voice low to frustrate any curious ears in the CID section.

He sat looking at the phone for a full half minute after he had put it down, wondering what the real purpose of this meeting could be. Perhaps he was to be vetted again for his role of Polonius. Perhaps he hadn't been as convincing as he'd hoped at the reading. Or perhaps it was something else altogether, something wider than his questionable dramatic talent.

Being a CID officer made you naturally suspicious.

Christine Lambert opened the front door to find her daughter outside with a suitcase. With her white, drawn face and the clothes she had thrown on without regard for appearance, she looked like a refugee. But to her mother, she looked more like one of those black and white pictures from 1940 of evacuee children, moved out of the cities and away from the bombing.

Christine's surprise must have shown in her face, for Jacky

said plaintively, 'Dad came to see me. He said it would be all right if I came home for a night or two.'

Christine liked the sound of that word 'home', though she knew the suffering which had prompted it. 'Of course it is, love. Come in. I've got the kettle on. We'll have a cup of tea, then get your old room ready for you.'

Jacky stood awkwardly in the hall, looking around her as if she had never been in the bungalow before. 'He didn't tell you, did he?'

'I expect he meant to, then got diverted by all kinds of other things as soon as he got back to the station at Oldford,' Christine said loyally. Typical bloody John, another part of her thought. But at least he'd been to see Jacky; at least he'd shown concern for his daughter's situation. And he'd told her to come here, to have her hurts soothed by her mother.

'It won't be for long,' said Jacky diffidently. Her mother sat her down in the big airy kitchen, which was so different from her own charming but darker little galley beneath the thatched eaves. Jacky looked down at her blue skirt and realized for the first time that it clashed horribly with the garish orange flashes in her top. She shouldn't have come here, she thought.

She said, 'I know you didn't like Jason. But please don't say, "I told you so". Not at this moment.'

'Oh, love, don't say that!' Christine found herself standing behind the chair, with her hands on her daughter's shoulders. She tried to pick her words and stumbled as a result into the hopelessly conventional. 'Jason wasn't exactly what we'd have chosen for you, but he was your choice, and we did our best to get on with him, for your sake.'

'He was a bastard!'

She put all of her accumulated bitterness into the word, so that it shocked mother and daughter alike with its vehemence. There was a little pause and then both of them were laughing together. It was a loud, high, echoing laughter, which had tears not far behind it.

'I got away without any charge on that shoplifting,' Becky Clegg said. 'I was lucky. I got a soft copper: I didn't think there were any of those around. No charges, just a caution and a direction to amend my ways. He seemed to think he could save my soul or something. Daft bugger!' Her Gloucestershire accent came out strongly on the last phrase, and she laughed as she heard it.

Jack Dawes said, 'You always bloody get away with it, you girls! After you'd been caught red-handed with the goods in your possession, too. I expect you fluttered your eyelashes and everything else at him.'

'You bet I did! I'd have given him a flash of anything he wanted, to get out of the nick! But I didn't have to, did I? He were more interested in my soul than my pants, silly old pig.' She felt a little guilty about her bravado, but she had an image to keep up with Dawes. People who lived by their wits had a certain code, and being impressed by any member of the fuzz wasn't part of it.

She certainly wouldn't tell Jack Dawes how that Detective Sergeant Hook had shaken her up and made her contemplate her future. She'd have quite fancied Jack Dawes if he hadn't been a villain who was going to end up inside. She didn't want her street-cred with this able, restless young man to disappear overnight just because she was trying to straighten out her life.

She quite certainly couldn't tell him that she was planning to appear in a play with the same stolid DS Hook who had persuaded her to change her ways. That would be unthinkable, with Jack Dawes.

He said, 'I had a result, too. Two young pigs who were still wet behind their ears came to see me about emptying the till at old man Joussef's shop. My mum said I was at home all night and we made 'em look pretty stupid!'

He'd wanted his news to come out with more triumph and more contempt for the enemy than it had. In truth, he was not very proud of getting away with the squalid little raid on a defenceless, frightened man. But he didn't want to show any of that, when he was trying to impress this confident, attractive, experienced thief.

As if she heard his doubts rather than his words, Becky said, 'That shopkeeper was roughed up, wasn't he? I don't like that.' She was surprised to hear her own words: last week she would never have dared to voice them.

Jack looked at her sharply. 'He was knocked about a bit because he resisted, at first. Whined on about trying to make an honest living and not being able to do it if he was constantly being robbed. The Paki bastard had it coming to him.' But his argument didn't seem convincing, even to himself. He said limply, 'I never touched him, myself. Wouldn't soil my hands with him, would I? We could have taken the money without hitting him, but the lads who were with me wanted to show the Paki who was boss.'

'I see. I'm glad it wasn't you who thumped him. But I still think you should leave old Joussef alone.' Becky Clegg stared at her plate, astonished by her boldness. Then she crushed the crumbs which had fallen off her cake between her fingers and thrust them vigorously into her mouth, as if it must be filled to prevent it from voicing further dangerous new thoughts.

Jack said quickly, 'He's a Christian, old Joussef. The pigs told me that. I didn't know you could be a Christian and a Paki. Anyway, we won't be going there again. Joussef is safe from us.' Then, feeling this assurance would be seen as a sign of weakness, he said roughly, 'Too dangerous, I mean. The rozzers will be watching the place from now on, won't they?'

'Yeah, I suppose so.' Becky spoke abstractedly, as if she had hardly heard him.

She wasn't looking at him, so he was able to watch her. She sipped her espresso in between her enthusiastic demolition of the huge cream cake she had brought from the counter when she came to sit with him. This was so vigorous that she flicked a blob of cream on to the side of her nose. In that moment, she became the girl he had known when he was at school, with a healthy appetite and a total disregard of calories. Some time in the future, he supposed, she'd be like his mum, watching for grey in her hair, studying her hips and her paunch in the mirror and moaning about putting on weight and needing to go on a diet.

Jack Dawes was seized with a feeling of tenderness for Becky's slimness, for her youth and her vulnerability. He felt very protective of her. He said without knowing he was going to say it, 'You should take what happened to you as a warning. Get yourself a proper job and change your friends. You've had a lucky escape and you should learn things from it.'

She looked up into his thin, handsome, intelligent face. 'I've already got myself a job.' She spoke tentatively. It was almost as if she was voicing a confession of failure.

'Good for you.' He reached across the table, took her small

hand in his, felt it sticky from the cake, but held on to it resolutely nevertheless. 'Hang on to that job. There's no future in the way you've been living, Becky. You can do better for yourself. You were a clever girl at school.'

She had been, too. She'd been a year ahead of him, seeming impossibly mature and out of reach in his early days at the comprehensive. It was only since they'd left and he'd got himself a reputation as the brains behind his raffish group of lawbreakers that he'd dared to swagger a little in front of her.

'You want to practise what you preach, Jack Dawes. You'd plenty of brains yourself, when you chose to use them.' That was all hearsay, because you didn't know anything about the people who were coming along behind you in the school, but she'd picked up bits from other, younger girls who fancied him. She slid her hot, sticky hand out of his grip. 'You should stop pestering people like Joussef, Jack. We're both worthy of better lives than the ones we're heading for now.'

He smiled at her earnestness. Girls were always saying things like that, even when they didn't change their own lives. But he found that he wanted to agree with this one. 'I was only saying the same thing myself, as it happens, after those two pigs had left the house yesterday.' He wouldn't tell her that the thought had come in the first place from his mother: honesty was all very well, but it had its limits, when you were trying to impress a girl.

He finished his coffee and squared his shoulders, rippling the studs on his leather jacket. 'If *you* can do it, Becky Clegg, so can Jack Dawes. We'll keep a check on each other – keep each other up to scratch, like.' He looked at her anxiously, fearing that she would mock this evident weakness in him.

But she was smiling and nodding. 'I enjoyed those plays we were in, when we were at school.' She spoke as if it had been in another life altogether, rather than four or five years ago.

He nodded. 'I was thinking I might give it another whirl. The drama thing, I mean. I've already volunteered, as a matter of fact.' He added quickly, as if in apology for such weakness, 'I thought it would occupy my evenings, see, get me away from the lads who'll want to be up to no good.'

She smiled at him, her eyes lighting up. This was the kind of happy coincidence that only happened in Mills and Boon.

'I'm doing that. I'm already into it. With the Mettlesham Players.'

'Bloody hell! Well, bloody, bloody hell, Becky Clegg! That's where I'm thinking of going!'

They gazed at each other, oblivious of the two women behind them who were casting their eyes towards heaven at Jack's loud exclamations. Then they both said together, 'It's Shakespeare, you know,' and promptly dissolved into laughter at this unrehearsed harmony.

When they recovered, she said, 'It's *Hamlet*. If everything works out, I'm apparently going to be mad and singing bawdy songs. And guess who's going to be directing it.'

'Logan the Lech.'

'Yes! He'll be glad to give you a part. He thought you were terrific, when he directed you in those school plays.'

'Maybe. I'm definitely going to give it a try, now that I know you're in it with me, Mad Becky!'

They went out into the busy street in Gloucester still talking about it, still in the early stages of enchantment with each other's company. They had walked quite some way in happy, giggling collusion, and were in the long autumn shadow of the city's great cathedral, before Jack Dawes struck the first jarring note.

He clenched his right hand into a fist, stroked it with the palm of his left, and said, with a return to his old harsh aggression, 'Old Logan will cast me in his play, if he knows what's good for him. And in due course, I've got a score to settle with our Mr Logan.'

Bert Hook was surprised at the size of the house which Terry Logan occupied.

It was on a slight rise at the edge of the picturesque Gloucestershire village of Mettlesham. It was a square, handsome house in mellow Cotswold stone. Quite possibly the house where the lord of the manor had resided in years past, Bert decided, though his knowledge of architecture was sketchy at best.

Scarcely the residence you'd expect for a schoolteacher, Bert thought, as he paused beside his car at the gate. The view towards the Black Mountains of Wales would be spectacular in daylight. There was no street lighting here and, even at this hour, Hook could see the dark outline of the hills beneath the stars and catch a glint of reflected light on a wide horseshoe bend of the Severn in the middle distance.

Logan was obviously well accustomed to being complimented on the house. 'It's far too big for me, of course. But I have a man who comes in to do the garden and a cleaner who keeps the house in order. And I have a treasure of a cook who comes in and does the food for me when I have guests. I inherited the house, and I couldn't bear to leave it after all these years.'

Private means, then, thought Bert Hook. He'd heard something to that effect, in the hushed, behind-the-hand tones which denoted the English reverence for money. There could hardly be a greater contrast to his own Barnardo's boy background, but envy had never been part of his make-up. His days in the home had bred into him the philosophy that there would always be inequalities, that they were a part of life you accepted as easily as the landscape around you. People had their virtues and their venalities, whatever the hand that life had dealt them; one of the things which CID work taught you was that the essence of humanity was very much the same, once you scratched away the surface veneers.

Terry Logan was as meticulous in his person as in the neatness of his elegant, child-free house. His plentifully waved and luxuriant grey hair spoke of an expensive hairdresser, and he was formally dressed, even in his own home after work, making Hook feel immediately scruffy in the sweater, cotton trousers and trainers he had thought appropriate for drama. Logan wore a lightweight grey suit and a blue shirt and silk tie; the whole ensemble oozed Savile Row to Bert, who in his entire life had not been within miles of that sartorial Mecca. As Logan brought Hook a Manzanilla sherry and set it upon a small antique table beside him, Bert caught an expensive but elusive odour from his host; possibly deodorant, possibly aftershave, possibly even eau de cologne. Bert Hook, who was more used to dealing with toughs with tattoos, was no expert on pleasant scents.

DS Hook went into many houses in the course of his work and had developed a sensitivity to the way people were feeling, beneath the polite introductions and the surface niceties of small talk. Terry Logan seemed to him unexpectedly and unaccountably rather nervous.

The man relaxed a little when they got on to the difficulties of playing Polonius. Logan talked a little about the character, and then they read part of the middle section of the play, where a supposedly mad Hamlet makes fun of Polonius and pretends to think him a fishmonger.

'You'll be fine,' Logan assured Bert. 'I could tell even from the reading last week that you were going to be all right. You understand the nuances of the text, and that's always a great start.'

Bert was emboldened by such approval to confess that he was nervous about being exposed on stage, since he had not been there since he was a boy.

'You'll be fine, after a few rehearsals. The moves won't be complicated, and if you're a little stiff at first, that's fine for the character. Polonius is full of himself and his plans, but a little out of touch with what is going on around him, what other people are thinking. He is unaware, for instance, of the pervading sense of decay, of the feeling the audience must have at the beginning of *Hamlet* that "something is rotten in the state of Denmark". You'll soon get the hang of it. And you'll have some seasoned amateur actors around you.'

'Yes, I suppose so,' said Bert gloomily. He found the prospect of rehearsals with these vastly more experienced people, and with Mrs Dalrymple in particular, quite daunting.

'Team work is important in Shakespeare.' Logan stated the truism with brisk confidence. 'Maggie Dalrymple you already know. Her bark is much worse than her bite. You'll need to remember that, in the play, you're brighter than she is.' Perhaps he saw the trepidation in Bert Hook's face, for he grinned and said, 'Believe me, you'll find it quite easy, once you both get into character.' He took a sip of his neglected sherry and said with unexpected tenderness, 'She's a good sort is Maggie, underneath her surface bluster. She'll look after you.'

Bert wasn't sure about that. He said, 'Mr Proudfoot seemed to know what he was about.'

Terry Logan glanced at him sharply. 'He's a very competent actor, Ian Proudfoot. Might even have made it in the professional theatre, though I'm not sure that he'd have had the stamina for it. He'll be a good Claudius. I've no doubts about that. You'll be working with him quite a lot on your scenes, and you may find him a little prickly, but he'll be a great help to you.' Logan looked guarded, and Hook thought he was going to leave it at that. Then he said, 'Don't take any notice of what Ian may say to you outside the play. He's a strange man in many respects.' His lips set in a thin line, as if to frustrate his tongue in any attempt at further words.

Bert felt as if he was in some strange dream, sitting here in the big armchair, sipping sherry, and discussing the playing of Shakespeare. He said, 'I was very impressed with the young chap you've got for the main part.' He didn't feel he could say 'the Prince' or 'the gloomy Dane' without claiming some relationship with the theatre which would have been wholly spurious.

'Michael Carey is pure gold for us. He was a bit of a protégé of mine, in the past, so I suppose I can't claim to be objective, but in my opinion, he'll do great things at RADA and have a fine career on the professional stage. We're lucky to get him before his career really begins. In a different way, he's lucky to have us: he'd never have got the chance to play Hamlet without us. If everything works out as it should, we should all benefit.' He hesitated. 'Again, I shouldn't pay too much attention to anything he says outside rehearsals. He's a gifted but rather blinkered young man, is Michael Carey.'

Hook thought he should reassure his host. 'Not many people want to say anything very important or personal to me. It's an inevitable part of being a policeman, I'm afraid. People are very guarded in what they say to you. I got used to that a long time ago.'

Logan nodded, looking curiously relieved at the thought. 'We're almost fully cast now. We've got a couple of quite promising youngsters for your children in the play, Ophelia and Laertes.'

Bert nodded. 'Becky Clegg came in at the end of last week's reading. You think she'll be fine, then?'

'She'll need a lot of work, but she could be sensational.' He hesitated. 'You know Becky Clegg, then?'

'Just a little. Not well at all.' He wouldn't say that their only meeting was a professional one, that in effect he'd saved her from a serious charge and put his own reputation on line at Oldford CID in doing so. 'I'm glad you think she could be good. She needs something like this.'

'So does the lad who's turned up for Laertes. Jack Dawes, he's called. I've directed him before, in a school production,

and he's good, if he wants to be. He's been in trouble with
the law since he left school. Bit of an Artful Dodger – perhaps
worse than that, for all I know. I'd like to think that he could
help us and that we could help him to save him from himself.'

Bert made a mental note to check on Jack Dawes when he
went into the station the next day. He didn't want to pry un-
necessarily, and he'd already been reminded by tonight's
exchanges that this venture ought to be totally divorced from
his working life, but if the young man should have a criminal record, it would be as well to be aware of it.

Terry Logan showed him a provisional rehearsal schedule,
with the pace steadily accelerating once they moved into the
new year: the nights where Bert would be required were efficiently picked out for him with a marker pen. For the first
time, he realized what a huge commitment, both in time and
in emotional resources, this production was going to be for
Terry Logan himself.

He said as much, and the man smiled at him. 'Hopefully
there'll be lots of pleasure to compensate for the moments of
pain. I did two years in professional rep, many years ago,
Bert. Nothing is as hard as that. To tell you the truth, I'm
quite excited about this. I never thought I'd get to direct
Shakespeare again, let alone the greatest play of all. And I
think we've got quality, in the important parts. We're going
to surprise a lot of people, if I'm any judge.'

It lifted Hook to see the man's enthusiasm bursting through
the slightly effete persona which was so alien to Bert's experience. Terry refilled the sherry glasses, and they chatted
amiably for a few minutes about the trials of Bert's work in
CID and Logan's work in school, themes which signified that
the business part of the evening was at an end.

Logan came down to the gate with his visitor as he left,
assuring him that he would enjoy a breath of the mild night
air. 'I look forward to working with you, Bert. I'll be delighted
to have your support and protection.' He closed the car door
as Bert put on his safety belt.

Bert drove carefully after the sherry. He had negotiated two
miles of winding lanes before he wondered why Terry Logan
had used the word 'protection'.

Seven

Wednesday the fifteenth of November was the date of the first proper rehearsal for *Hamlet*. The man who was to play the lead felt his pulse quickening as the clock ticked slowly through the afternoon.

Michael Carey was a graphics artist in a small company. The money wasn't great, but it was the kind of work he enjoyed and the kind of conditions he could live with. Because of his skills and his ability to deliver what was required at short notice, his employer allowed him a lot of autonomy. It was the best job he had had. There were even moments when he regretted the fact that he would have to abandon it, when he went off to RADA.

Michael had a room of his own on the top floor of the old building in Cheltenham, where there were extra windows in the roof and the light was good for his work on the big paper sheets. He used the computer for all the detail of his designs, but you still needed excellent light. He had more or less finished the advertising poster he was working on by four o'clock, as the early twilight dropped in and he switched on the powerful fluorescent lighting over his working table.

He wasn't going to achieve anything useful in the last hour of the working day: his thoughts were increasingly on the night's rehearsal and his part in it. He took the draft of the poster down two floors, to the more populated part of the building, and found it noisy with conversation and laughter. This sudden cacophony of human exchange was quite startling after the isolation of his studio room at the top of the building. He tapped on the door of the office in the corner, put the draft of his poster in front of his boss, and said, 'This is a first draft. I think it's quite promising, but I'd like you to have a look at it before I go any further.'

Without waiting for a reaction, Carey turned and left the

room and the building. The older man stared after his young worker, half-irritated and half-amused, wondering exactly what went on in that talented, eccentric, very private mind. He looked down at the first draft of the poster. It was both witty and striking, making its point in the spare, precise lines of the drawing, scarcely needing a caption to convey its message. It would need very few amendments before they went ahead and printed it.

Two girls from the office called greetings after Michael Carey as he moved out into the last dim light of the November day in the car park. With his fair hair and large, brilliant blue eyes, he attracted more than his measure of female attention. Usually he was polite and cheerful, but tonight he was too preoccupied to make more than a token acknowledgement of the young women.

The old Fiesta started readily enough. He'd paid very little for it, but it had been a good buy; Michael Carey breathed his usual silent prayer of thanks to the young man who had found it for him six months ago. It had been an advantage having a friend who worked in a garage; he wasn't usually able to turn his friendships to such useful ends.

Michael lived four miles west of Cheltenham, in the village of Norton. He was well before the rush hour traffic tonight and home within quarter of an hour of leaving work. He hadn't many possessions in the little flat; he had learned to travel light over the last few years. But he had been here for five months now, as long as he had spent in any one place in the last seven years, and he looked forward to reaching it in the evenings as his haven from the world.

It was really a granny annexe, built on to the end of a big detached house to accommodate a relative who had long since died. But it suited Michael Carey admirably, giving him the privacy he had long desired but failed to achieve. The rent was low, because the owner wanted someone reliable to keep an eye on the main house during his frequent trips abroad. Michael had no real idea what an appropriate rent for his comfortable retreat would be, but he was sure that he was paying much less than the economic price.

The owner was absent at present. The gaunt, irregular outline of the building was completely unlit as Michael drove around the curving drive and parked in front of his flat. He had made no plans when he left work, but by the time he reached Norton he knew what he was going to do. He did not bother with the mug of tea he often made himself whilst the place was warming up. Instead, he snatched a small drink of water and changed quickly into the dark blue track suit and the expensive trainers which were his one extravagant purchase since he came here.

He slipped his small torch into his pocket, but found there was just enough light left in the western sky for him to see the deserted country lane. He dropped easily into the steady, loping stride which covered the ground so quickly. He had never been much good at any of the sports they had made him play at school and had eventually developed many ingenious ways of avoiding them. But this was different. He had been introduced to jogging a year ago, and had taken to it with unexpected enthusiasm. It now seemed as natural to him to run as it was for the horses in the fields or the stags on the moors.

He wouldn't go very far tonight: three hours from now, he would need all his energy and concentration for the rehearsal, when he wanted to impress everyone and convince them that *Hamlet* was a realistic proposition. He couldn't have it snatched away from him now, when it was so nearly in his grasp. He dropped into the steady rhythm which was so important for running, using as usual lines from the play to beat time with his steps. Iambic pentameters were ideal for building up the rhythm of running. He'd used 'To be or not to be ...' for many weeks, pounding his way through the metre of the soliloquy, beating the rhythm of the verse into his subconscious with the dropping of his feet on the tarmac.

Tonight they'd be doing the first scenes of the play. He seized on that important early line which sets the tone of the first act. 'Something is rotten in the state of Denmark,' Michael Carey chanted softly and rhythmically, hammering it out over and over again as he ran, an invisible smile suffusing his face with pleasure in the darkness.

Ian Proudfoot tried to control his excitement and his rising sense of anticipation as he ate his evening meal with his wife. However, he found himself at a loss for conversational topics. He knew he must avoid any mention of the evening's activity if he was not to antagonize Angela, but his mind wouldn't settle genuinely upon anything else as being of comparable importance or interest.

He was confined to largely monosyllabic replies to his wife's unimaginative trivia. He found himself suddenly surprised by the realization that he wanted to tell her that he had loved her once, could love her again if she would only try to recapture some of the humour and flexibility and live-liness she had possessed in the first years of their marriage.

But she would take that as a criticism, and Angela didn't respond well to any form of criticism.

She said suddenly, throwing in the word she had thought up during the afternoon, 'I haven't forgotten you're going off posturing tonight, so there's no point in keeping quiet about it.'

For a lunatic, intoxicating moment he was tempted to tell her that he would be playing a king in control of his court, with a lascivious queen who could hardly keep her hands off him. Instead, he said, 'It will help to keep me sane, I suppose, dear. It might help me to escape from the drab world in which I have to exist from day to day into a little harmless excite-ment. My working world, I mean, of course!' he added hastily.

'It will be damp and draughty in that hall tonight,' said Angela, with undisguised relish.

'I expect it will.' He tried to be light and amusing. 'Still, we have to make sacrifices for the sake of our art, don't we?'

Where once she would have responded with a remark in a similar light, self-mocking vein, she merely said, 'I expect you'll be asking me if I've anything for a cold in a couple of days, and then snivelling all over the house and your clients at the bank. Peter bloody Pan!'

How could he tell her about the familiar surge of adrenalin he could get in this and in no other way? How could he convey that he would come alive in the next few hours of trial and error and progress, as he now did in no other section of his life?

He said mildly, allowing just a little of his excitement into the words, 'It might just be very good, this one, you know. You might yet be able to boast a little to your friends about your husband's triumph as the wicked king!'

Fortunately, the phone rang before she could reply. It was their youngest daughter, squeezing a phone call to her parents into the crowded schedule of her first year at university. Ian

Proudfoot noted how his wife's voice changed and softened as she responded to her daughter's account of her life, how it seemed to change her back into the woman he had known and loved and still wished to love.

He changed into his casual clothes for the rehearsal, found Angela still in animated conversation when he came down the stairs, had time for the briefest exchange with his daughter himself before she rang off. He left the house before the pleasure in the contact with her daughter could drain away from his wife's face.

In Bert Hook's house, the anticipation of the first important rehearsal was very different.

His two boisterous boys were intrigued by this new departure in a parent they thought they had safely summed up and filed away. Eleven-year-old Luke said, 'I expect if this goes well, you could be "discovered", Dad. This year Shakespeare, next year a pop idol!' He strummed an imaginary guitar and leapt about the room grotesquely in his imitation of a boys' band leader.

Jack studied his younger brother's efforts dismissively. 'I see Dad as a serious artist. Discovering talents that he and the world never knew he had. Perhaps throwing up his dull life in the police and going off somewhere quite different.' He leapt across the room to place an imaginary microphone two inches from his mother's mouth and intoned in an unnaturally deep voice, 'Eleanor Hook, how do you react to this alarming development in your middle-aged husband?'

His mother sighed. 'I shall just have to come to terms with it, I suppose. As I have had to come to terms with having lunatic children in a crazy world.'

Bert contented himself with a portentous diatribe about homework and left the trio with a wry smile. It was only after he had driven two miles through the autumn darkness that his trepidation about what he had committed himself to returned.

Jack Dawes's mother was full of encouragement. 'It's just what you need, son. It will get you in with a better set.' She leaned towards him as if to impart some startling original thought. 'It's who you know, not what you know, that's important in this life.'

Jack set out with a brave face and considerable inner apprehension. At school, amateur dramatics had all been a bit of a
lark. Now that he was going to have to mix with older and
very different people, he wondered whether he would be up
to it. He decided to stop off at the empty shop where he knew
his mates would be. A spliff of pot was what he needed.

The back door was open as he knew it would be, and the
three of them were sitting on the floor, backs against the wall,
with the sweet smell of the cannabis dominating the room. He
took his spliff, hesitated for a moment, then sat down on the
floor opposite them, feeling against his back the sharp edge of
the hole where the plaster had dropped away. A boy who was
a year younger than him watched Jack's every movement, then
sniffed hungrily at his cannabis, as if he was reluctant to let
even the thin smoke from it get away from him. He kept all
expression out of his old-young face as he said with affected
indifference, 'You coming out with us tonight, Jack?'

Dawes said, 'I got other plans for tonight. I told you that
yesterday.'

'I thought you might have changed your mind. There's a
chance of a rumble, tonight. Other people are muscling in on
our patch. We might need you.'

For a moment, he was tempted by the prospect of continuing his leadership of this disreputable, dangerous group, by
the excitements of what the night might bring for them. The
status of leader and the thrills of breaking the law seemed
much more attractive than the uncertainties of the effete world
of amateur theatre. Then he said, 'No, I've got other plans for
tonight, like I said.'

'I thought you were going to batter that Logan man. Thought
you were going to see him off.' The boy did not look at Jack
now; he watched the smoke from his spliff wreathing up past
the bulb towards the invisible ceiling.

Jack couldn't remember telling him about the play and his
plans. But word got round quickly among a group like this, with
mischief on their minds and too much time on their hands. He
said carefully, 'That was when we were kids. I might still batter
him, but I'll make sure the filth can't pin it on me, if I do.'

'If you say so.' His follower allowed himself a secret,
knowing grin.

'That's exactly what I do say!' Jack Dawes stormed out of

the empty shop. He stood panting in the night air, until he felt his breathing slow and he had control of his anger.

Then he threw himself across the Yamaha 350 which was the envy of his peers and flung out a few pebbles behind him as he roared impressively away. He still wasn't sure that he was doing the right thing.

Maggie Dalrymple was trying to reassure a man who was never going to accept reassurance. 'I don't expect to be very late, but you can never be sure how long these first rehearsals are going to last,' she said apprehensively.

'Too long. They always do. But you'll be enjoying every minute of it, I expect,' grunted her husband. During the day, he had been determined to be relaxed, even gracious, but now that the moment had come his resentment had come bubbling to the surface.

'I wouldn't go if it didn't give me pleasure, would I, Andrew? You know I enjoy the Players, and I'll never get another chance to act in Shakespeare. That's what you said when you hired the hall for us.' She went over to where he had slumped with the paper and perched herself on the side of his armchair. 'You'll be proud of me, when it all comes off. We're a long way from discussing costumes, but I suspect I might even be wearing a nightie in one scene. You might even quite fancy me.' She dragged her hand seductively across his chest like some latter-day Delilah.

It was the wrong approach. 'Prancing about on stage for all the world to see!' he said, his outrage only a little exaggerated. 'You're not twenty-one any more, you know!'

'Neither of us is, unfortunately, Andrew.' She ran the back of her fingers across his forehead, took a deep breath, and plunged on recklessly. 'But I seem to remember from last night that someone retains all his old vigour and enthusiasm!'

He smiled a little, despite himself. She surely couldn't have forgotten the clumsy fumblings before he had got into his stride or how quickly it had all been over. But Andrew Dalrymple, like many middle-aged men, was not and did not want to be objective about his sexual performance. He took her hand in his, pressed his lips briefly against the back of it, and said, 'Well, don't be late, then. And don't come back exhausted from your efforts.'

They giggled amicably for a moment, and then she kissed him, suddenly and passionately. She left him without another word. It was only after she had gone that Andrew Dalrymple fell to wondering why Maggie should seem to be sexually stimulated by the prospect of her evening's labours.

Becky Clegg said firmly, 'I'll be moving out at the end of the month.' Now was as good a time as any to tell them, when she was going to be safely out of the way for the rest of the evening.

'This is part of your new life, is it?' The boy with the lank yellow hair threw the sneer from his face into his voice.

'I've got myself a proper job. It's the right time to move on, that's all.'

'Not good enough for you any more, are we?' The girl on the stained sofa looked at her resentfully.

It was so nearly true that she didn't deny it. 'You'll get someone else to share the rent easily enough. It's not much, though it's plenty for this place.' She looked at the paint peeling from the ceiling, the smears of beer and wine on the wallpaper, and congratulated herself anew on her decision to get out now.

'And who's going to help us to lift stuff?'

Becky hesitated. 'You can take over yourself, if you want to, Carol. And Wayne will take care of the rough stuff.' It didn't sound convincing, because she wasn't convinced of it herself.

'We'll come unstuck without you. The bloody pigs'll have us.'

The boy bestirred himself. 'It's true, girl. You're the best, when it comes to lifting stuff and getting away.' He hadn't had a lot of practice at flattery, and it showed.

Becky sighed. 'No one gets away with it for ever. I always meant to stop before I ended up inside. You should do the same.'

The girl said with a resentful whine, 'It's all right for you, Becky Clegg. You've got brains. You've got options the rest of us don't have.'

'Anyone can get a job, nowadays. You can get a job in the supermarket, if you want one.' But even as she said it, she knew that the girl wouldn't do that. She'd never be able to hold a job down, with the drugs and the sort of life she'd got used to leading. She'd never accept the discipline of long hours and taking orders. Becky was finding it hard herself, but she was going to stick at it. She looked at her expensive watch which was a reminder of that former life. 'I've got to be on my way. I've got a lift.'

Her companions continued to sit and stare sullenly ahead of them. She was glad to be out of the place and away from them. She'd move out as soon as she could – before the end of the month if she could find somewhere to go.

She heard the noise of the engine before the motor cycle turned the corner of the street. She put on the helmet he gave her and threw her right leg over the pillion as if she had been travelling like this all her life. She mustn't let him know how nervous she was. She shut her eyes and clasped her hands tightly around Jack Dawes's waist. He twisted the grip and the big Yamaha leapt away beneath them.

Terence Logan was savouring the buzz he always got before the first major rehearsal.

Until now, he hadn't really believed in his heart of hearts that this project would ever get off the ground. As he'd kept insisting all along, it was a hugely ambitious undertaking for amateurs, a production of *Hamlet*. It remained so, even with the fairly savage cuts they'd now agreed upon. But he had a cast which was stronger in all the major roles than he'd been able to envisage when the Mettlesham Players had first approached him with the idea.

He acknowledged to himself that he was in fact delighted with the cast he'd assembled. There was no denying that he'd got serious history with most of his principals; there were some of them he'd cross the street to avoid in the rest of his life. But that didn't matter: the play was the thing. As long as they were good in the parts they were playing on stage, that was all that mattered. No doubt they felt something similar about him as director.

He'd directed all of them before, though not in the immediate past. Well, all except that lumpish detective fellow, who'd come to the house the other night and proved unexpectedly intelligent. He'd make an excellent Polonius, with a few pointers from his director. And it might even be good to have an experienced policeman around in case any of his old enemies cherished ideas of revenge.

He didn't think they would. They all seemed as surprised and delighted by the idea of *Hamlet* as he was. They'd soon realize that if they were going to succeed in this, they'd need to forget any previous differences and work together as a team. All the same, he decided at the very last minute to take his own precautions.

He had reached the front door of his handsome house before he turned abruptly and went back up the stairs. He entered the bedroom which he used as a study, unlocked the bottom door of the desk, and picked out the object wrapped carefully in an old linen serviette.

The Beretta pistol with the ivory handle was small: a weapon more suited to a woman, he had always thought. It wouldn't blow a man's head away, like the Smith and Wesson which featured in so many films. But it would kill a man or a woman easily enough, if the occasion arose. The probability was that it never would, of course.

But Terry Logan liked to be prepared.

Eight

John Lambert had been alone in the bungalow for half an hour before he heard their voices in the hall. Jacky and her mother were animated, noisy, suffused by a small and harmless hilarity. He divined that for the first time in years, mother and daughter had been on a shopping expedition together.

Christine Lambert was an unusual lady, in the view of the modern media. She resented hours wasted on shopping, had to force herself to expend upon it time she grudged because she would rather have used it for other things. It wasn't just the weekly grind of the supermarket visit she found trying: even more adventurous sorties to purchase clothes, which most of her friends anticipated eagerly, were anathema to Christine Lambert. She normally postponed such expeditions for as long as possible. For your children, all things change.

As the two came into the room still animated with the excitement of their purchases, Lambert felt himself suffused with a petty resentment. Why should Jacky be able to lift her mother out of herself and her normal habits? It should be him who could raise Christine's spirits like this. This alien daughter who had long flown the Lambert nest had no right to come back and lift his wife so effortlessly on to another plane.

Jacky flew across the room to plant a kiss on his forehead, and then there were plastic bags flying on to every chair, in what had two minutes ago been a tidy, peaceful room. John Lambert tried and failed to join in the brouhaha of female animation over the myriad small and unremarkable additions to their respective wardrobes. His bonhomie was as false and forced as theirs was spontaneous and joyful.

Eventually he put on his broadest smile and said, 'Well, I was just on my way out to the garden when you two arrived. I must go and move a few of the autumn leaves.'

His wife understood him and his falsities, as wives

irritatingly tend to do. She followed him through the kitchen door. 'You should be pleased to see Jacky showing an interest in life. She's having to be brave to do it. This separation's bitten deeper than either of us realized it would.'

'I know. I'm sorry. I'm an old curmudgeon. I just wasn't coping very well in there. I was afraid of saying the wrong thing.'

'Just be yourself, John. It's her dad she wants to see, not some diplomat afraid to open his mouth for fear of offending her.'

He couldn't tell her that it was her laughter, not Jacky's, which had upset him, that there was an unseemly jealousy within him that it should be his daughter and not himself who was touching this part of Christine. He said, 'I'm glad to hear Jacky laughing, glad to see her happy again. I am really.' He spoke as if he was trying to convince himself of that, rather than Christine.

'Make the most of it, then. Your daughter's cheerfulness is very brittle.'

Everyone was apprehensive at the first proper rehearsal. That was natural enough: the beginning of every amateur production is fraught with angst, as each member of the cast begins to appreciate the difficulties of what has seemed great fun until now, as everyone abruptly wonders if these distraught fumblings with lines and cues and casting will ever develop into a performance. Something which they might put on stage; something which they might expect people to come and watch, and perhaps even to enjoy.

But there was an additional massive thought which lingered unspoken in the minds of everyone in Mettlesham's village hall. This was *Shakespeare*. It was surely ridiculous for amateurs even to aspire to put a great tragedy on stage, surely folly for them to expect an audience to attend to their efforts with anything more than derision.

All of this was vaguely understood among the people who assembled in that unpretentious wooden building on a still and chilly November evening. The place was full of a brittle laughter as they greeted each other; of vague, unconnected, incomplete conversations as each of them realized that the fear they had brought with them into the hall was translating itself into a collective anxiety about what they had taken on together.

Bert Hook had a greater fear about the exposure of his personal inadequacies as an actor than anyone else present. Everyone save him had recent experience of being on stage; that included even the two youngest members of the seven who had assembled for this first active evening of preparation. And by all accounts, they had all been successful. Beneath Bert Hook's calm and stoical exterior, his heart was pounding as the young toughs of Gloucestershire and Herefordshire never caused it to pound. A small, panic-stricken part of DS Hook was insisting that it was still not too late to get out of this.

The two younger people seemed to Bert to be preoccupied with each other, though Becky Clegg had given him a friendly, uncharacteristically shy, greeting when she had seen him come in. At least she had acknowledged him: many youngsters seemed to find that their code forbade them to display any sort of friendliness towards a police officer. The lad with her seemed to be bound by that code: he denied himself any communication with Bert, who learned only from listening to his exchanges with their director that he was Jack Dawes and had been provisionally assigned the role of Laertes.

Ian Proudfoot and Maggie Dalrymple, veterans of many successful Mettlesham Players' productions, gravitated naturally towards each other in this nervous prelude to the business of the evening. Bert found himself spared any of Maggie's well-meant but cringe-inducing eulogies about his potential as an actor. This wasn't a moment when he wanted his supposed triumphs as a boy-soprano urchin in the chorus of *Oliver* thirty years ago to be recalled in Mrs Dalrymple's stentorian tones.

Bert watched Maggie talking to Proudfoot, snatching glances at the text of the play, flinging quick looks of encouragement in his direction, and keeping a nervous eye upon their director as he prepared to call the meeting to order. Her body language gave him a moment of cheer as his stomach threatened to reject his evening meal. Bert realized in a sudden bright shaft of illumination that in a different way the formidable Mrs Dalrymple was almost as nervous as he was.

The only person who spoke to no one was the man who was the original spur to all this activity. Michael Carey sat alone at the edge of the hall, his fair hair dropping over his forehead, his nose looking a little longer in the poorly lit spot he had chosen, his blue eyes cast steadily down upon the text of the play. If he had nerves, he did not show them. Cocooned in concentration, he seemed to be already within the play, already to be calculating the effects he might make by nuances of voice, movement and reaction.

When Terry Logan rapped his pen against his clipboard and told them briskly that it was time to make a beginning, it was a bitter-sweet moment for Bert Hook. There was relief that the stomach-churning minutes of waiting were over, and at the same time a panic that the moment had finally arrived when a staid policeman feared he was about to make a laughing-stock of himself. He told himself that this must be a perfectly natural reaction, that the others were probably nervous as well, but he did not dare look at them to check on this.

He became dimly conscious of Logan explaining that this was a first rehearsal for principals only, that although not all of the bit parts had even been cast as yet, it was time to make a start. He gave a short pep talk on the commitment involved, stressing the fact that non-attendance at rehearsals would be a grave blow to the team involved in this most complex of the Players' enterprises. In the winter months, colds and chills were inevitable, but he hoped everyone concerned would make supreme efforts to keep to the rehearsal schedule. Even death, he pointed out, would be accepted as an excuse only with some reluctance. There were a few nervous titters at this. Bert Hook, who hadn't been entirely sure that this had been intended as a witticism, joined in with them belatedly.

Terry Logan announced that they would make a start with the first court scene, in which all the principals save Ophelia were involved, and then move on to the domestic scene in Polonius's house, where the father gives his famous advice to Laertes and then questions his daughter about her relation-ship with Hamlet. That would be quite enough for a first evening, he told them, with an experienced twinkle in his eye. Bert realized with a sinking heart that he had a lot of lines to deliver in the next two or three hours.

The director spent some time positioning them on stage, and then gave them a single important thought for the first court scene. 'Everyone is relaxing, brilliantly dressed in a court newly released from mourning. Everyone save one figure, who is obstinately and insultingly clad in black: Hamlet, bringing to the revelry his conviction from the earlier scene that "something is rotten in the state of Denmark". All the tensions in the scene proceed from this single visual anomaly.'

It worked. Their progress was halting, of course, and they were still reading from their books. But even a very nervous Bert Hook could feel the tension crackling as Hamlet made his bitter jokes and Claudius, knowing very well what was going on, chose to ignore them and deliver his avuncular, face-saving homilies to a Prince increasingly frustrated by his refusal to take offence. He wasn't bad, this Shakespeare bloke. Hook began to feel the thrill of being involved in something very special.

Michael Carey was the only one who didn't need a script. He knew his every line and his every cue already, and he roamed the stage like a feral cat, darting his verbal claws at anyone who claimed his attention. Bert, and no doubt the others on stage with him, felt a resentment at this dazzling control, exercised without seeming effort, whilst others fumbled desperately towards some sort of effect.

Yet Carey's uneasy brilliance was indisputably raising the performances of those around him. The reactions to the Prince's attacks upon hypocrisy and his puncturings of pomposity became sharper as his bitter ironies struck at the others on stage. Even Bert Hook, when he delivered the elaborate circum-locutions and self-satisfactions of Polonius, realized now that he was part of a larger whole, setting off the razor-sharp perceptions of the central figure in the play with his verbosity and his delusions.

It felt as if everyone save Hamlet had staggered through the scene, yet Logan at the end of it was plainly now as excited as everyone else. He pronounced this an excellent start, gave them a few general pointers, said that he would have more moves to suggest to them by the time they came back to the scene at the next rehearsal. He did not comment directly upon the dazzling exhibition from his central character, contenting himself with pointing out how all their performances would be lifted once they knew their words, when they would be able to move properly and react to others on stage more natu-rally. Perhaps that was a subtle way of telling them that he expected all their performances eventually to rise towards the level already being displayed by the eponymous hero.

They had a short break and a swift cup of tea, which the young girl whom Logan had introduced as his stage manager and general dogsbody had made for them. Then, with a few encouraging words about the start they had made, the director dismissed all save Bert Hook and the two youngest members of the company. Bert wondered if this was a subtle plan to work with the least experienced members of the cast without the embarrassment of more experienced observers. His estimation of Logan as a director was rising with each minute of the evening.

It was quite a relief to move into the lower key of the domestic scene for Polonius and his son and daughter. During the opening speeches, Bert was comforted to hear in their voices that Becky Clegg and Jack Dawes were almost as nervous as he was. But Terry Logan stopped them and explained the more light-hearted nature of this scene, encouraging them to relax. Bert realized as the scene proceeded that these two young people who were playing his children were good, both together and individually.

Their youth sparkled, and they began to enjoy their humorous but tender mocking of their parent. It was almost like having an older version of his two sons at home, having fun at the expense of their out-of-date old dad; some things did not change very much over four hundred years. He'd have to be on his toes, to keep up with Becky and Jack. Their developing confidence reminded him again that both of them had been on stage before. Whether it was from natural talent, or previous experience, or a combination of the two, they knew what they were about.

When their director told them that that was enough for the evening, Bert was amazed to see that three hours had passed. Terry Logan said that he'd just like a word with Jack Dawes, which wouldn't take long. The other two could go.

For a moment, Becky Clegg looked from the director to the young man who had starred for him in a school production five years ago, wondering what this could be about. Then she turned abruptly and went out of the village hall with Bert Hook. She chatted happily enough, not feeling the cold, gazing up at the clear navy sky, still full of the joy and excitement of their successful rehearsal. Bert understood her animation: he felt that it would take even a staid middle-aged man like himself some time to wind down.

When he could get a word in, Bert said awkwardly, 'Do you want a lift home? I go quite near to where you live, I think.'

'No thanks, I'll wait for Jack Dawes. I came with him on his motorbike, you see. And Terry Logan said he wouldn't be long, didn't he?'

Bert Hook went away smiling. As he pressed his remote control to unlock the doors of his Ford Focus, Becky Clegg took a step or two after him. Then she called tentatively through the darkness, 'I got that job, by the way. Thanks for everything.'

Chris Rushton spent the last twenty minutes of the film wondering what he should do afterwards. He was still old-fashioned enough to wonder what was expected of him rather than to plan how to achieve exactly what he wanted to do. For a handsome young man who had made Detective Inspector by the age of thirty, he was in many ways an anomaly. But his modesty and uncertainty were precisely what had attracted Anne Jackson to him.

She chatted about the film as they walked arm-in-arm towards his car. 'I knew it wasn't going to work for them after the first half an hour.'

'Did you? I was hoping they'd come through everything and make it together by the final scene.'

Anne smiled and squeezed his hand. 'You're a sucker for the old Hollywood happy ending, Chris Rushton! You're a sentimentalist at heart.' She sounded quite happy with the idea.

'I suppose I am.' Without realizing that he was going to do it, he suddenly turned her towards him and kissed her. She was taken by surprise, but she responded strongly, until they both emerged breathless and a little shocked by the strength of their feelings.

'Well!' was all she said. He didn't think he had ever heard such a variety of pleasurable emotions compressed into one syllable. He giggled, and surprised them both anew. Chris Rushton was not a natural giggler.

He kissed her again and more predictably when they were in the car. She said into his ear, 'I'd better get back. I've got thirty eight-year-olds to face first thing in the morning.' But she sounded reluctant, so Chris didn't mind. He was getting quite used to the delicious idea that Anne Jackson was really rather fond of him. He kissed her again before she got out of the car and hurried into her digs. She waved to him shyly from the doorway after she had turned her key in the lock.

It was only when she had gone and he was basking in a joyous moment of self-content that he realized that he had never mentioned his golfing scheme to her.

Terence Logan was pleased with the way the rehearsal had gone. The central heating had switched itself off half an hour ago, but still he sat in the village hall, digesting the experience of the evening, adding yet another reminder to himself at the end of the copious notes he had made for future reference.

An excellent start. He had always known that Carey was going to scintillate, but that didn't dilute his exultation over the man's performance this evening. He could see how impressed the others had been, how this central figure was eventually going to raise the standard of all the people around him. Whatever his personal difficulties with Michael Carey, he was certainly a man on whom you could centre a production. He had looks as well as a formidable stage presence, and he understood the subtleties of this most complex of plays. Terry knew that it was part of a director's brief to cut out any personal problems he had with his cast. Well, this director had always been good at doing that.

He went through the other people who had been there tonight and found that he was giving mental ticks to all of them. They would need licking into shape, but he was confident he could do that; he knew when to offer the carrot and when the stick to the people in his productions. The ones he had been confident about were going to be as good as he had hoped: the ones about whom he had had reservations all had the potential to be good, perhaps even very good. The exchange he'd had with Dawes, after the others had left, could only improve his performance over the next couple of weeks. Perhaps he'd compare notes with the girl and spur her on as well. He was glad he'd kept tabs on the two of them over the last few years. Good research was never wasted.

He felt the first shiver of cold, and noticed for the first time

quite how late it was. Reluctantly, for he was loath to frac-
ture the feeling of well-being which had suffused him by the
end of the rehearsal, he shut the folder on his notes and picked
up his clipboard. The evening could hardly have gone better,
he told himself again, as he took a last look at the deserted
stage before switching off the lights and making sure the door
locked securely as he pulled it to behind him.

It was very dark outside after the brilliance of the interior.
Most of the sky was clear of cloud, but there was no moon
visible tonight. As his eyes gradually adjusted, he perceived
the dark outline of his Mercedes at the end of the car park,
the only vehicle now left in the area.

Terry Logan glanced away to the west, where he would
normally have glimpsed the local landmark of May Hill, with
its copse of firs at the top. It wasn't high, but you could see
it from many miles around and it was a much-loved local
landmark. Terry remembered an octogenarian telling him of
how when he came home from Hitler's war half a century
earlier, May Hill had been the beacon which told him that he
was home and all was well with a battered but defiant Britain
and with his Gloucestershire world.

Tonight, although he knew exactly where the hill lay, he
could not see it.

The car park was unpaved. He picked his way carefully
across its uneven surface in the darkness. Ten yards from his
car, he pressed his key pad to open the doors, and the sudden
flashes of orange illumination seemed unnaturally brilliant in
the prevailing darkness, showing him exactly where he should
place his feet for the last few steps to the driver's door.

He had his hand on the handle before he heard the first soft
footstep behind him. He was turning his head when he felt
the steel blade of a knife against his throat. The human brain
works with amazing speed under pressure. Terry Logan's brain
told him in the same split second in which it registered the
arrival of the blade that he was going to die.

Then, as the knife slashed swiftly across his throat, his brain
ceased to function even as it registered the final swift agony
of death.

Nine

B ert Hook took his time over his morning shave. He was happy to have the bathroom to himself, with the door safely locked for a few minutes. It would give him time to prepare for the inevitable banter of his family at breakfast and his colleagues at the station. This was an aspect of amateur dramatics which he had not anticipated amongst his other trepidations.

It was scarcely eight o'clock when the phone rang. 'It's John Lambert for you,' said Eleanor from the kitchen. 'I expect he wants to hear about your triumph at the rehearsal last night.'

Bert smiled his most elaborately tolerant smile and went to the phone. His expression changed very quickly. Lambert was as usual terse and informative. 'We have a suspicious death, Bert. I haven't seen the stiff yet, but from what I hear this sounds like murder.'

'Where and when?' The two automatic initial questions. How would be the next one, but that could wait until they had the corpse in front of them. Why would come much later.

'In the car park behind the village hall in Mettlesham. I've no idea yet exactly when – some time last night.' Chief Superintendent Lambert stopped, uncharacteristically hesitant about how to communicate the next piece of information to his old friend and colleague.

'I was out there myself last night. It was our first proper rehearsal for *Hamlet*.'

'I know you were. I'm afraid it seems likely that the deceased is one of your colleagues at that rehearsal.'

Hook's mind flew first, for some reason he did not care to analyse, to Mrs Dalrymple. Surely that majestic voice which had first dictated to him that he should involve himself with the Players had not been stilled forever? Then he thought it must probably be their enigmatic star, that handsome, gifted loner who he was sure had the capacity to infuriate many people. These thoughts took him no more than two seconds, at the end of which he was telling himself that such speculation was entirely inappropriate for a man who called himself a detective. But he heard the tremor in his voice as he asked, 'Do we know yet who the victim is?'

Lambert noticed that his sergeant had already accepted his suggestion that this was murder. 'It's a man called Terry Logan. I'm not sure exactly what part he was playing in your *Hamlet*.'

Bert tried to control his shock. He had never had a personal involvement as close as this in a serious crime. He said woodenly, 'Terry Logan wasn't going to be on stage. He was directing the whole thing.' And now he was going to be the central figure in a wholly different real-life drama.

'You knew him.'

'Not well.'

'Well enough to have any idea who did this?'

'No. I don't know much more about his background than you do. He lives – lived – in a beautiful old manor house.' Bert heard himself make the mistake in tenses which he had so often heard the newly bereaved make in shock. 'Terry Logan had private money, I believe. He worked in a school, but I don't think his income from there was very important to him. He'd directed plays in school, as well as amateur dramatics outside it, for many years. He was very experienced in all of that. That's about all I know.'

At the other end of the phone, Lambert was smiling. 'That's quite a lot, for a man who knew no more about him than I did.'

'We'll need to check it out. I'm not sure where I got it from – most of it was probably just hearsay.'

'It's more than we usually know at this stage. I'll meet you in that car park in half an hour, if you can make that.'

'I'll be there.'

Bert Hook put down the phone and went back to an immediately sobered breakfast table. He hadn't known Logan well, but he'd been to his house and drunk his drink. The man had been full of life and his plans for it.

Bert Hook was feeling the kind of shock he often had to cope with in the relatives and friends of victims.

* * *

Becky Clegg was eating her cereal in an unwonted, hostile silence. Since she had announced last night that she was leaving this squalid flat, her two companions had scarcely spoken to her. More than that, they had rejected her sporadic attempts at conversation. Her male companion had rebuffed her with mono-syllabic grunts, whilst the female one had not deigned to reply at all, but had walked over and turned up the volume on the battered little radio by the sink.

The radio was tuned to their local station, Gloucester Radio. The music was raucous and the fact that the set was not accu-rately tuned made the sound excruciating even to their young ears, but none of them went over to adjust the tuning or turn down the volume. In the complex code of their adoles-cent tensions, that would somehow have meant a loss of face.

The announcer had that chatty, falsely cheerful voice which local radio seems to think is the appropriate way to thrust you into the trials of a new day. She gave the silent trio at the battered table the benefit of her opinions and reactions on a variety of trivia. Then her voice dropped into the deeper and more portentous tones which Becky remembered national radio using to convey the news of Princess Diana's death when she had been a schoolgirl.

The presenter intoned, 'We have some disturbing late news. Police have just announced the discovery of the body of a middle-aged man in the car park behind the village hall in Mettlesham, near Ross-on-Wye. It is understood that the man, who has not been named, was suffering from knife wounds. The police are treating the death as suspicious and anyone with any information is asked to get in touch with the CID section at Oldford Police Station immediately.'

She gave them a number to ring, but the trio who had avoided each other's eyes for twenty minutes were looking at each other long before the last digit was pronounced. The girl broke her self imposed silence. She said with undisguised relish, 'Mettlesham Village Hall. That's where you were last night, Becky Clegg.'

The girl had used her full name, as the teacher had been used to do years ago when you were in trouble at primary school. Becky stared not at her but at the spoon she had suddenly dropped into her cereal bowl. 'It's Terence Logan.' She hadn't known she was going to say anything at all: the words sounded in her ears as if they were coming from someone else.

The boy who had been about to leave the room stared at her bowed head. 'And how would you know that?'

'I don't. But that's who it will be. You'll see.'

'He's right. How could you know that?' This time it was the girl, coming in right on the heel of Becky's words.

Becky didn't reply to that. She said dully, 'He was going to be our director in this play.'

'So who killed him?'

'How would I know?'

'You seem to know who's been killed before it's been announced. You might know who did it.' The girl was enjoying this. 'You didn't do it yourself, did you?'

'Of course I didn't.' For the first time, she registered the malevolence of the girl on the other side of the table. 'We had a rehearsal. We had notes on the rehearsal from the director. We came home. All right?'

'If you say so. Not me you've got to convince though, is it?' The girl's small eyes narrowed in amused hostility at the thought. 'The police will be wanting words with you. And this time you might not get the soft tosser you got last week. And you can't expect support from us, now that you've decided we're not good enough for you. That right, Wayne?'

The boy looked from one to the other of the women in the room, then nodded weakly. His will was no match for that of this virago.

Becky said, 'I might be wrong. They only said a body in the car park. It might be nothing to do with us.' Yet the uncertainty in her voice said that she was certain that it was.

Her rejected flatmate picked up this weak shot and volleyed it back across the net with delight. 'It will be. And the police will have you in for questioning before long.' She nodded in happy anticipation.

Becky thrust her arms resolutely into the sleeves of her coat, took a deep breath, and said briskly, 'I must be off to work. Can't be late at this stage of my career, whatever's going on in the rest of the world!'

The girl had been planning some caustic remark about the desertion of her friends, but now she had better weapons at her disposal. She gathered herself for her final thrust. 'I wouldn't like to be in your position, Becky Clegg. Not if I had your record with knives!'

Hook turned his Focus carefully into the car park behind Lambert's old Vauxhall Senator. They filled the last two spaces of a parking area which was now cut down to half its normal size by the blue and white ribbons which formed a rough rectangle around the crime scene.

The SOCO officer was a civilian, but he knew this duo well enough. 'A man walking his dog when it was barely daylight found the body this morning. We had the police surgeon out here at seven-thirty, just to confirm death. Bit of a waste of time, as our man was as cold as ice. The pathologist arrived about ten minutes ago. He might be able to tell you a little more.'

They donned the paper overalls, slid the plastic coverings over their shoes, and picked their way down the three-feet-wide strip which had been designated as the entry for all personnel into the central area of the crime scene. As they passed between the screens which had been erected to give the corpse its final privacy from the vulgar gaze of a curious public, Bert Hook halted involuntarily in shock.

It was true enough, what people said. However many bodies you had seen, it was different when you knew the deceased. And this death was pretty dramatic, he told himself, as he swallowed hard and followed his chief forward.

Terry Logan lay sprawled upon his back beside his Mercedes, so close to it that the palm of his outstretched left hand was underneath the body of the car, near to the driver's door. His throat had a deep cut which ran almost from ear to ear. His expensive light blue leisure shirt was now crimson-brown for most of its length, with the blood from the wound. His eyes were open, staring at a new day they would never see. The features were not rigid with horror; they had relaxed into an inappropriate surprised smile.

Lambert stood impassively above the body and stared down into these unrevealing features, wishing for the umpteenth time in his career that the old myth about the eyeballs retaining an impression of their killer had any truth in it. But that would have made life far too easy for detectives. He said grimly, 'I suppose this is Logan, is it, Bert?'

'It's him all right,' said Hook, still trying to recover his normal equanimity. He said stupidly to the pathologist, 'He's lost an awful lot of blood.'

'Less than it looks, really,' said the man whose business it was to handle human remains. Like many of his kind, he seemed quite cheerful, as if treating such things as everyday occurrences was part of his professional patina. 'He'd have lost a lot more blood from a wound like this, if death hadn't been instantaneous. This man died within a second or two of being attacked.'

'When?'

'Several hours ago, at least: he's quite cold.' He looked down calmly at the awful, gashed throat. 'Probably late last night or early this morning – some time around midnight. The stomach contents may give a little more guidance, but only if you can establish when he last ate.'

'Did he put up a fight?'

The pathologist was about to say that he couldn't give an opinion about that after a cursory on-site examination. Then he glanced at Lambert's intense, concentrated face. 'My guess at this stage would be that he didn't have the chance to do that. I'll need to have him on the slab to see if there is suggestive bruising or any traces of skin under the nails. There's nothing visible here. I'd say it's probable that he was taken from behind by surprise and killed before he could offer any real resistance.'

'Or that he knew his assailant and wasn't expecting to be killed.'

The small man with the neatly trimmed red beard considered this. 'That's more your field than mine. It's a possibility, but I'd have expected the victim at least to get his hands up and take some damage on them if he was facing his attacker, even if someone pulled a knife on him when he wasn't expecting it. The surprise attack from behind seems more probable to me.'

'Will the assailant have blood on his clothes?'

Criminals are always "he" initially, a concession to statistical probability.

The pathologist gave the matter a little thought, lifting his hand to touch his beard in a mannerism Lambert remembered from previous encounters with him in the Home Office Laboratory at Chepstow. 'Impossible to say for certain. The blood from a wound like this would certainly spurt. If he was killed as I suspect he was, it would probably have wet the killer's sleeve. But it's possible it didn't touch him at all: he might have had just a little on his hands, which could be easily washed away. Sorry.'

Lambert answered his wry smile, recognizing that they were two professionals applying very different skills in the pursuit of the same goal. 'I suppose we're right to assume this was a male.'

The pathologist shook his head. 'Can't even help you there, I'm afraid. You know better than I do that a huge majority of knife crimes are perpetrated by males. But there's no reason why this killing shouldn't have been inflicted by a woman, once you accept the element of surprise. He's not a tall man, and with the sharp blade which was used here, no great physical strength was needed.'

Hook found himself wanting to contribute something to the discussion to show that he was not still in shock. He said dully, 'More and more women and girls have begun to carry knives over the last two years. Becky Clegg, the girl who was playing Ophelia, has assault with a knife on her record. Two years ago, I think.'

There was the sound of another vehicle arriving, then of an engine changing into reverse as it manoeuvred as close as possible to the screens. The pathologist glanced towards the roof of the van and said, 'The meat wagon's arrived. I'll get him on the table as soon as I can and see what else I can find that's going to be useful to you. Don't hold your breaths. I've a totally unscientific gut feeling that I'm not going to find a lot more on this one that will be helpful to you.'

As the photographer took a last shot of the body where it lay, he went back to his car, nodding a greeting to the driver of the van and his companion, as they brought in the plastic body shell and prepared to load the remains into the back of the van.

Lambert went back to the SOCO officer, watching the two men who were combing the site on hands and knees, laboriously gathering anything with tweezers which might have a possible bearing on this crime. There is a well-documented theory that there is always an "exchange" between criminal and victim at the scene of a crime, that however careful the criminal might be, he will leave behind some evidence of his presence at the spot. Apart from assisting detection, the evidence gathered by the SOCO team is often instrumental in

preparing a case for the Crown Prosecution Service to take
to court.

'Had he been robbed?' Lambert asked without much hope.
A mugging which had gone wrong, a thief panicking and
killing in the face of unexpected resistance, would be a much
easier crime to solve than one with more complex motives.

The civilian officer shook his head. 'His wallet's still intact.
Credit cards untouched, as far as I can see. We can't be
absolutely sure of this, but I doubt if his pockets have even
been searched. What is almost certainly his house key is still
in his trouser pocket. And his car keys were on the ground
beside him: the most valuable thing around here is that
Mercedes, but no one attempted to drive it away.'

In spite of his carapace of professional calm, the SOCO
chief was animated and involved. He hadn't been in charge
of things very long. After a series of squalid minor crimes,
investigating seedy flats and alleys smelling of urine, this was
his first murder. He didn't want to get anything wrong, to
miss even the slightest, most innocent-looking clue.

He knew he had one unusual thing to report to the revered
Chief Superintendent Lambert, and he couldn't quite keep the
excitement out of his voice as he said, 'We found just one
thing we wouldn't have expected to find. It was in the right-
hand pocket of his jacket.'

'And what was that?'

The SOCO chief led them across to the little portable table
which he had set up to receive the gatherings from the area of
the death. He pointed to the central item in its carefully sealed
plastic bag, trying not to feel like a conjurer completing a trick.

The small Beretta pistol looked almost like a toy or a stage
prop in a more modern production than *Hamlet*. As if to assure
them that it was something more genuine and dangerous,
the SOCO man said softly, 'It's loaded. It hasn't been fired.'
He looked across to the point where the legs of the corpse
were disappearing without much dignity into the van. 'Probably
the poor bugger never had a chance to use it.'

'But it does mean that he was probably expecting trouble,'
said Lambert.

Ten

Andrew Dalrymple opened the wide oak door at the top of the three stone steps. The detached Edwardian house with the Virginia creeper clothing its walls was one of the tangible proofs of his success as a businessman. Normally he enjoyed strolling through its high rooms and corridors, but today was different. He looked down at the two CID men below him. His gaze was not welcoming.

Andrew had heard of this man Lambert, who was something of a local legend, but he'd never seen him before. He couldn't have said what his image of a successful detective was, but this wasn't it. He decided that he'd been expecting someone shorter and more powerful, and certainly squatter of feature and less intelligent-looking. The man who now introduced himself as Chief Superintendent Lambert was tall and slim, with a long, lined face and grey eyes which seemed to see more than you wanted to offer him. He seemed to be already assessing Dalrymple, who wasn't even the person he had come here to see.

Andrew turned his attention to the shorter, less threatening figure whom his chief designated as Detective Sergeant Hook. He managed to give this man with the weather-beaten outdoor face a smile before he said, 'Maggie already knows you, doesn't she?'

'Mrs Dalrymple was the one who got me involved in the play,' said Bert Hook. He had meant this merely as an explanation, but it had emerged sounding rather like a complaint.

'Yes.' Andrew smiled again, more genuinely this time. 'Maggie's a bit of an organizer, isn't she? And she's a habit of getting her own way. But she was pleased she'd got you involved. She said you were going to be good.'

Lambert said impatiently, 'We need to see Mrs Dalrymple, as DS Hook explained on the phone.'

'She's not fit to see anyone. She's – well, as you'd expect, she's shocked and upset at the moment.'

Hook said, 'Everyone involved in the play will be shocked and upset by what happened to Terry Logan last night, Mr Dalrymple. Nevertheless, we need to speak to your wife now, whilst anything from last night which may be relevant remains fresh in her mind.'

Andrew Dalrymple gave Hook a look of distrust. He said firmly, 'You'll have to come back again. Perhaps this evening, perhaps tomorrow. I'll let you know later today when you can—'

He stopped at the sound of a door opening in the hall behind him. Margaret Dalrymple came forward and spoke with a quietness which was unusual for her. 'It's all right, Andrew, I'll see them now. They have a job to do. Just the same as you have a business to run.'

It sounded like an appeal for him to be on his way out of the house, but he said stubbornly, 'If you're going to insist on being brave, I'm going to insist on staying with you for this meeting.'

She shrugged, as if she hadn't the strength or the will to argue further, or to overrule him with her usual forcefulness. She turned away and led them through the first door off the hall and into a front room which was obviously used as a dining room. There she invited them to sit down. They pulled out upright chairs and sat down facing her across the antique mahogany table. After a moment's hesitation, her husband sat down awkwardly beside her.

She jutted her jaw at her visitors and said with a suggestion of her normal assertiveness, 'I shan't be able to help you, but fire away with your questions. I understand why you're here. I know a little about the law and the way you operate. I realize that you have to follow your usual procedures and go through the formalities of questioning me.'

Lambert let that pass. 'How long had you known Mr Logan?'

A quick, instinctive glance between the two people opposite him. Then Margaret Dalrymple looked back at him with a slightly guilty air. 'A long time. Fifteen to twenty years, I suppose. You must understand that I'm very much involved in local affairs. I'm a JP and a parish councillor, and have chaired various committees. I come across a lot of people.

Most of them I don't know very well.' She stopped abruptly, seemingly aware that she was talking too much in answer to a simple opening question.

'Mrs Dalrymple, can you—?'

'Call me Maggie. Everyone else seems to. I'll feel easier if you do. DS Hook already knows me as Maggie from the play. And I've got used to calling him Bert.' Her little, uncharacteristic giggle emphasized how nervous she was. She gave another involuntary glance at her husband.

Lambert relaxed his own intensity with a small answering smile. 'How did you meet Mr Logan?'

'Let me see. I was on his school governing body, many years ago. I came across him because of the plays he produced there. He was excellent at drawing good work from children, you know.'

Bert Hook said, 'He was a good director in any context, I should think. I appreciated that much, even from my very limited experience with him. Was it you who recruited him for the Mettlesham Players?'

'No.' The negative came too promptly and too vehemently on the heels of his question. 'I don't know who did that. It might have been anyone concerned with the group. Terry was, as you say, Bert, a very talented man. He acted quite a bit in his early days with the Players, and he was very good. But I think we all realized that his greatest talent was for direction, and we were always happy to persuade him to exercise it. In amateur dramatics, a lot of people want to be on stage; there are not many people who are both able and willing to direct productions.'

Her husband reached across and put his hand briefly on top of hers; he seemed to be trying to stop her saying too much for it to seem like a natural reaction to a simple question. She was plainly in shock; she stared down at his hand as if she could not fathom how it had come to be there. They could see by the hollowness of her eyes and the swelling of her cheeks that she had been crying.

'You were clearly very fond of Mr Logan,' Lambert said.

She looked up at him as if that were an accusation. 'We had known each other a long time. When you work as a team in the theatre, it brings you very close. His death is a great shock to me.'

Lambert studied her for a moment, in the dispassionate, objective way which people always found disconcerting. 'It must have been a great shock to everyone who was at Mettlesham Village Hall last night. Except for one person. Or perhaps two, if we decide that this killing was a joint crime.'

'I can't believe that it was one of us who did this.' Her voice faltered a little.

Hook could scarcely recognize in this suffering woman the dominant middle-class female whom he had found so intimidating as she had dragooned him into *Hamlet*.

Lambert said, 'It's theoretically possible that the killer could be someone outside that group, but a random killing does not seem likely. Nothing seems to have been removed from the body, so we can rule out theft as a motive.'

Andrew Dalrymple resisted the temptation to look at his wife. 'Logan was a man with many enemies. You shouldn't just assume that it was one of the people involved in the play. Someone else could have known that he was going to be in the village hall and waited for his opportunity.'

Lambert did not take his eyes off the woman beside him. 'Would you agree with that, Mrs Dalrymple?'

She glanced from one to the other of the detectives, and Hook thought for a moment that she was going to insist again on being addressed as Maggie. Then she dropped her eyes to the table and said, 'Andrew's right. Of course he is. Terry was a very talented man, but he went his own way. I'm sure he made enemies along that way.'

Lambert knew that silence could only work in his favour with a woman as much on edge as this one. He allowed several seconds to stretch out before he spoke again. 'Indeed. And of the people who were with you last night, which ones do you think hated him enough to kill him?'

Andrew Dalrymple was about to intervene again, but she raised her hand no more than three inches, in a strangely moving and compelling gesture which all of their eyes followed. 'That's an impossible question, Mr Lambert. I scarcely know some of the people there.'

'You know more than I do, Maggie.' For the first time, he used the name she had asked him to use. 'One of the problems with murder is that the victim can never speak for himself. We are left to build up a picture of his life and his relationships

with the people around him through the statements of those
who are left. You have told us that you had known this victim
for many years. We are asking you to help us to construct the
picture we need to have.'

'I understand that. But I am as shocked by this death as
anyone. I can't think straight at the moment. It seems inconceivable that anyone who was in that hall last night could
have been planning to kill Terry.'

'It didn't seem so unlikely to Mr Logan. We think he knew
that his life was in danger.'

She stared straight at him, her brown eyes widening in
horrified speculation. 'What do you mean?'

'He was carrying a loaded pistol in his jacket pocket. Unless
someone convinces us that he was planning aggression towards
someone else, we must presume that he felt that he might
need to defend himself.'

She stared at him for so long that he thought she was not
going to react. Then she said, 'How did he die?'

It was a question which the innocent should have asked
much earlier in the interview. He watched her closely as he
said, 'His throat was cut. It appears that he was probably taken
by surprise from behind. The pathologist tells us that his
assailant could have been a man or a woman.'

She looked as if she had been struck in the face. Lambert
remembered how Hook had told him on the way here that she
had surprised him by her competence as an actress. He had
no means of knowing whether she was exercising that talent
now. She dropped her eyes to the table again, said only, 'Poor
Terry!' in a voice that they could scarcely hear.

Hook, who had his notebook at the ready, said apologetically, 'We need an account of your own movements last night,
Maggie.'

An outraged Andrew Dalrymple was about to intervene, but
she stilled him again by that oddly effective minimal raising
of the back of her hand. 'We rehearsed the opening court
scene in *Hamlet*, in which all of the people there were involved.
Then Terry gave us some notes and dismissed all of his cast
except Polonius, Laertes and Ophelia. That is to say, yourself
and Becky Clegg and Jack Dawes. I went out and drove away.
I was home before ten o'clock.'

It was delivered in a flat monotone. Almost as if it had been carefully prepared before they arrived, thought Hook. But this was plainly a woman in shock – though he supposed you might well be suffering from the aftershock if you had committed a premeditated murder ten hours or so earlier.

Andrew Dalrymple spoke a little too hastily. 'I can confirm that. It means, of course, that my wife was nowhere near the scene of this crime at the time when it happened.'

Lambert said dryly, 'We do not have a precise time for this death as yet. But I take your point. We shall probably need to speak to both of you again at a later stage of our investigation. In the meantime, I remind you that if you should recall anything which might have a bearing upon this killing, it is your duty to inform us of it immediately.'

Maggie Dalrymple allowed her husband to leave her at the table as he saw them out of the house. He shut the door of the dining room carefully behind him and led them to the front door. 'Logan was a man with a lot of enemies,' he insisted again. 'You're going to have a wide field for this crime.'

He watched the CID men as they got into their car, then remained standing on the doorstep for a full minute until he saw it disappearing round a bend in the lane four hundred yards away and was assured that they had gone. Then he went slowly back into the dining room and found that his wife had not moved. She was staring fixedly at the table and looking quite exhausted.

He spoke awkwardly, for he was not used to being the dominant one in this home. 'I could use a drink, but I suppose it's a bit early in the day for that. If you go into the sitting room, I'll make us a coffee and bring it through.'

Still she did not move. Eventually he went over and stood behind her, putting his hands on her shoulders. She remained motionless, not even reacting to his touch.

He was wondering what to do next when she said, 'You don't know what time I came in from the rehearsal last night. You weren't here when I got home.'

Eleven

'The identity of the man found dead in rural Gloucestershire last night has now been released. He was Terry Logan, a schoolteacher and a leading figure in local amateur dramatics. We understand that he was directing rehearsals for a production by the Mettlesham Players at the time of his death. Police are treating the death as suspicious.'

Sally Dawes left the radio on, but there wasn't any other reference to the death. She stared at the battered black set as if it were a live thing, deliberately choosing to hold information from her. Jack had been out at Mettlesham last night. And she didn't know when he had come home. It must have been after she'd gone to bed and gone to sleep. When was that? She ran a hand through her peroxided hair, feeling it stiff against her fingers, pressing her knuckles into the scalp beneath. She couldn't be sure of times: she'd had a few drinks last night – surprise, surprise!

She heard the front door slamming hard and went back to her magazine. Jack came in, looked hard at the radio, then at his mother. 'You don't usually listen to Radio Four. Trying to educate yourself, are you?'

She didn't want his cruel mood. Not the sneering and the insults about the life she led. Not today: she hadn't the strength to fight with him today. She said to him as though it were an accusation, 'It's made the national news now, Logan's death. Foul play is suspected.'

Sally didn't know why she used that official, legal, old-fashioned phrase. It was probably because of the nightmare of speculation in which she had lived her morning. Her son had gone out as soon as they'd heard it on the local radio, without even finishing his toast. Early for Jack, it had been: he was usually still in bed at that time. He hadn't wanted to be with her, to talk with her about the news. Now, three hours later, he was back, and he was in one of those excited, reckless moods which she feared most.

'You must be glad Logan's dead,' he said. 'You'd have killed him yourself, at one time, if you'd thought you could have got away with it.'

She didn't want to talk about that. There was something vicious in his tone. She wanted only to be assured that the odd, dangerous young man whom she loved was not involved in this death. After the welter of different emotions which had beset her during the morning, she now felt bewilderment descending upon her. Sometimes she felt she didn't even want to love Jack, really, yet she knew that she did.

Not for the first time, Sally Dawes found the mysteries of motherhood beyond her. Feeling the words dragged from her against her inclination, she said, 'You were out there yourself last night. In Mettlesham.'

'Yes. Joining the cast in a Shakespeare play. Making the kinds of contacts my dear mother thought were appropriate for me.' He made it into an accusation, enjoyed watching the hurt it brought to that pretty, vacuous face which was running so fast into middle age.

'They obviously think Logan was murdered.'

'They? Oh, the police, I expect you mean. Well, they often do, when a man's found with his throat cut from ear to ear and no knife in his hand. Even the pigs begin to suspect things, when they come upon something like that.'

Her blue eyes widened in horror. She wanted to turn them upon her son, to see innocence proclaiming itself in his thin, astute, handsome face. But she could not do it. She stared at the worn patch in the carpet for two, three, four long seconds. Her voice was scarcely more than a whisper as she said, 'There's been nothing on the radio about the way he died. I've been listening all morning.'

'Yes, I expect you have. That's what I'd have expected. You're very predictable.'

'Is that how he died?'

'Ask no questions and you'll be told no lies.' He swept across the room to where she sat at the table and brushed his thumb playfully across her nose. 'Cor, it's hot in here, Mum. You should open a window and let in some fresh air!' He busied himself with freeing the rickety catch on the dusty wooden window frame.

She looked at his muscular back and the black hair at the nape of his neck and forced out the words she did not want to voice. 'Jack, how do you know the way he died, when there's been nothing to tell you about it on the radio or the television?'

He whirled on her, and she flinched at the suddenness of his movement. Then he controlled himself, smiled, looked at her with the affection which was another part of his complex make-up. It was important to him that he should convince her of this. He tapped the side of his nose, preparing the clichés he needed, and said, 'Wheels within wheels, Mum. I have my contacts. You get to know things on the grapevine, when you move in the circles I do.'

She looked at him, wanting to be convinced, responding automatically to the cheeky, boyish grin he had fixed upon his face. It was a little while before she said weakly, 'You'd tell me, wouldn't you, if there was anything wrong? I've not been a good mother to you, but it's not always been easy, with being on my own, and—'

'You've been the best.' He took into his arms the body which was running a little to seed, which men like him must once have found so desirable, and he was suddenly full of an uncomplicated love for her, alongside the guilt for himself and the things he did to her.

It was one of those moments when he was surprised by tenderness, and as usual it did not last long. He said roughly, 'You won't be bothered by Logan again. He's wiped from the face of the earth!' He could feel her body stiffening beneath his hands with each word he spoke.

She pulled herself away from him, looking up anxiously into the sharp, unlined features which she knew so well and could read so little. 'You didn't kill him, did you, Jack?'

He grinned down at her, that wolfish, alien grin which had come between them in the last year or two. For a moment, she feared that he was going to tell her again that she should ask no questions and be told no lies. But he looked down into the dark roots of the blonde hair and the anxious, vapid, loving face and was beset with pity as sharp as a physical pain.

He knew that he must reassure her, that that was partly what he had come back to the house to do. He had lost that urge, as the febrile excitement and the desire to taunt and hurt her had taken him over. He said as firmly as he could, 'No,

I didn't kill him, Mum. Don't you worry your pretty little head about that!' Then he ran his hand through the dry yellow hair, bending her head so that she could not look at him, and tried to make a joke of the preposterous idea.

It was nearly one o'clock. He stayed to eat with her, trying to calm himself and think clearly. She bisected a pork pie from the fridge and put tomatoes with it. She cut several thin slices from the good loaf she had got from the bakery on the previous evening and spread them with butter. Then she watched him eat, trying to get the pleasure from it which she had derived from seeing him feed well when he was an infant. She wasn't hungry herself, though she forced a little down to try to keep up with him. She couldn't eat all of her pork pie and he took it eagerly when she offered it, clearing his plate with that swift, animal speed which he always had when he was excited by life outside this house.

He downed his mug of tea at the end of it, then said, 'That was good, Mum. You know how to keep a lad happy!'

But despite the phrasing, it was the ritual, automatic thanks of a stranger, and she knew it. In spite of her knowledge of how he would react, she found herself saying, 'You should keep up with your better friends and get rid of the bad ones, Jack. I only want the best for you.'

As always, he shied away from her pleading. 'I have to be off now. I shouldn't have stayed as long as this.'

Sally wanted to ask him where he was going, but she knew that it would be a mistake, that he would only shut her even further out. 'I want you to get a proper job,' she said weakly, 'the way we said. You're a bright boy, Jack, and I don't like seeing others leaving you behind.'

'You don't mind seeing Terry Logan lying dead, though, do you?' His laugh was a harsh, alien sound in her ears. 'I bet you've been listening to the news all morning. Can't get enough of it, can you, the thought of him being out of your life?' His eyes glittered with a febrile passion.

She was frightened again by his aggression and his excitement. She said quietly, trying to calm him, 'Logan was out of my life a long time ago, Jack.'

Jack Dawes was annoyed by that. She should have been more grateful to him for the sentiment. But he needed her. He forced himself to be calm, to bathe her again in that affectionate smile he knew she could not resist. He gripped her shoulders, kneading the soft flesh at the top of her arms with his strong fingers. 'Just in case the cops ask you, I was in here by eleven o'clock last night. A boy's best friend is his mum, eh?'

Ian Proudfoot led the two big men into the manager's office. 'We'll be private in here,' he said. 'It's one of the few perks of being a branch manager – there don't seem to be many others left nowadays.' He heard the little laugh with which he followed that complaint, and knew in that moment that he was very nervous.

Lambert went quickly through the formalities of introducing himself, then turned to Bert. 'I believe that you already know Detective Sergeant Hook.'

'Bert and I have already suffered together on the boards, yes!' He checked his smile as he remembered why they were here. 'Though I don't know whether the production will proceed, now that we lack a director.'

'I should have thought it unlikely, with a murderer hiding himself in the cast,' said Lambert acerbically.

'I can't get my head round that one, as the youngsters say.' Ian Proudfoot glanced at the twelve-year-old photograph of himself and his children which he kept on his desk and thought how quickly the years had passed, how quickly he had aged. 'It seems inconceivable to me that anyone who was rehearsing *Hamlet* in that village hall last night could have committed murder. We seemed to be a happy bunch. And it was such a good start to the most exciting project most of us have ever had the chance to put on stage.'

This man seemed more concerned with the loss of his dream than with brutal murder. But Lambert did not show his irritation. 'How long had you known Terry Logan?'

'Terry and I go back quite a long way. It's difficult to be certain how far.'

'Try.'

Ian felt the hostility in this quiet, watchful man. He was used to being in control in his own office, but this tall man with the intense grey eyes and the absence of any polite small talk seemed to have taken it over. 'I suppose it must be twenty years since I first met Terry.'

'Tell us precisely where and when, please.'

He knew the exact answers to both those questions. But he wasn't going to be too accurate: it would argue an unhealthy preoccupation with the man and his movements. 'It was probably in amateur dramatics. We were both of us great enthusiasts. I think Terry had been in the professional theatre for a couple of years in his youth.' Ian tried not to sound jealous of that. 'He had private means, of course. He could afford to take chances with his life.'

'Which you couldn't?'

'Oh, I never really considered trying to become a professional.' A lie, and a clumsy and a needless one; he was losing the calm he had been determined to keep. 'I was planning marriage and a career in banking at the time when Terry was indulging himself with a venture into rep. And shortly after that, I had a young family to think about. In any case, I'm sure that I wouldn't have been good enough to be a professional.'

The lightness of his tone was a little forced and Hook was an expert on tones after thirty years of questioning people. 'So, united by this common interest in the stage, you became good friends with Terry Logan.'

'No!' He knew that the monosyllable was too loud and too insistent, but it was out before he knew it was coming. 'I had family concerns, as you know. My wife has never been as enthusiastic about amateur dramatics as I am.' *That's a whopping understatement, but it shows I'm getting back my control,* he thought. 'It's a very time-consuming hobby. When you have a young family, you have to ration out your leisure time carefully.'

'You're saying that you weren't a close friend of Logan's?' Lambert asked.

'That's it! I met him quite a lot off and on over the years, but we were never particularly close. We had completely different lifestyles for one thing. He was a bachelor with private means and lots of time on his hands, whilst for a long time I was watching every penny and very busy with work and family.'

'Did your wife know him?'

'No.' He wondered if the negative had again come a little too promptly. 'Not really,' he said. This was new to him: in his professional life as a bank branch manager he didn't have to think much about the effects he was making on people.

'Angela has no interest in the theatre, as I said. We didn't meet up with Terry socially; so when she met him at all it would be at parties after productions, which I'm afraid are usually more enjoyable for those who have been involved than for their spouses and partners. Insofar as she knew him at all, she probably resented him as a figure from a world which was taking up too much of my time.'

'Did you have any professional dealings with him?'

The question had come suddenly, when he was busy trying to distance himself from Logan. He told himself that he had always expected it, had prepared himself to answer it. Perhaps he wasn't as good at remembering lines as he had been in his youth, for the precise phrases he had devised wouldn't come to him now. 'I think he was once a customer of the bank, but that was before my time. Perhaps he transferred his funds when he heard I was becoming manager of the local branch. Many people don't like to bank with someone who knows them, because they don't like them knowing the details of their financial background. But I can't be sure about that, and I wouldn't like to indulge in speculation.' That was better: those were a couple of the phrases he'd prepared for this. He gave them a deprecating smile.

Lambert had a response for that. 'And who do you think killed Mr Logan?' The question flew like an arrow across the bank manager's big desk, the more effective for its almost casual delivery.

'I don't know.' Ian fumbled for something stronger. 'I've no idea. You can't expect me to have any idea.'

'On the contrary, I think you wouldn't be human if you hadn't been speculating about exactly that ever since you heard of this death.'

When Ian Proudfoot looked for some relief from Bert Hook, the DS merely reinforced the logic of this with a small smile and the slightest affirmatory shrug of his broad shoulders. Then Bert said thoughtfully, 'Unless you killed him yourself, of course, Ian. In which case you'd have had no need of speculation; you'd have been much more concerned to cover your tracks.'

This was unexpected from the calm and unthreatening man whom he had been thinking of as a friend. Ian glared at him, but he produced nothing but a lame, 'I trust that's a joke.'

Hook flicked to a new page in his notebook and said, 'We'll need you to account for your movements last night.'

'That's ridiculous. You were with me for most of the evening. Are you going to provide a record of your own movements?'

'If it is required of me, of course I shall. You were with me until just after nine o'clock, by my reckoning. Please tell us your movements after that.'

Ian knew that he must not be rattled. Apart from any other implications, he wouldn't want to give them the satisfaction of that. 'As you know, I wasn't required for the final section of the rehearsal. I left Terry Logan alone in Mettlesham Village Hall with you and the two young people.' He enjoyed saying that.

Hook nodded, taking an irritatingly long time to record this in his round hand. 'What then?'

'I left the hall, opened my car, and drove carefully home. I must have arrived there by half past nine or just after that.' He spoke slowly and with exaggerated clarity, like one instructing a child.

Hook nodded, not troubling to look up from his notes. 'Presumably there is someone who can confirm this?'

'Angela, my wife, will confirm it.' She owed him that much at least, however bitchy she'd been about him going out last night.

Again it seemed to take Hook an inordinate number of seconds to make a note of the time and the name. Then he looked up and smiled brightly. 'You still haven't responded to Chief Superintendent Lambert's inquiry about who you think might have committed this appalling crime.'

Ian almost snapped at Hook that he wouldn't think it so appalling if he'd known Logan as well as he had. Then he realized what a mistake that would have been, undoing all his previous attempts to distance himself from the dead man. This Bert Hook was much more dangerous than you would conclude from his village-bobby exterior.

Ian said stiffly, 'You were right when you pointed out that it would be natural for me to speculate about who might have done this. I have been doing just that in what few spare moments I have had during the day. But I have to tell you that I can offer you nothing useful. At this moment, I am as baffled as you seem to be yourselves.' He looked from one to the other of his questioners with a thin little smile, enjoying delivering this small barb of his own.

'We know virtually nothing yet about our murder victim,' Lambert said. 'No doubt you are anxious to see his murderer arrested quickly.'

Ian hoped that was an assumption, not a question. He knew exactly what he thought about this death, knew also that he mustn't let them see his satisfaction that Logan had been removed from the world for ever. He said tersely, 'Of course. That goes without saying.'

'Then tell us about him. Tell us about the sort of man he was. Tell us above all about the enemies he had.'

'I didn't know him well. But I take your point that I knew him better than you. My children passed through his hands at the school. He taught some English in the lower school. But his main interest was drama. He . . . he was unusual for a teacher, in having private means. He wasn't much interested in promotion or in what others thought of him, I think. That gave him a certain independence. He certainly wasn't a typical teacher.'

Lambert, whose wife had been a teacher and still did part-time work in schools, wondered quite what a typical teacher might be. 'All right. But what were the consequences of this? How might it have a bearing on his death?'

'I can't tell you that. But I think his sexual preferences might have made him a few enemies. As far as I know, he's never been married. But he's had a string of women over the years. Some fairly serious, some more casual.' Ian realized that he was speaking as if the man were still alive. Well, that was all right: probably a lot of people did that, after a sudden death. He was doing the right thing.

Lambert watched him closely, then gave him a wry smile. 'People of that kind usually acquire enemies. Were any of the people who were with you last night sexually involved with him?'

'Not as far as I know,' said Ian stiffly. He wasn't going to fall into the trap of pointing the finger at others, just to divert attention from himself. He hesitated. 'You will understand that this is mostly hearsay. I don't enjoy spreading gossip about a dead man.'

Lambert thought that he had been very content to do just

that. But he gave his stock response. 'In a murder inquiry, we encourage speculation. It need go no further, if it proves to have no bearing on our investigation.'

'I'm relieved to hear it. In the light of that assurance, perhaps I should add that I've heard . . . well, rumours.' He looked as if he wanted to be prompted, but they said nothing and he had to press on himself. 'I believe there were men as well as women, but I can't offer chapter and verse.'

He looked thoroughly uncomfortable, but his body language indicated that he had wanted them to have this information. They pressed him for details, but he said he could give them none. 'Perhaps I shouldn't even have voiced the idea,' he said unconvincingly as they prepared to leave.

The CID men were back in their car and a mile away from Ian Proudfoot before Hook said, 'He was holding something back, despite what he told us about Logan. Something about himself and his own relationship with the man.'

'I agree. We'll be back to see him again, when we've talked to other people and got a fuller picture,' said Lambert grimly. 'In the meantime, he's given us a problem with what he *has* told us about our murder victim. A man who can't keep it in his trousers usually makes a lot of enemies. A bisexual Lothario is going to have made even more.'

Twelve

Michael Carey didn't let his excitement affect his work. He was rather proud of that.

A holiday camp which now called itself a leisure park had asked the firm for some advertising material and Michael was roughing out some possibilities for them. He enjoyed playing with nineteen thirties advertising posters from railway stations. If you were clever, you could at once gently send them up and evoke a little nostalgia for the more relaxed days of the past.

He moved things about rapidly on his computer screen, amusing himself as well as throwing up some interesting possibilities for the commission. If their designs for this were accepted, his boss had said it could lead to lucrative future contracts. He hadn't mentioned the death at Mettlesham. He hadn't yet associated his bright young worker with the rehearsal which had preceded the murder and Michael chose not to enlighten him. As the day went on, he hugged his excitement to himself like a delicious secret, wondering how long it would be before any one of the thirty other people in the building connected him with the sensational events of the previous night.

Michael was called to the phone at lunch time, but it wasn't the police, as he had half-expected it to be. Perhaps they were taking time to find where he worked and lived: that was one of the advantages of keeping yourself to yourself. Being a bit of a loner had a lot to be said for it.

He recognized the voice on the other end of the line immediately. It said nervously, 'I've just heard about this death at Mettlesham.'

'Yes. Bit of excitement, isn't it? Plenty of deaths in *Hamlet*, but we weren't anticipating a real one.'

'Is it Logan?'

'I believe it is. Just been announced on local radio, the girls in the office tell me.'

A long pause; he could hear uneven breathing for several seconds. Then the voice said, 'Are you involved, Mike?'

He considered the question for a moment, enjoying his calm in the face of the other's discomfort. 'Of course I'm involved. I was at the rehearsal immediately before it happened.'

'You know I don't mean that.'

'Ah! You meant did I kill him, didn't you?'

'Well, did you? God knows, from what little you've told me, you've ample reason to wish him out of the way.'

'I suppose God does know, if He exists at all, which I very much doubt. He'd also know whether I killed him, wouldn't He?' He grinned at the mouthpiece, enjoying his teasing, visualizing the puzzled face above that other phone. Then he said seriously, 'As a matter of fact I didn't. Murder's not my style.'

'I'm glad to hear it.'

'Are you? Yes, I suppose you are, really. Though to be the friend of a murderer would give you a certain cachet among your circle, wouldn't it? But I suppose you will have to consider the fact that even if I had killed him, I'd be bound to declare to you that I hadn't, wouldn't I?'

'I have to go now. My friends are waiting.'

'Run along then. Must be nice to be a gregarious soul and have friends to support you.' Michael put the phone down and smiled.

The call from the police still didn't come, though he waited for it all through the afternoon. Nor did anyone at work yet realize how close their talented and rather secretive young colleague was to the sensational event which they were all talking about at breaks. That was almost a disappointment, he thought, as he drove home in the reliable old Fiesta.

He went for a run in the dark, using his torch to light his path along the deserted lane, exulting in the physical release which came with vigorous exercise. He was getting very fit, he realized with a delicious surprise. Even when he stepped up the pace and pounded hard over the last four hundred yards of his two-mile stretch, his breathing remained even, the movement of his limbs rhythmical and steady. He breasted an imaginary tape and slowed to a walk, watching the long

funnels of his breath disappearing into the darkness above
the hedgerows as he turned into the drive and made for his
flat at the end of the house.

The phone was ringing as he turned his key in the lock. He
loped quickly across the room to it and said, 'Michael Carey.'

'It's Bert Hook, Michael. Polonius. Detective Sergeant Hook
now, I'm afraid. You've no doubt heard about Terry's death.
We'd like to speak to you about it in the morning.'

It was almost a relief that the call he had been waiting for
all day had finally arrived.

DS Hook was wondering quite how to play out a situation
with a very different suspect. He was aware that he had something of a special relationship with Becky Clegg, as a result
of sending her out of the station when they could clearly have
held her on a shoplifting charge. He smiled at her and said
tentatively, 'Thanks for coming in here.'

'It suited me. I didn't want big ears listening to pigs questioning me in my pad. And I didn't want CID men coming
into my place of work, when I've only been there two days.'

'You got the job, then.'

'I'm giving it a try.' She wouldn't tell him that she was
delighted with the work and with herself or thank him for his
encouragement. Old habits die hard, and police stations made
her nervous. So the man she had rehearsed with last night
was back to being a copper. It was the first time in her life
that she had volunteered to come into a police station and she
was reverting to type; her instinct was to call these people
pigs and give them nothing.

Hook grinned at her. 'It's working, isn't it?'

She looked at him and felt suddenly guilty. He didn't look
like a copper, with his slightly out-of-date sweater and his
brown shoes and his innocent, open, lived-in face. Bert Hook
might be a soft touch, as she'd boasted to her friends at the
time, but he'd given her a chance and set her off on a new
road which she was finding quite exciting. 'Yes, it's working.
I like the job and so far they seem to like me. I'm moving
out of my flat at the end of the month. Everything was going
fine, until I became a murder suspect.'

She waited for him to deny that and tell her that she had
nothing to worry about, that this was just a tiresome formality.

Instead, he nodded his head thoughtfully. Perhaps he wasn't a soft touch after all.

At that moment, a tall man with a long face and grey, speculative eyes came into the little box of the interview room, and she suddenly felt hemmed in and under threat. Hook introduced the newcomer as Chief Superintendent Lambert and Becky Clegg was back in that familiar world where the barriers were up and the police were the enemy.

'You were very close to a man who was murdered last night,' said Lambert. 'Tell us about the latter part of your evening, please.'

Becky glanced at Bert Hook, who gave her the slightest of nods. 'There isn't much to tell. I spent the last hour of the rehearsal with Jack Dawes and with Bert here. We were concentrating on what we were doing.'

'And what you were doing was being directed by Terry Logan. Did you notice anything abnormal in his conduct or his attitude?'

'No. I wouldn't know what was normal for him, would I? I hadn't seen him before last night. Well, not since I was at school.' She glanced nervously at Bert Hook, hoping that he would confirm that all three of them had been too anxious about the scene to observe their director. They had been concerned only with doing what he wanted them to do on stage, concerned a hundred per cent with their own actions, anxious only not to make fools of themselves. She had sensed at the time that they were all preoccupied with themselves, even this older man who seemed so unlikely a candidate for amateur dramatics.

Lambert studied her for a moment before he said, 'You didn't notice any sign of fear or nervousness in Mr Logan?'

'No. You must already have asked Bert about this.' She was delighted to see Hook a little discomforted when she threw in his first name again.

'I have. Now I'm asking you, Miss Clegg.'

'And I'm telling you that I didn't see anything strange in old Logan – sorry, that's what we called him at school. But I was concerned with making sense of my lines, of trying to be the naïve girl Logan said he wanted me to be, not with looking at him. He was in charge, and he knew what he was doing. We didn't: we were scared stiff we'd make a bollocks of it.'

'And did you?'

That threw her. He surely couldn't be interested in the quality
of the rehearsal. Becky realized with a pang of fear that what
he was interested in was *her*. 'I don't know.' She glanced
desperately at Bert Hook and received no help there. 'We were
muddling through. It seemed to go reasonably well, I suppose.
Terry Logan said it was good for a first reading. Very promising, I think he said. The time seemed to flash past very
quickly. I couldn't believe it when he said that it was well
after ten and we must finish for the night. Terry was full of
himself and *Hamlet* – quite excited, I'd say, but only because
of the play. We were all pretty excited, I suppose, but only
on account of having got the first night of rehearsals out of
the way.' She looked again for Bert Hook to confirm that, and
this time he nodded and gave her a small smile.

'Tell us what happened then.'

Lambert had never taken his eyes off her; Becky felt that
he didn't believe a word she was saying. And yet so far she
had told him nothing but the truth as she recalled it. She said
carefully, 'We all left more or less together, as I remember
it,' and looked again at Hook.

'To be accurate,' Bert said, 'I think that you and I left before
the other two, Becky. Mr Dawes stayed behind with our
director. I offered you a lift, but you said you'd arrived with
Jack and you'd wait to go home with him.'

'That's right. I watched you drive away. Then Jack came
out and we put on our helmets and went off on his motorbike.'

Hook nodded slowly. 'How long was it before Mr Dawes
came out?'

'No more than a minute or two after you'd gone.' She kept
her eyes steadily on Bert's face, preferring that to the cold,
unblinking scrutiny of his companion.

'And did Terry Logan come out with Jack?'

She pretended to give the matter some thought. 'No, I don't
think he did. We'd have seen him when we were putting on
our gear for the bike, wouldn't we? I'm sure he was still in
the hall when Jack started the bike and we roared off. Yes, I
remember, the lights were still on in there when we pulled
out of the car park.'

Lambert said, 'Did you see anyone else in the car park or
the surrounding area?'

It was an advantage having been interrogated by the police so many times in the past. This might be more serious, but it wasn't a new situation for her. Again she made a pretence of considering the question very seriously, a small frown momentarily creasing her smooth forehead. 'No. I'm sorry, because I realize how important it would be if I had. It was very dark, of course: the only real light was the bit spilling out from the hall.'

'I see. Who do you think might have killed Mr Logan?'

She felt her pulses racing at the sudden rawness of the question. This is where she must keep her head. 'I don't know. Not Jack or me, obviously.'

'You mean you alibi each other.'

'If you want to put it like that. I prefer to think that we are fortunate to have arrived and left together.'

'Indeed. An alternative theory would be that two people with a previous history of crime carried out a murder together and are now providing each other with convenient alibis. But then I'm an experienced CID man, and experience tends to make you cynical.'

Lambert delivered this almost affably, but that did not affect her rage. 'You're a pig, you mean. And with pigs, it's once a villain always a villain, isn't it? You never give the benefit of the doubt to anyone, do you?'

Lambert gave her a grim smile. 'It's our business to investigate any doubts we have, not to give or deny benefits. I didn't ask you to deny your own guilt. I asked you to tell me any thoughts you had about who killed Terry Logan. If it wasn't you, you must have been thinking about who it was.'

She knew she must control her anger. Anger, like any other emotion, made you vulnerable with men like this. When you were emotional, you were not rational: you needed to keep your cool with the pigs. 'If I have thought about it, I haven't come up with anything useful,' she said calmly. 'It could have been someone not involved in the rehearsal at all, someone who knew Terry was going to be there and just waited for him outside.'

Lambert gave her again the thin smile she was beginning to hate. 'Which would be very convenient for you, of course. But I have to agree that it is a possibility; we shall need to investigate it. Nevertheless, the probability remains that it was one of the people who had been working with Mr Logan during the evening who waited for him in the darkness outside.'

Becky was beset by a sudden involuntary shiver. She thrust her hands against her sides, seeking control of her slim body. 'Some of the others who were there knew him much better than me. I think they did, anyway, from odd things they let drop when we were talking to each other beforehand.'

Lambert, despite the stress he had put upon her, had decided by now that this was a shrewd and resourceful young woman. He said tersely, 'Two pieces of advice, Miss Clegg. First, you should go on thinking about last night, trying to recall any remark or action which might seem to be significant in relation to this murder: that is in your own interest. Secondly, if you are in any way acting to protect Mr Dawes, you should immediately cease to do so.' He stood up. 'We shall need to speak again, in due course.' He made it sound like a threat.

Becky Clegg wandered along the street outside the police station, which was still busy with the last of the evening rush-hour traffic. She was happy to lose herself amongst the other pedestrians, to recover the anonymity which suddenly seemed so necessary to her. She looked at the displays in the brightly lit shop windows without registering them, walking slowly until she was a good quarter of a mile from the police station.

Only then did she take the mobile phone from her bag. Turning a corner into sudden darkness, she listened to the ring of the other mobile phone, and gave her first smile in a long time as the familiar voice said, 'Jack Dawes here.'

'I've just spoken to the filth. They'll be round to see you before long. I told them we left together as soon as you came out. Make sure you tell them exactly the same story. Keep it simple, Jack. Whatever they think, they won't be able to break that one down.'

Thirteen

'You need to eat properly. I know you're upset, but things will only get worse if you don't eat.'

The mother's perennial advice. The advice and sympathy you had to give, even when you knew they wouldn't be welcomed. Christine Lambert had been determined to say nothing, and yet the words came tumbling out as if propelled by some unseen force within her.

'I'm doing my best, Mum. I'm afraid I'm just not very hungry.' Jacky stared at the table and spoke like one in a trance.

'You'll be telling her to eat her sprouts up next, to make her big and strong!' John Lambert glanced conspiratorially at his daughter, and won a wan smile in response, though she did not look at him either.

Christine told herself grudgingly that her husband was trying to help. But she resented the old partnership between father and daughter, was taken back twenty years to the small defiances which had undermined her attempts at discipline. She stacked Jacky's almost untouched meal on top of the two empty plates, watching her stricken daughter carefully whilst pretending not to watch her at all.

'There's strawberries and cream to follow.'

'Not for me, Mum. Sorry.'

Christine wanted to scream at her, to tell her to make an effort, to respond to the other efforts that were being made all around her. It was her daughter's favourite dessert and she'd paid a lot for the out of season strawberries.

'I'll have yours, then!' John said with desperate cheerfulness.

Christine threw him a withering look and went silently into the kitchen.

The flushed and artificial excitement of yesterday's shopping expedition hadn't carried over into today. That laughing daughter had departed; Jacky was listless and isolated again, retreating into that cave of depression where no one would be able to reach her.

In the dining room there was a silence which father and daughter understood, which both of them accepted as being better than useless speech. They listened to the sounds from the kitchen. John Lambert eventually said, 'Your mum's not used to being unable to help. It's in her nature to offer distressed people comfort and she's usually been successful.'

'She won't be successful this time.' She spoke like one determined upon her misery. John Lambert wanted to take her on his knee as he had done when she was a child, to make her laugh against her wishes, to banish her depression with a fit of the giggles he had once been able to induce. But those days were gone: this was a more crushing and dangerous blackness than those childish heartbreaks which had passed so quickly.

He said with all the confidence he could muster, 'What you need is a whisky!' and went to get the bottle from the cupboard in the sideboard. He poured two generous measures, splashed in a little water to disguise the depth of the whisky, set the glass down firmly in front of her, and took a sizeable mouthful of his own allocation. He was surprised how welcome the taste was upon his tongue; when you were out of your depth, the patient wasn't the only one who needed a crutch.

He wasn't sure how many of his words Jacky had heard. She looked at the glass as if she didn't understand how it came to be in front of her, then raised it to her lips and took a stiff pull at it. Her face puckered in distress, for a moment, as if this was a sour-tasting medicine, and Lambert was reminded again of the little girl who had gone for ever. Minutes later, the glass was empty, and she slid it towards John and the bottle at his elbow.

She hadn't looked at her father's face throughout all this, and she did not do so now. He hesitated for a moment, then poured another stiff measure into the glass. Before he could add water, she raised it to her lips and drank half of it immediately. Again there was that wincing of the cheeks which denoted pain rather than pleasure, and a part of John Lambert thought that this was a terrible way to treat good Scotch. Jacky downed the rest of the spirit, with determination but no sign of enjoyment, and slid her glass towards him again.

He gave her another measure. They weren't coping with her despair, any of them, and oblivion might be better than consciousness for her, at this moment. He put the bottle back in its cupboard, sensing that she would not stop until he halted this. He sipped at his own drink, feeling the helplessness about his shoulders like a heavy blanket. He could no longer think of anything to say; even the clichés wouldn't come now.

Jacky emptied her glass, pressed her palms upon the table, stood up, and looked at her father in puzzlement, as if he was a stranger and she was in a strange place. Then she staggered, would have fallen if he hadn't leapt to support her. John Lambert, caught in this strange mixture of tragedy and farce, glanced at the door to the kitchen, wondering what Christine would say to him when this strange, unreal interlude was over.

He said, 'I think you'd better have a lie down, love, don't you?' and draped Jacky's arm around his shoulders.

She did not giggle, as other drunks had done in the past, as he half-hoped she would do now. They made a difficult and halting progress along the hall, lurching against first the wall and then the telephone table as he fought to ensure that she did not fall backwards. 'Good job there's no stairs in a bungalow!' she slurred, and became even more helpless with laughter.

Her room was untidy, with her purchases from the previous day spread across the floor, a bra across the back of a chair, and unused cosmetics and hairbrushes upon the dressing table.

John Lambert felt a searing moment of pain and helplessness: Jacky had always been a tidy girl; even in adolescence, she had kept her surroundings meticulously neat, sometimes to the irritation of those around her. How had that well-organized and loving daughter been replaced by this creature so heavy upon his arm, by this suffering, desperate, drunken woman?

He slid his shoulder from beneath her torso and put her head gently upon the pillow, then lifted her feet carefully on to the bed. Perhaps he would send Christine up to undress her; but even as the thought entered his mind, he knew that he would not do that. Jacky opened her eyes briefly, but she did not look at him. She stared at the ceiling for a moment with a little private frown, then shut them with a soundless sigh.

He placed the duvet over the unresisting body and drew the curtains upon the blackness outside.

CID pigs were a different proposition from those uniformed tyros who'd been here ten days earlier. Jack Dawes decided

that within thirty seconds of their arrival in his mother's shab-
bily furnished living room.

He was confident he could handle Bert Hook, that amiable,
ruddy-faced, slightly bumbling man who had made such a good
Polonius when they had rehearsed together on the previous night.
But he didn't like the look of the younger man he introduced
as Detective Inspector Rushton, who seemed bent on hostility
from the moment he entered the room. He was one of the few
CID men Jack had met who did not look like a policeman in
plain clothes. In his sharply cut dark blue suit, he might have
been a senior executive who had come here to inspect the efficiency of his staff. He was probably in his early thirties, Jack
decided. He had dark, carefully parted hair, clean-cut features,
and brown eyes which glittered with enmity.

'We need to talk to you about last night,' said Hook.

'Your companion has already been into the station to give
her account of what happened,' said Rushton. He made it
sound as if Jack's failure to do the same thing was already a
suspicious act.

'My companion?' Jack decided that it would be best to deny
any close connection with the girl who had ridden on his
pillion on the previous night.

Bert Hook smiled at him. 'Becky Clegg. She gave
Superintendent Lambert and me the distinct impression this
evening that there was something between you.'

'We were acting together in the play, that's all. With some
older bugger who was playing my dad. Though I don't feel
any filial attachments with him at this moment!' Jack tried
hard not to smile and look smug; he'd enjoyed taunting Hook,
and he was particularly proud of that word 'filial'. That would
show the pigs that he wasn't just an ignorant yobbo, that they
needed to treat him with respect.

Bert answered his smile. 'And I'm sure that you won't
expect me to show any fatherly tenderness towards you, Jack
Dawes. You're in the midst of a murder inquiry, lad, and the
sooner you realize that the better. At the moment, you're the
last person known to be with the victim when he was still
alive.' Hook looked at him with his head a little on one side
and allowed himself the suggestion of a smile at the young
man's predicament.

'You mean the last person other than his murderer, I think.'

Jack tried to remain calm and dismissive, but he realized with a shock what he should have acknowledged to himself much earlier: this was a much more serious affair than anything he had been involved in before.

Chris Rushton said thoughtfully, 'The two might be one and the same, of course. We have to consider that possibility.'

'And what happened to innocent until proved guilty?'

'Nothing happened to it, Mr Dawes. It still applies. We simply have to consider all possibilities, as DS Hook has already indicated to you. And it will be self-evident to anyone as sharp as you that someone with a previous history of law-breaking and violence is more likely to perpetrate murder than more law-abiding citizens.'

'So you're not given a chance if you've tangled with the filth before. That's it, isn't it? If you've got a bit of previous, you're—'

'Statistics, Mr Dawes. Cold and objective. Much better than emotions, when it comes to making decisions. Statistics tell us that people who have offended in the past are more likely to do so again, particularly when there is a steady history of transgressions.'

Jack was beginning to hate this composed, self-contained man, with his immaculate hair and his smart collar and tie, who seemed not to feel the heat in this stuffy, ill-ventilated room. He had intended to treat the CID men with contempt, scorning to defend himself, leaving them frustrated by his cold refusal to discuss any involvement in the demise of Terry Logan.

Now he heard himself saying defensively, 'I might have stepped out of line a bit, in the past. I don't have convictions for violence.'

'Oh, but you have, Mr Dawes. I could give you the dates of those convictions, if I wanted to, but we don't wish to waste our time with that when we have your involvement in a murder investigation to pursue. I will merely remind you that you beat up an innocent shopkeeper, only last week.'

'I didn't do that. You pricks have already been told that I was here with my mother when old Joussef got what was coming to him.' He glanced at the kitchen door, knowing that his mother would be listening behind it.

Rushton looked at him with open contempt, enjoying this discomfort of a sharp rogue who was only around ten years younger than himself. 'No, that hasn't been established, Mr Dawes. The case may never come to court. That will depend on Mr Joussef and how much louts like you have managed to scare him. But we know and you know that you were involved in the injuries to Mr Joussef.'

'I told you, I wasn't there. My mother's already confirmed to your PC Plods that I was here at the time of that attack.' He glanced at Bert Hook and found no relief this time in that unthreatening face. The DS was studying him with undisguised curiosity and suspicion.

Bert said quietly, 'I think you'd better tell us exactly what happened last night, Jack.'

'You know most of it. I was rehearsing with you and Becky for the last part of the evening. With Terry Logan directing.' He kept his voice perfectly level. 'Then we finished and went home.'

'Not quite. Terry kept you behind when everyone else left. I talked briefly with Becky in the car park outside. Offered her a lift home, in fact. She said she preferred to wait for you.'

'And she told you what happened after that. I don't know why you're asking me about it when you could be—'

'Because we want your version of how the evening ended, Jack. Just as we are collecting the version of everyone else who was in the Mettlesham Village Hall last night.'

Jack took a deep breath, forcing himself to be calm, to deal with this on his terms rather than theirs. It was at that moment that the kitchen door burst open and his mother stumbled into the room. 'He was in here at half past ten last night, my Jack. So don't you go accusing him.'

'Accusing him of what, Mrs Dawes? I assume that is who you are.'

This was Rushton, and he threw Sally Dawes off balance immediately. Tall and handsome men usually did, and this one was also unsmiling and hostile. 'Anything. My Jack hasn't done anything.' She looked desperately at her son, then back at the unsmiling official face. 'You lot are always coming here and saying he's done bad things when he hasn't.'

Hook had not taken his eyes from his young quarry's face. 'How long were you in the hall after Becky Clegg and I left?'

'Hardly any time at all. You were just driving away when I came out. I saw your rear lights on the lane.' They might not believe that, but they couldn't disprove it. 'I knew Becky would be waiting in the cold outside and I'd promised her a lift, so I couldn't be long, could I?'

'Very considerate of you. What were you discussing with Terry Logan?'

'He was giving me a few pointers about my performance. Telling me how Laertes would develop through the play. I haven't even read *Hamlet*. I didn't even know that he kills the hero at the end of the play, until Terry Logan told me.'

'And why did he dismiss Becky and me whilst he did this? Why did he need to have you on your own to tell you these things?'

'I don't know, do I? You'd need to ask him about that. Except that you can't do that now, can you?'

Bert Hook did not take his eyes from the boy's face or change the tone of his voice even fractionally as he said, 'What time did Jack really come in last night, Mrs Dawes?'

The swift, fearful glance she shot at her son spoke louder than many words. 'Half past ten. I just told you.'

'It must have been later than that. Unless he broke the speed limit on that bike of his.'

Another significant glance passed from her to Jack. 'It might have been a bit later than that. I wasn't watching the clock, was I?'

'Was it perhaps much later than that, do you think? Half an hour later? An hour later?'

Jack almost shouted. 'No, it wasn't! It might have been half an hour later, but no more than that.' He forced himself to speak more calmly. 'I dropped Becky off and came straight home. I didn't notice the time, because none of us thought it was important then, did we? Mum likes a drink at night, so she was a bit pissed when I got in. But it was somewhere about the time she said. All right?'

Rushton studied mother and son for a moment, as if he was reluctant to leave it there. But he knew they wouldn't get any more out of either of them tonight, that they would merely retreat into their shells and stubbornly reiterate the story he fancied they had agreed beforehand. 'Who do you think killed Mr Logan, if you didn't?'

'I don't know, do I? If I knew anything like that, I'd tell you about it, wouldn't I?'

'You'd behave like a good citizen and help the police with

their inquiries, would you, Mr Dawes? Well, I suspect it would be for the first time in your life, if you did. But I see that you have a high regard for your own miserable skin. You will realize that it is very much in your own interest to come forward with any information you have or any thoughts which occur to you in the next day or two. Until we have other candidates for this murder and some real evidence, you will remain firmly in the frame for this one. Don't think of leaving the area without informing us of any plans, will you?'

He nodded the briefest of goodnights to the anxious face of Sally Dawes and led his colleague out of the house.

At one thirty in the morning, Christine Lambert was still awake.

She had been thoroughly exhausted when she came to bed, yet she hadn't slept. And now, two hours later and with her eyes sore and dry within their sockets, she knew that she would be awake for hours longer yet. She switched on the light and tried to read, but her eyes were too tired for that; she was soon rubbing them in irritation and closing her novel in frustration.

Her mind kept coming back to her daughter and the agony of her isolation. She had felt isolated herself, twenty years ago, when that girl in the next room was a toddler. But she had never had to contend with that bitter and unhinging sense of betrayal which Jacky now felt. John's mistress had been his work, a faceless and impersonal rival. She had never felt the bitter sense of personal failure and disconnection she had seen in her daughter's suffering, bewildered face over the last two days.

She listened to the regular breathing of her husband beside her and felt the sharp, illogical hostility which the sleepless always feel towards the sleeping. It was silly and selfish, she told herself: John needed his sleep to cope not only with the situation at home but with this murder which was already exciting the media. Knife crimes were always more sensational than poisonings or gunshots, he had told her, and it was true that even she was more appalled by the grisly visions of blood and gore which a slash across the throat aroused.

He should have let her go in to see her daughter before she came to bed, Christine decided. He'd popped in himself, said she was out to the world, that she was sleeping and best left undisturbed. As if Christine didn't know that Jacky had been drinking too much; as if she needed to be preserved from the reek of whisky or the possibility of vomit. Hadn't she known much worse? Hadn't he left her to cope with much worse during the children's illnesses all those years ago, when she was at the end of her resources and yearning for his sympathy and his support?

Yet she knew that John had been protecting her not against the possibility of physical mess but the evidence of Jacky's disintegration. She was grateful to him for his care, surprised by the empathy he had shown for his daughter in her crisis and by the way she had responded to him. But why should she be surprised, and even a little jealous? Hadn't John always been good in a crisis, even in their darkest days? Hadn't he always found it difficult to show his love in the routine of day-to-day living, and easiest to show how much he cared for her and for the children when there was some real emergency?

Christine looked again at the time on the bedside clock; it had crept forward to one forty. Before the idea had clearly formed itself in her mind, she had slid softly from between the warm sheets. The heating had switched off hours ago. She stood shivering in the November chill for a second, then snatched her dressing gown from the back of her door.

She'd check on Jacky. She'd find her sound asleep, perhaps tidy the sheets a little around her chin, as she had done when she was a child, then come straight back to bed. She'd be able to sleep then. That's what she needed. John had meant well, no doubt. How little men knew about the way life worked! Christine crept on to the landing, turned the handle on the door of Jacky's room carefully. She mustn't disturb her husband: John needed his sleep.

Thirty seconds later, she was back at his bedside, shaking him roughly awake, shrieking at his insensible, insensitive, ignorant male face. 'She's taken pills! I can't wake her! John, I felt her wrist, and she's cold!'

He was dialling 999 before she knew he was awake, saying with authority and apparent calm, 'Ambulance, please. It's extremely urgent.'

Always good in a crisis, John Lambert.

Fourteen

Michael Carey had a thought over his breakfast cereal which both amused and excited him.

He would treat this interview with the police as an acting exercise. He would play the gauche young man who was preoccupied with his own dreams and not very much aware of the world around him. That wasn't at all how he saw himself. But it would be good practice for an alert realist who intended to make his living from the stage.

A smile flickered over his face as he cut up his banana and apple with the antique fruit knife he kept specially for the purpose. It was as sharp as a surgeon's scalpel; he always enjoyed slicing through the flesh of the fruit with the effort-less precision afforded by this razor-sharp tool. By the time he was finishing his muesli, the smile had taken over his face: he found it difficult not to giggle at the prospect of what he had now designated his little brush with the law.

When the bell rang and he opened the door, he found the man he had rehearsed with on his doorstep, the man who had made such a good fist of Polonius in the opening court scene. He brought with him a tall man, whose plentiful dark hair was grizzled with grey, whose long, lined grey face looked drawn with tension. Bert Hook introduced him as Chief Superintendent Lambert. Michael was pleased to meet this local detective legend, but surprised to see him looking so pale and strained. The challenges of the job must be catching up with him; the man looked as if he must be due for retirement before long.

Lambert wouldn't have argued with that description of himself this morning. He had not slept since his wife had awakened him with the news of his daughter's condition. You did not get much rest in the brightly lit corridors of hospitals, as the night crawled slowly towards morning.

It was curious how mental illness of any kind still carried its own taboos. He would have said he had no secrets from his old friend Bert Hook. They had shared much together over the last ten years, in their family as well as their professional lives. Yet he had said nothing to him of Jacky's crisis and the events of the small hours as they had driven here today. A few months earlier, he had felt Hook's agony as Bert's son had almost died from meningitis; now he felt himself unable to speak about the sufferings of his own child.

He tried to concentrate whilst Bert Hook took Michael Carey through the details of the rehearsal and his movements on that fatal Wednesday evening. He noted a febrile excitement in the young man, an animation in the fresh face beneath the striking golden hair, which might or might not be characteristic, and thus normal behaviour for him.

Bert concluded the interview with, 'So you left the rehearsal at around nine o'clock.'

Michael Carey grinned, as if they were playing a game together. 'You know I did. Terry Logan gave us some notes on the scene we'd just rehearsed, and then dismissed us, apart from you, Becky Clegg and Jack Dawes.' He was pleased that he'd remembered the full names of the two other young people in the cast. 'Good thing that boy isn't going into the professional theatre. He might not get far, with a name like Jack Dawes! He could play petty thieves, I suppose. Or perhaps Autolycus in *All's Well that Ends Well*, that snapper up of unconsidered trifles.' Michael sniggered a little. Whether his mirth was at that thought or at the notion of leading this PC Plod out beyond his depth, he was not quite clear himself.

'I think you'll find Autolycus is in *The Winter's Tale*,' said Hook, without looking up from his notes. 'What did you do after you left the village hall?'

Michael tried not to show how nettled he was at being corrected on his Shakespeare by this lumpen figure. 'I got into my faithful little Fiesta and drove home. Then I took an hour or so to wind down after the excitements of the rehearsal and went to bed to be ready for a hard day's work on Thursday. My mother would have been proud of me.' He gave them a modest smile: not too dazzling and not too vacant. He saw himself as a young Kenneth Branagh rather than a Bertie Wooster.

Lambert had watched the performance without a smile. 'And are there any witnesses to this admirably dutiful conduct?'

'There are not, Chief Superintendent Lambert. I live here alone.' He looked with satisfaction around the neat flat, with its prints of Aubrey Beardsley cartoons and the etching of Henry Irving at Stratford on its walls. 'That is an arrangement which normally suits me well. However, on this occasion, I presume that it leaves me "in the frame" for this killing. Is that still the term you use, Chief Superintendent Lambert?'

'We find it useful sometimes, yes. It may be a cliché, but at least people usually know what you mean when you use clichés. How long had you known Terry Logan, Mr Carey?'

Michael kept his smile for a second or so: Mr Branagh would not be shaken by this abruptness. 'I've only known him through our mutual love of the theatre. We were in two or three productions together, between seven and four years ago. I hadn't seen him for almost four years. About two months ago, he got in touch with me about his production of *Hamlet*.'

'That is admirably precise.'

'Thank you. I thought so myself, as a matter of fact. I'd anticipated that you would ask me the question, you see.'

'How well did you know him?'

'Not well at all. As I say, we had a mutual love of the theatre, and enjoyed chatting about any production we'd both seen. We hadn't much else in common.'

'By all accounts, including that of DS Hook here, you're a very talented performer. Mr Logan has directed several productions in the last four years. Didn't you wish to be involved in any of them?'

'I was working in a different area of the country until recently. It was my loss not to be involved: Terry is – was – a very gifted director. Imaginative, but practical as well; that's not a common combination.'

'So you had no hesitation in joining him when he asked you to be in *Hamlet*.'

Michael smiled his widest, most winning smile and gave a little, humorous, self-deprecating shrug of his shoulders. He enjoyed that: only a man who was going to be a professional could act with his shoulders. 'He offered me the Prince. Even in an amateur production, I wasn't going to refuse that, was I? A man can spend a whole lifetime without getting the chance to play the gloomy Dane. Many fine actors have never had that opportunity.'

Lambert glanced through the window at the drift of yellow leaves at the end of the lawn. 'What time would you say that you got back here last night?'

'About twenty past nine, I should think. But no one saw me. Even my landlords, who occupy the main house next door, are away at the moment.' He decided to tease them a little. 'In any case, I could always have stolen out, driven back to Mettlesham, and waited my moment to kill Terry as he came out of the hall, couldn't I? I've no witnesses to corroborate the account of my virtuous mediocrity.'

'If you did do what you suggest and went out again, there's every possibility that someone in the area will have spotted a black Fiesta. House to house inquiries in a rural area are very dull for the officers involved, but they throw up the occasional fact which is quite vital to an arrest and an eventual court case. Who do you think killed Mr Logan?'

As sudden as a bolt from a crossbow. That was probably one of their techniques. Michael was pleased to find himself so unruffled by it. 'One of the cast, I should think, wouldn't you? Some of them knew him far more intimately than I did. And where there is intimacy, there is often passion, isn't there? And passion can lead to violence. Sorry, I'm just thinking aloud, not teaching Granny to suck eggs. Of course, other people as well as our cast probably knew where he was going to be on Wednesday night. Someone I don't even know, from another area of his life entirely, could have been waiting for him to come out of the hall after everyone had left.'

'That is a possibility that will be thoroughly investigated. I notice that you have not answered my question, except in general terms. Is there a member of your cast who you think might have killed your director?'

'I don't know, and I've more sense than to speculate, in something as serious as this. I think you'll find that some of them have previous close associations with the victim.' He gave them a small, helpful smile, enjoying the way he had selected his words as he played the helpful, rather naïve young man.

He was good in the role, very good. But Lambert's experience told him that there was more here than was being offered to them. He found himself enjoying the contest with this

intelligent, hyperactive young brain, happy that he was setting
his own troubles aside as he concentrated upon their exchanges.
'No doubt you chose that word "association" carefully. What
exactly did you mean by it?'

Michael Carey grinned, ruefully and winningly, as if some
small ploy had been rumbled. 'I intended it to cover a variety
of relationships. From that enjoyed by Becky Clegg and Jack
Dawes when they were pupils of Terry's at school to the more
mature connections undertaken with Logan by the admirable
Maggie Dalrymple and Ian Proudfoot in quite different contexts.
There, I said I wouldn't speculate, and now I have, haven't I?'

He was not just good but very good, Lambert decided. His
fresh face merely looked a little embarrassed. It was impossible to tell whether he was merely stating what he thought
was obvious or whether he was deliberately implanting ideas
of deeper and more sinister connections between Logan and
the two older people mentioned. 'You're saying that Mrs
Dalrymple and Mr Logan had some sort of liaison outside
amateur dramatics?'

'Oh, I'm saying nothing of the sort, Chief Superintendent.
I've heard a few rumours, that's all. No more than that. Don't
forget I've been out of this area for several years.'

He was playing with them, and they could do little about
it. He was a member of the public voluntarily helping them
with their inquiries, not a man who had been arrested and taken
in to custody for a grilling. Lambert glanced at Hook, who
said, 'How close was your own association with the deceased,
Michael?'

He noticed that the man who had corrected him about
Autolycus had now picked up his own word 'association' and
thrown it back at him, with a hint of irony in his Herefordshire
tones. He was brighter than a DS had any right to be, this man.

'It didn't go beyond the theatre,' Michael said cautiously,
'I was grateful for the chances and the training he'd given me
in the past. I was even more grateful when he gave me the
chance to play the lead in *Hamlet*.'

'And you're going off to RADA next summer.'

'If all goes to plan, yes. I've had the interview and been
accepted.'

'Did you use Mr Logan as a referee when you applied to
RADA?'

Michael had thought carefully about what they would ask him, but this was a question he hadn't anticipated. 'No, I didn't.'

'It would have been natural to do so, wouldn't it? Terry clearly had a high regard for your abilities, and I understand he has both a considerable reputation and contacts within the world of drama.'

'I had other referees. I hadn't been in touch with Terry for several years.' Michael gave them a smile: show them you're relaxed; don't let them see that you're thinking on your feet, picking your way prudently through this. Think of this man Hook as Claudius, not Polonius, because he's clever and potentially very dangerous to you. 'Terry had known me as a callow young man. I wanted people who would speak of me as I am now, more mature as an actor and a person than I was four years ago.' He gave them a modest, deprecating smile, slipping securely back into the part he wanted to play.

Lambert was irritated by the control of this handsome young man, by the sense that he was playing a game with them. He said brusquely, 'It's a pity that you haven't any witness to your movements after you left Mettlesham Village Hall on Wednesday night.'

Michael Carey caught his opponent's pique and rode upon it. 'From your point of view as well as mine, I expect. It would be nice for you as well as me if you could eliminate me from your inquiries.' He managed to produce the phrase with just the slightest hint of contempt for their mundane affairs. 'But that is often the way with the innocent. It may be inconvenient, but they don't see the need for alibis.'

Lambert was far too professional to allow his dislike for this brilliant young creature to affect his conduct. He said evenly, 'We shall almost certainly need to speak to you again, Mr Carey. If you propose to leave the area, you must let us know. And if anything—'

'I shall be away this weekend, actually. Only in Warwick. Do let me know if there are any exciting developments. I haven't played in melodrama and I should hate to miss any new experience.'

He gave them an address and a telephone number, watched Bert Hook write them down in his clear, round hand, then saw them off the premises with the open and friendly smile which betokened his complete innocence.

Michael Carey stared thoughtfully at the quiet autumn scene outside, with its myriad hues of orange and yellow in the trees, and then went indoors and picked up his mobile.

'I'll be with you this evening as planned. I've got some tales to tell which will engage even your erratic attention.'

The psychiatrist told himself not to look at his watch. He was a busy man and this was routine stuff, as far as he was concerned. He had more urgent and tragic cases to deal with and he was anxious to be away. But he reminded himself that for the white-faced couple in front of him this was a unique experience.

'Your daughter is in no physical danger, Mr and Mrs Lambert. I have talked to her myself and I do not think she is clinically depressed. I have asked one of my colleagues to see her later today, but I am sure that he will confirm this. I anticipate that we shall keep her here for another few hours and then send her home.'

'You don't think she is clinically depressed? After what happened last night?' Christine Lambert knew that she should be relieved, but her first reaction was outrage that her daughter's trauma should be downgraded like this. It must surely be more serious than this awkward man in the white cotton jacket was saying it was.

The psychiatrist dropped into his more urbane mode. He used this a lot; sometimes he felt he spent half his life reassuring people. 'That wasn't a suicide attempt last night. It wasn't even what people like to call a cry for help.' He scratched his brain hard and was delighted when he came up with a name. 'Jacky drank rather a lot and became confused, that's all.'

Christine glanced furiously sideways at her husband, who was nodding a little guiltily amidst his relief. Turning her eyes back to the doctor, she said, 'But she took an overdose.'

'No, she didn't, Mrs Lambert. She was very drunk and probably not very conscious of what she was doing. She took three sleeping pills. The combination of barbiturates and alcohol made her insensible for a short time. It is not a combination which we would advise for anyone; on the contrary, we would absolutely forbid it. But it was not fatal, nor ever likely to be in the case of a healthy young woman. And it was certainly not an attempt at suicide.'

An uncharacteristically embarrassed John Lambert spoke for the first time. 'May we see her?'

'Yes. She may well be asleep, but there's no reason why you shouldn't wake her if she is.'

Jacky wasn't asleep. Her small, white, almost childish face turned towards them as they went into the ward. Her mother took the blue-veined hand she slid from beneath the bedclothes and said foolishly, 'You look very tired, love.'

'They pumped me out.' She looked like a girl filled with the importance of an experience which they had never had. She transferred her attention to the lined face beyond her mother's shoulder. 'I'm sorry, Dad.'

Christine said, 'It's not your fault. Your dad should never have plied you with whisky like that.'

'It was me, Mum. I kept asking for it. And then later on I took the pills. I didn't know what the effects would be.'

'All the same, he should have had more sense than to push spirits at an inexperienced young—'

'I'm not inexperienced, Mum. And I'm not as young as you think I am. But I'm what Dad used to call a bit of a twerp, years ago.'

All three of them giggled a little at the word, letting out a little of their tension. Then Jacky said, 'Anyway, I think I'm going to be all right, now.'

They took that assurance away with them, revolved it in their minds as the old car slowly warmed up on their way home. Christine was so preoccupied with it that she forgot to berate John over his foolishness with the whisky bottle.

Fifteen

A ndrew Dalrymple chose to see the CID men at his works. No doubt the office staff would gossip a little about the detective visitors, but they were full of excitement already about the murder at Mettlesham and the boss's wife's proximity to it. The fact that Margaret Dalrymple was a local luminary, a councillor and a JP, meant that the press had already made her the most prominent figure among the cast of the ill-starred *Hamlet*.

The journalists managed to convey that there was something faintly louche about a Conservative councillor involving herself in amateur dramatics, especially as a randy and adulterous Shakespearean queen. Now local radio and a salivating local press could imply, however obliquely, that Councillor Margaret Dalrymple, JP, was a suspect in a murder inquiry.

Aware of watching eyes in the building behind them, Andrew greeted Lambert and Hook like old friends in the car park of the small plastics factory. Let them see that you had nothing to hide, that you positively welcomed detectives into your life. Let both your staff and the CID see that you were anxious to clear up this shocking business as quickly as possible.

'How is the investigation going?' he said earnestly, as he led the two men through to his office and instructed his secretary rather imperiously that they should not be disturbed.

'It's progressing,' said Lambert enigmatically, and refused the offer of coffee. 'We now know more about all members of the cast than we did yesterday morning. Including many things which they chose to conceal from us initially.'

Andrew nodded, flicking a smile on to his rather florid face, and delivered the sentiments he had rehearsed in the minutes before they arrived. 'I'm glad to hear it. The sooner this mystery is solved the better. Particularly for my wife, who is suffering attention from the media at a time when she is naturally very distressed.'

'I see. Well, we would be nearer to a solution if you hadn't withheld information from us yesterday.'

Andrew felt himself flushing; he wondered how much of that would be apparent to this calmly challenging man with the lined, experienced face and the all-seeing grey eyes. He was the head of a prosperous business. It was a long time since anyone had challenged him directly, insultingly, like this, and he found himself unprepared for it. He sensed a blunt denial would only increase his problems. 'My wife has a lot to lose. You can't blame us for trying to avoid embarrassment.'

'I made it clear to you that in a murder inquiry there can be no secrets. You chose to ignore that. You have a chance to retrieve things now.' Lambert looked at the clearly distressed man behind the big desk. 'Wherever possible, confidences are respected. Unless it proves to be evidence in a murder trial, what you say to us here need go no further.'

Andrew Dalrymple stared hard at the leather panel in the centre of his desk, at the art deco pen set with its glass ink containers which he never used. He could see every facet of the cut glass and the silver decoration, every irrelevant detail he had never noticed before, as he forced himself into the most painful words he had ever uttered. 'Logan had an affair with Maggie. Five years ago. About that, anyway.' He still wasn't sure how long it had been going on when he found out about it.

Lambert said quietly, 'How long did this affair last?'

'About a year.' He didn't want these dispassionate, unfeeling men accusing him of inaccuracy, did he? Andrew studied the empty surface of his desk still, as if it was suddenly of intense interest to him.

'How deep was the relationship between them?'

Now at last he did look up into the man's face and stared at it with hate. 'How the hell do I know? What sort of question is that?'

'An important one, Mr Dalrymple. I'm sorry I have to ask it, but it's necessary, I assure you. A passing fling may have little significance for either party. A deeper relationship may leave passions which are still very strong, even five years later.'

'You're saying that my wife may have killed Logan.'

'I'm saying that we need to know the facts about how she felt about him at the time of his death. Just as we need to know similar facts about anyone else who was involved with Terry Logan.'

'Oh, there were plenty of those!' His snarling contempt was a relief to him. He wished there were more phrases he could fling at them, to release his pain and frustration. 'Logan had no loyalty to anyone, least of all Maggie. I told her that, but she wouldn't listen to me!'

'Mr Logan was a single man. We've already heard that he had many liaisons.'

'That's what you call them, is it? Well, you're right. Anyone who took his fancy got his full attention, for the time being at least. And he didn't care whether they wore trousers or skirts. Oh, he was very versatile, was Mr bloody Logan!'

Lambert studied the suffering man dispassionately, then gave the slightest of nods to Hook, who took up the questioning. Bert said quietly, almost apologetically, 'We have to take these things into account, Andrew. You must see that this gives Maggie a possible motive for murder.'

'She didn't kill him.'

The denial was automatic, unthinking.

'You're sure that this affair was all over?' Hook asked. 'Sure that the passions which no doubt went with it and the resentment at the way that it ended are now just history?'

'How do you know how it ended?'

Bert smiled at him, a psychotherapist encouraging talk and the release it would bring. 'We don't know, Andrew. And we don't need all the detail, but we do need to be assured that—'

'I'll tell you how it ended. He was going off to meet someone else when he left her. Not even a woman, but a mere boy! Oh, I don't mean he was under age – our Mr Logan was far too fly for that. But he was two-timing Maggie with a young man of nineteen or twenty. He said he needed innocence in his life as well as his Cleopatra, when she caught him out and challenged him! He laughed at her, told her she should try tipping the velvet with her own sex once in a while.'

Andrew found it a relief, once he had started. He had thought he would never be able to humiliate himself like this, but now he had difficulty in closing his mouth on the bile he wished to pour from it. He fought to control himself, knowing that this kind of self-exposure was dangerous with these men, that even this sergeant who seemed so sympathetic was trying to lure from him things which he might later regret.

Hook waited for a moment, then said quietly, 'The team trying to discover who killed Terry Logan have to be interested in all his relationships. You are right to tell us whatever you know about the man.'

'I'll tell you one thing, for a start. I hope whoever killed him gets away with it! The world will be a better place without Logan. So I hope he gets away with it, whoever he is!'

'Or whoever she is.'

'You're saying that Maggie did this?'

'We're saying nothing of the sort, though you've just informed us that she had a motive. The woman scorned – hell hath no fury like hers, we're told. But you have also told us that Mr Logan was bisexual, and so have others. Now that he is a murder victim, all his associations, whether frivolous or more serious, have acquired an importance for us. You must see that.'

Dalrymple paused for so long that they wondered if he was going to speak. The desire to pour out his invective about Logan had left Andrew now, and a belated desire to protect himself and his wife had taken over. Eventually he said slowly and with a surprising dignity, 'You may not see my wife as attractive. I still do. When Logan got his hands on her, she was a beautiful woman in her early forties. No doubt Maggie's maturity and the fact that she was a prominent local figure had its appeal for him.'

A spasm of pain flickered across the florid features, revealing to them how vulnerable were the heart and the emotions of this unlikely, slightly ridiculous figure. 'Maggie found out a lot about Logan in the course of that year – far more than she wanted to know. He had a fascination with youngsters. He kept track of the people who'd been in his school productions after they left the school. I'm sure he enjoyed a succession of squalid little romps with them, among others. I can't give you any details.'

Bert was at his most understanding as he said softly, 'You can't have been very happy when Maggie told you she was going to be in *Hamlet*.'

'I wasn't. Not when I found who was going to direct it. But she was very determined. It was she who got you involved, wasn't it?'

Hook grinned ruefully. 'Mrs Dalrymple can be very persuasive when she's set on something.'

Andrew Dalrymple smiled, for the first time since the meaningless smiles of his formal greetings to them when they arrived at his factory. 'I told you yesterday, she gets things done, does Maggie. And I believed her, when she said the affair with Logan was long over.' He tried not to think of those photographs which she had kept for five years in her secret drawer.

Hook said, 'You were less than frank with us when we saw you yesterday, which was foolish of you, if understandable. Are you now concealing anything else?'

'No. I've told you everything.' He certainly looked as if he had: his normally florid face had a grey, exhausted look.

Hook nodded. Then as if he were merely concluding the formalities, he said, 'We had better have the name of this young man who caused Maggie so much pain. The one she found he was seeing at the same time as her.'

'I thought you knew that.' Andrew felt bewildered. It was as if they had outwitted him, without him being aware of how they had done it. He said limply, 'It was Michael Carey, of course.'

Back at Oldford Police Station, DI Rushton had the full post-mortem report on Terry Logan.

It clarified a few factors, but revealed little that was new or useful. Logan had died where he had fallen, in the car park behind the village hall. In other words, he had not been killed elsewhere, with the body dumped in the car park to confuse matters. He had died many hours before the body was found by the dog-walker in the first light of Thursday morning. Between ten and two on the previous night was as precise as the pathologist was prepared to be.

It looked more and more certain that Logan had been killed as he approached his car, but how long he had stayed in the hall after the rehearsal was over, no one seemed to know. Intensive house to house inquiries in Mettlesham village and the scattered housing around there had thrown up no one who had passed the village hall on foot after ten thirty. The pub was at the other end of the village, and so far none of its customers had admitted to passing the village hall after the last drinks of the evening. It seemed that apart from the cast very few people even knew that there had been the first rehearsal of a play that night.

Various 'foreign' fibres had been found on the dead man's clothing and sent to the forensic laboratory. They would be retained there: if clothing fibres could later be matched with apparel which a murder suspect had been wearing on that night, they might eventually become evidence in court. But Bert Hook was not hopeful about that. He recalled that during the first scene rehearsed, where everyone in the cast had been involved, Terry Logan had frequently moved among his players, pushing actors into the positions he thought they should adopt upon a crowded stage. Fibres from the sweaters which most of them had worn might well be found quite innocently upon the victim's clothing.

The murder weapon was simply a very sharp knife. Forensics had not even committed themselves yet on whether the blade was a double-edged one. In crimes involving multiple stab wounds, all sorts of statistics about the length and construction of the knife employed could be deduced; with the single fatal wound to the throat in this case, no more details could be expected. A detailed search of the area had revealed no sign of the weapon at the scene. This again was what the CID team expected: probably the knife which had killed Terry Logan was now at the bottom of a pond or a river, where it would never be discovered.

It was the expected picture, but a bleak one. 'We don't have much from the house to house as yet,' Chris Rushton said. 'We'd have a better chance if it was June. People are not only out more in summer, but they notice more. If suspects are driving around in cars in November, all most people see is the lights of the car. It's only policemen who occasionally notice registration numbers.'

Lambert nodded. 'If it was Maggie Dalrymple or Ian Proudfoot or Michael Carey who did this, they're not telling us the truth about their movements.'

'Or Andrew Dalrymple,' said Hook.

'Or Andrew Dalrymple,' agreed Lambert ruefully, admitting another candidate on to their short list. 'Either they didn't drive home as they said they did, or they came out again and drove back to Mettlesham to commit murder. Becky Clegg or Jack Dawes, on the other hand, could have simply waited for

Logan to come out of the hall, slit his throat, and then zoomed away on that motorbike, merely arriving home a little later than they claim they did.'

'Which is what Dawes seems to have done,' Rushton said eagerly. 'We caught his mother out on the time he came in. She was trying to tell Bert and me that it was earlier than it was.'

'She then claimed she'd been drinking and was a little fuzzy,' said Hook. 'We'd have difficulty making much out of it in court without more tangible evidence.'

'It's emerging that most of the people involved are hiding things,' said Lambert wearily. 'Over the next day or two, we'll have to find out which of them is also concealing murder.'

'Or which combination of them,' said Hook reluctantly. 'Becky Clegg and Jack Dawes could have done this together. Or one could be covering for the other. At the moment the only convincing alibi which either of them has rests with the other's account of events.' There was still a part of him which fervently hoped that Becky Clegg, the young woman he had pointed towards a better life, wasn't involved in a vicious murder.

Rushton nodded. 'We have to remember that both of them have records and both of them have carried knives in the past. The Clegg girl actually assaulted another girl with a knife.'

'But she didn't seriously injure her,' Hook said. 'I'm not saying we should ignore it, but knives are almost standard equipment, amongst the people they've operated with in the last few years.'

'Which means they might well have been carrying blades on Wednesday night, whether or not they planned to use them at the outset of the evening,' Rushton said with satisfaction.

Lambert tried to reject the uncharacteristic lassitude he felt stealing through his limbs. It had been a taxing day, after a trying night at the hospital. He really was getting old, he thought: he might even have to begin listening to his wife and start taking life more easily if things went on like this. He looked at his watch. 'Bert and I will see what Ian Proudfoot has to say for himself, in the light of what we now know about his dealings with Logan. Then I shall be calling it a day. I've got problems at home.'

Rushton was startled by this unaccustomed acknowledgement

of frailty in his chief. This might be the moment to implement his scheme. 'You need a break from the case, John,' he said. He tried not to let himself be thrown off course by his daring use of the chief's forename. Lambert insisted upon it in informal contexts, but Chris, with his inclination to play everything by the rulebook, always found it difficult to call him John. As though the thought had just occurred to him, he said, 'I think we should all go out for a game of golf over the weekend.'

The old-established duo looked at him curiously. Chris was a beginner at the game. They had enjoyed a memorable evening when the peacock splendour of his brand-new golfing attire had disintegrated into sweaty raggedness under the pressure of their relentless scrutiny and even more relentless advice. They hadn't expected him to volunteer them more amusement as easily as this.

Rushton tried to conceal his eagerness as he said, 'Sunday afternoon would be a good time for me.'

Lambert looked at Hook and Hook looked back at Lambert; they sensed comic relief in the midst of a trying case. 'All right,' said the Chief Superintendent, carefully not looking too eager. 'We can't really be doing much on a Sunday afternoon, I suppose. And we need to prise this lad away from his computer, Bert.'

The thirty-two-year-old 'lad' looked at the ceiling. 'I might be able to get someone to make up a four, if you like.'

'Ah! We told you the game would help you to make friends, didn't we, Bert?'

'Indeed we did. Is this chap anyone we know, Chris?'

'It's a woman, actually.' Chris dropped it in as casually as he could, but he was sure that he was blushing like a schoolboy. 'And you do know her, actually, from a previous case. You may not remember her, though. Her name's Anne Jackson.'

The two older men looked at each other again, this time with the knowing smiles which Chris found quite infuriating.

'Of course we remember,' said Lambert. 'Women like Ms Jackson are not easily forgotten, even by men in such demand from the gentler sex as Bert and I. But are you sure you wish to deliver her into the hands of men like us? Golfing hands, I hasten to add.'

'Oh, Anne won't mind, if you don't. She's played a bit of golf, I believe.'

'Well, I suppose she'll get a lot of shots. And we're always prepared to help women and beginners along, aren't we, Bert?'

'We are indeed. I well remember having the benefit of your advice myself, John, when I was a tyro,' said Hook – rather grimly, John Lambert thought.

'I'm sure we'll both be glad of your sympathy and assistance,' said Rushton.

He didn't permit himself a quiet giggle until he was safely out of the room.

Sixteen

'Did you have to get them to come here?' Angela Proudfoot said petulantly.

Her husband tried to be patient, knowing that he needed her support. 'I asked them to see me at the bank, as they did yesterday. They said they wouldn't want to detain me there, after hours. They seemed to want to come here. Perhaps they like to see where people live, for all I know. I didn't want it any more than you do, but I didn't have much choice.'

'And you still want me to lie for you?'

Ian Proudfoot forced a boyish grin. It sat oddly on the careworn face beneath the balding pate. 'It's not really a lie, is it? You're just confirming the time when I came in – doing the police a service really; eliminating me from their inquiries.' He didn't have to force the nervous laugh, which came unbidden to his lips. 'Unless you think I killed the bugger, of course, in which case you'd be perverting the course of justice, I suppose.'

Angela didn't share his amusement at that preposterous idea. She said, 'It's justice that Logan's been killed at last, if you ask me.'

'Yes. That wouldn't be a very wise thing to say to CID men though, would it?' Ian wanted to take her by the shoulders and shake some sense into her, but he knew that her days of unthinking allegiance were gone. Nowadays he had to persuade her, not direct her.

'I won't know what to do or where to look. I've never been questioned by the police before.' She made it very clear that it was yet another of his failings that was threatening to besmirch this immaculate record.

'They probably won't even want to speak to you, Angela. I'll take them into the front room where we can be private. I wouldn't risk listening at the door, if I were you. I expect they watch out for that sort of thing and spring out suddenly to catch people.'

Like most of his attempts at marital humour, it fell flat. 'I'm not in the habit of eavesdropping, thank you,' Angela said haughtily.

The CID officers came at exactly the time they had agreed. He took them into the dining room which had scarcely been used in the last three months, feeling the winter chill in the room despite the central heating radiator he had switched on an hour earlier when he came into the house. He was careful to sit with the light full on his face and behind his visitors: it would never do to let them deduce from arrangement of the seating positions that he had anything to hide from them. He said nervously, 'I hope what I told you about Terry Logan yesterday has been of some use to you. I didn't like speaking ill of the dead.'

Lambert was in no hurry. He looked at the lean figure who was holding himself so still and nodded slowly. 'You pointed us towards some of his possible liaisons, with both sexes. You also attempted to point us away from yourself and your own relationship with the murder victim.'

It was a calm statement, not a question. Ian's first instinct was to deny it, but the man seemed very confident. He went for a more oblique dismissal. 'My own relationship with Logan is of no possible interest to you, because it had no bearing upon his death.'

'We are the people who will decide that, when we know a lot more about that relationship. That is knowledge which, in your own interest, should be in our possession when we leave here, Mr Proudfoot.'

Ian had expected at least a little preliminary fencing rather than this frontal attack. 'I think I made it clear that Logan and I were not bosom pals. We had a common interest in the theatre, that was all.'

'And a history of sharp differences in your professional life, which you deliberately concealed from us when we spoke yesterday.'

'I told you that he removed his account from my branch, shortly after I became manager there. That is hardly concealment.' He was playing for time, trying to organize his thoughts and decide exactly what to concede to them. Play it like Claudius, he told himself, the king he should have played in *Hamlet*, the role which might now be denied to him. That 'smiling damned villain', who frustrated Hamlet with his knowledge of the way the world worked. Claudius showed how much you could get away with, if you remained both calm and bold.

'You did not tell us that Mr Logan made a complaint to your head office, that he made a written attack upon your professional standing.'

He wanted to minimize it, to write it off as the spite of a deluded man. Then he thought of these two talking to Angela, of her pouring out her bile about Logan and all he had done to their lives. He said tersely, 'We complained to the school about him. But he didn't take things lying down, Terry Logan. He tried to strike back at my own professional life.'

Keep calm, defend yourself where you must, but with dignity. Be Claudius: retain your control of the situation. Ian Proudfoot gave them a cool, considered, regretful smile. The smile said that this sort of spite was what you had to deal with, when you met human nature at its basest, in men like Logan.

Lambert said, 'Why did you complain to the school?'

He had this ready. They'd expect him to be upset and confused: Claudius wouldn't be. 'It's a long time ago. It doesn't look as serious now as it did then. Sophie, our eldest daughter, was in one of his plays. He humiliated her. He let her learn the whole part and then dropped her from the play entirely, two weeks before the performance.'

'That is unfortunate. I can see how it would upset her, and you through her. But it is surely a director's right to change his cast.'

'It wasn't the actual decision, it was Logan's manner of implementing it which caused the trouble. He humiliated a sixteen-year-old girl in front of the whole of a large cast. In effect, he ridiculed her efforts and championed those of the girl who was to take her place. It was calculated cruelty. Sophie had a minor breakdown; she was off school for seven weeks of her GCSE year.'

'It sounds like some sort of personal attack on his part. Was it?'

'You would need to ask him about that. But unfortunately, of course, you can't grill him as you are now grilling me.

Murder victims become paragons of virtue, don't they, as soon
as they die? At least, as far as our admirable press are concerned
they do. I've noticed that often.'

Keep it measured, ironic, acerbic but controlled. King
Claudius was always controlled in public. Ian gave them the
sardonic smile he had rehearsed in front of the mirror for the
king.

'We can't ask him, as you say. It couldn't have been usual
conduct for him or he wouldn't have been so successful in
his work in the school.'

'He was a good director: I've never disputed that, have I?
I've asserted it, in fact. I told you yesterday, that's the only
reason why I considered working with the man in *Hamlet*.'

Lambert reflected that it wasn't just in the professional
theatre that actors had huge egos. Bert had told him that
Proudfoot was going to be very good in the play, and he
suspected that he would have taken the part whatever he thought
of Logan, because he desperately wanted to play the role.

Lambert tried to conceal his irritation with the man as he
pressed him. 'Tell us more about Logan's work in the school
and his relationships with his adolescent players, please.'

Ian pursed his lips, furrowed his brow, took his time, as if
he was formulating his thoughts on the spot. It wouldn't do
to look too eager over this. 'He wanted to get his hands on
selected members of his various casts. Oh, I don't mean he
was a paedophile. He would never have lasted as long as he
did in the school if he'd laid hands on under-age boys and
girls or even sixth-form pupils. He played a longer and cleverer game than that. He made them his protégés, encouraged
them to think that they might have a future in the professional
theatre if they let him guide them. Then, when they were over
eighteen and had left school, several of them ended up in his
bed.'

Both the CID men felt the familiar frustration of a murder
case: you could never have the victim's views. They would
have liked now to take this stuff back to Terry Logan, to see
his reactions to some of the accusations being thrown at him
by the people who had surrounded him. Instead, Lambert said
a little sourly, 'And how did the school react to your complaints?'

'The then head teacher pretended to investigate and then
said they were much exaggerated. He retreated behind the old

smoke-screen of making allowances for the artistic tempera-
ment. He said that Logan had no doubt acted a little insensi-
tively, but that he was a talented and valued member of staff,
who must be allowed to make his own decisions when it came
to school productions. He pointed out that the girl who had
taken my daughter's place was in fact very good, that she had
enjoyed what he called a triumph in the part when the play
was actually staged.'

Bert Hook came in now, his soft Herefordshire tones
sounding less threatening than Lambert's more urgent questioning. 'You said earlier that what happened in the bank was
connected with your complaints to the school.'

'It was a direct reaction to it. You must understand that
Logan was difficult to attack in his school persona. He wasn't
interested in promotion, or in anything beyond the teaching
of drama and his school productions, because he had private
money. So long as he could keep his job and exploit the contacts
with young people which it gave him, he was quite content.
Because most parents only knew him through the plays and
musicals he produced, he had made himself a considerable
reputation; he was both popular and successful.'

Ian let a little of his frustration come out in the bitter pronun-
ciation of the adjectives; there could surely be nothing wrong
with that, now that he had declared his hatred of the man.
Hook brought him back patiently to the bank. 'But he didn't
accept your complaints meekly, did he?'

'No. I was just pointing out that he was pretty well invulnerable in his own professional life, because he was clever
and talented and because he had money. But a couple of
months after the incident at the school, I found that he could
also be spiteful. He claimed that I had given him bad advice
on a share purchase.'

'And had you?'

Ian Proudfoot hadn't expected any challenge so direct from
affable Bert Hook, but he controlled his anger by forcing it
into a bitter smile. 'I hadn't given him any advice at all,
because he hadn't asked for any. But he had bought the shares
shortly after his account had been lodged with us and sold
them a few months later at a substantial loss, so that he had
the documentation to back up his vile remarks. He even
suggested that I had been unloading the shares from other

customers on to him, before the price fell. It was all lies, but
it made life very difficult for me. He knew one of the bank's
directors and he dropped all sorts of nasty innuendos about
me into his ears as well as writing in to complain.'

'But you kept your job.'

'Of course I did. I hadn't done anything wrong and, whatever Logan might claim, no one could prove that I had. But
it was a bad time. I had four children who were still dependent
on me and I needed the job that was being put in jeopardy. I
kept my job as a branch manager, as you say. But I've never
been promoted to anything beyond that. I might have had a
much more important post in the investment department of
the bank by now if it hadn't been for Terence Logan's efforts.'
His resentment hissed out on the sibilants.

Hook nodded thoughtfully. 'And yet despite this very serious
difference between you, you chose to volunteer yourself for
a production of *Hamlet* which was to be directed by this same
Terry Logan.'

It was exactly what Angela had said to him so often over
the last few weeks, in terms which were considerably less
polite. At least he could respond honestly to this one – and
shouldn't Hook, as a fellow thespian, understand his eagerness? He ignored the keen-eyed Lambert and addressed his
remarks to the DS. 'Amateur dramatics have been more than
a hobby to me, when I look back over the years; they've been
something nearer to a passion, Bert. There's a small part of
me that still wishes I'd had a go at becoming a professional
when I was a young man, before my family responsibilities
made that impossible.'

Hook stubbornly reiterated his point. 'You're saying that
your desire to perform on stage overcame even your dislike
and distrust of the man you suspected of damaging your
career?'

Put in these calm, questioning phrases, the argument which
Angela had hurled at him so stridently seemed to have more
weight. Ian strove desperately to convince this more objective listener. 'I've never had the chance to play Shakespeare,
apart from a couple of the comedies whilst I was still at school.
Hamlet was a dream come true for me. Claudius is a wonderful
role, which I never thought I'd get the chance to play. It may
not reflect well on me, but I suspect I'd have taken it on

whoever was directing the production. The fact that I knew that Terry Logan was an excellent director, whatever the state of his personal life, only made the opportunity seem more valuable.'

Bert Hook, who in his single evening of rehearsal had caught the merest whisper of the excitement which Proudfoot was voicing, judged that this yearning to play the role, this jettisoning of the normal moral canons of behaviour, was quite genuine. He was surprised at the depth of the passion in this man, who in his professional life was necessarily so quiet and reserved. Bert nodded a couple of times over his notebook, then said calmly, 'What time did you get back here after the rehearsal on Wednesday night?'

'About half past nine. I told you that yesterday.' Ian hesitated. 'My wife will confirm that for you.'

It was Lambert who now said, 'We wondered if you might wish to change that time.'

Suddenly, after keeping calm so far, Ian was beset by panic. He could see Angela's face, see her letting him down if they chose to press her on this. 'I . . . I might have got it wrong, I suppose.'

'One of our team has found a witness who says that you were in the Crown Inn in Calford at around ten o'clock on Wednesday night,' Lambert said. 'Are you saying that this man has made a mistake, that you were in fact in this house at that time?'

Ian felt as if the blood was draining from his sallow face. 'No. I was in the Crown as you say.'

'You'd forgotten that?'

'No. I've just been telling you that I hated Logan. I wanted an alibi for the time of his death. That's why I told you I was home earlier than I was.' He found that he was calm again now that the moment of his exposure had arrived. 'I didn't kill him, but I knew you'd have me down as a suspect once you discovered what had gone on between us in the past.'

'Which you also attempted to conceal from us yesterday.'

'Yes.'

'In fact, very little of what you told us yesterday was true, was it?'

'I suppose not. I can only say that I saw it as concealing embarrassing facts, rather than telling you lies.'

'A rather peculiar moral viewpoint. And one which has now landed you deep in trouble. When did you leave the Crown on Wednesday night?'

Ian wondered how closely this anonymous observer had monitored his movements in the pub. He had sat alone in one of the alcoves and had spoken to no one. Perhaps he should have realized that a stranger would always be remembered on a quiet Wednesday night in a country pub. 'About half past ten. I don't think the landlord had called last orders.'

'And what were your movements then?'

'I drove straight back here. I'm pretty sure I was in before eleven – the exact time didn't seem important, at the time.' He was glad he had put that phrase in: it was surely what an innocent man would have said. He had more sense than to say that Angela would confirm this, when he had earlier in effect asserted that his wife was prepared to lie for him.

Lambert stared at him for a long, unembarrassed moment. 'It would obviously be in your interest to produce someone who can confirm that you were nowhere near Mettlesham Village Hall at the time when Terry Logan died. I imagine that that might be difficult for you.' He spoke in a carefully neutral tone as he and Hook stood up. Then, using a favourite technique of throwing in a key question just when a man was relaxing in the thought of their departure, he said, 'What was the name of the girl who took over from your daughter when she was dumped from that school play, Mr Proudfoot?'

Ian had thought they might already have known that. Perhaps they did; perhaps they just wanted to trip him up in yet another lie. Well, they wouldn't do that. He had nothing to lose by being completely honest on this one. Rather the reverse, in fact, when he thought about it.

'It was Becky Clegg,' he said with a wan smile.

Seventeen

There were still roses blooming in John Lambert's garden in this mildest of autumns. His headlights picked them out, unnaturally large on top of the bushes in the darkness.

On other nights he would have savoured these late blooms. Tonight he scarcely noticed them as he eased the spacious old Vauxhall into the garage. Normally, he would have savoured being home after a trying day. Over the last few years, he had taught himself to appreciate domesticity, to enjoy his isolation in the comfort of his home from the teeming and often harsh world outside it.

Tonight was different. He was beset by an overwhelming weariness, a reluctance to open the familiar door and join this smaller world beyond it. The selfish part of his psyche, which he felt was never far from the surface, told him that he had a right to expect calmness here, that he should not be having to deal with another crisis after the various stresses of his working day. A crisis which he had not prepared for, an emergency where he would have to improvise to meet the particular demands of a daughter whose life had been thrown into turmoil through no fault of his. In fact, if Jacky had listened to him all those months ago . . .

Lambert was taken over now by another more familiar emotion in his domestic life: an overwhelming sense of guilt that he should even be able to entertain such thoughts. He took a deep breath, summoned the false cheerfulness of a smile to his lips, and went through the front door and into his home.

Christine was in the sitting room and what he saw there made him stop dead at the door. It was like a scene from a nineteen-fifties women's magazine, where wives were encouraged to be homemakers and to see their roles as ensuring maximum comfort for the breadwinner of the house. Lambert remembered seeing pictures of such scenes in his mother's *Woman's Own*, and wondering as a six-year-old why she sniffed so derisively at them.

Christine was sitting as if carefully posed in an armchair. His own chair was ready for him on the other side of the fireplace, with a bottle of beer and a glass on the small table beside it. Save for the absence of slippers and the flames of a coal fire in the hearth, it could have been that same vintage illustration he remembered. 'I heard you putting the car away,' said his wife with a cheerful smile. 'Mine's a gin and tonic, but I thought my old man might appreciate a beer.'

John Lambert sat down wonderingly. This couldn't be true. It was some elaborate and tasteless period caricature conjured up by Christine to mock him. He realized that the prepared smile was still on his lips. He decided that he might as well play along with this. He sat down, poured the beer into his tilted glass with elaborate care to avoid excessive foam, and took the long, appreciative pull at it which the scene demanded.

'Dinner nearly ready?' he asked at length. He looked across at the gin and tonic and his wife's elegant dress and wondered anew at this strange tableau. 'I can give you a hand with things, if you like.'

'No need for that. Jacky's getting the meal tonight.'

'She's home from the hospital?'

Christine looked at her watch. 'Three hours ago now. She insisted that she was going to cook tonight. I decided that it might be good therapy for her. Anyway, I'm not complaining, after what she's put us through over the last day or two.'

An implied criticism of her beloved daughter from Christine Lambert? Lambert had more sense than to endorse it. 'She's been through a lot in a short time, since that bastard walked out on her.' He glanced towards the kitchen. 'Should I go in there and offer to help her?'

'I'd leave her to it. I think concentrating on something ordinary like food is exactly what she needs.'

He ignored Christine of course, sauntering into the kitchen as casually as he could with his tankard of beer in his hand, trying to behave as if finding Jacky cooking the family evening meal for the first time in ten years was exactly what he had expected. She glanced up at him, gave him the wide smile which had once been her childhood recognition of his arrival.

She gave no hint of the effort this was costing her. 'How's the world of detection, Dad?'

He dropped into an awful parody of black and white gangster movies which had been a joke between them when she was fourteen. 'I'm playing a hunch, kid. Nobody ain't saying nuttin' to no one, but when you been in this game as long as I have, you gotta play your hunches.'

'You ask me, that doll's hidin' something. You gotta go for the doll. With curves like that, it's gonna be the blonde that did it, Mister.' Jacky sashayed across from cooker to sink with a pan of potatoes, then dissolved into laughter that was a little too near to hysteria. 'Your Bogart isn't what it was, Dad!'

'It was meant to be Robert Mitchum. At least I think it was. You won't believe it, but those blokes were even before my time.' He went and put his arms round her waist as she stood draining the water from the potatoes into the sink. 'You're going to be all right now, aren't you, Jacky?'

It was half a question and half an order. She set down the pan on the side of the sink and turned round to him, managing a smaller but this time completely genuine smile. 'I'm going to be all right, Dad. I'm not going to let the bastard grind me down, am I?'

He'd forgotten that he'd ever delivered that police cliché to her. It had been when she had left home to set up house with the man who had now deserted her. He had felt guilty for spoiling her happiness at the time, but his warning now seemed wholly justified. 'That's the spirit, girl!' He tousled her hair and was stupidly comforted to find it still so glossy and healthy.

She sent him out whilst she dished up the food. The meal was, surprisingly, reassuringly good. Christine made the right conventional noises about how nice it was to be waited upon for once and John opened a bottle of claret to go with the braised beef, studiously avoiding his wife's warning eye as he filled the glasses. Jacky drank very little of hers, then put her hand over the top of her glass when her father went to refill it. She grinned sardonically at Christine. 'You needn't worry, Mum, I'm not about to become a lush. Last night was a one-off, and the consequences were so embarrassing that I am duly contrite.'

'It was your dad's fault, if you ask me,' said Christine

Lambert, as if delivering a well-rehearsed line of dialogue.
The happy trio all knew it wasn't, but they were content to
let mother have the closing words on the matter.

At ten o'clock, with the meal long over and a happy somno-
lence descending upon the diners, Lambert said he needed a
breath of air and wandered round his garden with a torch. The
night was still uncharacteristically mild for the second half of
November. There was not a breath of wind to disturb the clear,
moonless Gloucestershire darkness, but there was no danger
of a frost.

John Lambert knew now that his daughter was going to be
all right and the world seemed suddenly not such a bad place
after all. He wondered why all the detectives he glimpsed on
television seemed to be such tortured, insecure figures in their
private lives.

'There are still roses in bloom out there,' he announced
when he went back indoors.

Friday night and the end of the working week.

The cities of Gloucester and Cheltenham become noisy
places, with young minds determined upon celebration and
young bodies beset by booze and drugs. A busy night for the
city police, who handle the routine noise and violence with
practised hands and a slightly world-weary efficiency.

Away from the city, in a rural Gloucestershire many miles
from the illumination of street lighting, things are so quiet that
you would scarcely suspect a police presence. Nevertheless,
the rule of law is represented here. It is admittedly represented
so minimally, almost apologetically, that you would hardly
register its presence, but it is here nonetheless.

PC Alan Jones is young and inexperienced. Indeed, he has
been allotted the Friday night work which falls as naturally
as autumn leaves to the young and the inexperienced, which
the sergeant in charge of the duty rosters sees as wholly appropriate for the latest addition to his work force.

PC Jones is not even guarding a crime scene, with the
blue and white strands marking its limits. He is one remove
further from the action than that. He is stationed not where
a murder victim met his end, but at the house of the deceased.
Scarcely worth the waste of even this minimal manpower in
the station sergeant's view, but the edict had come down

from the mountain where dwelt CID, and whatever his views of that august body, he wasn't going to risk ignoring it.

So PC Alan Jones, with his torch and his asp and his apprehension about the dark which he could never admit, found himself at the former manor house which had been the residence of Terry Charles Logan. It was an impressive place, very dark and square against the blue-black, moonless sky as PC Jones looked up at it from the wrought-iron gates.

He just wished that the spot was a little less isolated.

It seemed to Jones a long time since he had heard even a passing car on the lane below the house. He had watched the orange light from the car's headlamps between the hedges, until the last faint glimmer had disappeared into the woods of the valley; then he had listened to the car's engine note for a good couple of minutes after this, until its last sound had died away into the night. He thought for a second or two that he caught an echo of the engine sound from the other direction entirely, but the sound died in his ears as abruptly as it had entered them.

The night and its stillness no doubt played tricks with sounds as it did with other things.

'Patrol the site,' the sergeant had told him. 'Walk round the perimeter from time to time and flash your torch into every dark corner. It's straightforward work, lad, even for someone as wet behind the ears as you are. Don't think you can sit inside with your feet up all night, but feel free to vary the routine of your patrols, so that anyone watching in the darkness cannot anticipate your movements.'

Alan had joined in the station sergeant's mirth at that melodramatic idea at the time. Now, in the blackness and the silence which surrounded the square stone building, it did not seem funny at all. Jones had grown up in a terrace of houses in Cardiff, where the sound of human voices was never far away. He wondered now why Terry Logan, a man who by all accounts could have chosen exactly the house he wanted, had sought out such isolation for his dwelling.

PC Jones could not dismiss from his mind the knowledge that the man who had lived in this house had had his throat cut from ear to ear two nights ago, in a stillness and an isolation less profound than this one. He tried to control his erratic breathing by whistling, sporadically and tunelessly, as he walked along beside the wall at the front of the garden, feeling less threatened here on more open ground. A screeching owl rent the air with its raucous call half a mile away, down the valley, as if in response to his whistling, and Alan was glad of even that eldritch sound.

He went reluctantly back up the garden path towards the great mass of stone above him, playing his torch on every angle of the building, telling himself like a parent comforting a child that the bright white light showed that there was nothing to fear. He went into the kitchen at the back of the house which was his base for the night, hesitated for a moment, and then locked the door behind him. It was against regulations, but who was going to know?

At least now he could settle down for a while in comfort, knowing that no one could surprise him. It might be a totally ridiculous idea that someone with a knife was going to spring upon him, but if he locked the door it couldn't happen, could it? And no one would be any the wiser in the morning, when the bright light of the dawn would make all such notions absurd.

Alan Jones looked at his watch. Twenty past one. How slowly the time seemed to pass, when you were on your own in a place like this. He couldn't open his thermos flask and have a cup of coffee until three. That is what he had decreed at ten o'clock, when his stint here had begun. Well, you had to adapt to circumstances, the police training course had taught him. He would have a cup now. And perhaps one of his biscuits. Save the main snack for three o'clock, as planned, but demonstrate your flexibility.

He sat down at the table and undid his greatcoat. Might as well relax; no need to go back outside for another half an hour or so. He nibbled his digestive biscuit very slowly and deliberately, making it last as he had done when he was a child. He wondered what time the dawn would come. Not much before seven, at this time in November, but out in the country like this you would be able to see the grey streaks in the east well before you were aware of them in the town.

He was halfway through his coffee, savouring the sharp heat at the back of his throat, when he heard the sound which set his heart pounding. It was at the other end of the house. A distant, muffled scratching. He told himself that he was imagining things, but he did not believe himself for even a moment. And sure enough, no more than three seconds later, the sound came again. The front door, it must surely be. Well, probably the front door: from the other end of the house, you couldn't really be sure.

The scratching was there again, persistently, now, and then abruptly it stopped. There was another sound, a sort of click. And then perhaps a footfall. But he couldn't be sure of that.

His first thought was that he should be out there, tackling the intruder, if intruder it was. Then he remembered his orders, the orders no one had paid much attention to, because the possibility of anyone coming here was surely so remote. You radioed in for help. You did nothing but maintain a watch, until reinforcements arrived. Until a car full of powerful, confident, experienced officers came and took over.

Thank God for the rule book.

Jones spoke softly into his radio, fearful in case that sinister, unseen presence at the other end of the house should hear his tremulous tones. To his immense relief, he heard a calm, answering voice, redolent with the warmth and safety and camaraderie of the station. He was told to maintain a watching brief, to do nothing unless the suspected intruders tried to leave the premises.

PC Alan Jones prayed fervently that they would not do that.

They? Had he already decided that there was more than one of them? He found himself wondering absurdly whether it would make him less of a wimp if there were several of them rather than a single felon. But he wasn't a wimp at all, he told himself firmly. Much as he would have liked to make an arrest single-handed, he was simply observing tedious police routine. He had no choice about that.

Unless of course the burglars got what they wanted and left before the cavalry arrived. He heard another sound, almost above his head, and welcomed it. He switched off the light in the kitchen, went to the door into the hall and listened intently. Whoever was out there had gone upstairs. They weren't going to leave in a hurry, unless they were disturbed. And they certainly weren't going to be disturbed by PC Alan Jones.

He went on listening. He heard other muffled, indeterminate sounds. Sounds he would never have heard if he had not had young, efficient, hyperactive ears. They were definitely upstairs now, moving from room to room up there. He could not tell whether it was one person or more than one, but they seemed to be going through the house.

Alan Jones, with his head pressed hard against the edge of the closed door, wondered how long it would take them to reach the kitchen.

He heard the sound of the squad car coming rapidly up the valley, held his breath as it came nearer and nearer, until it was certain that this was his colleagues and that they were coming here. He thought that he had never heard a more welcome sound than that engine racing through the gears.

Jones had feared that they would come with sirens blaring, alerting the anonymous presence upstairs to their arrival long before they were here, compelling some reaction from him to prevent their escape. They did not do that. You would have thought they were innocent revellers, returning late to some house further along the valley. They were at the gates of Terry Logan's house before those who were within it illegally were even aware of the danger.

PC Jones hastily unlocked the back door of the house, peered out at the shadowy figures who were moving up the slope of the long front garden, flashed his torch briefly and blindingly towards them, congratulated himself that there seemed to be several large and powerful officers.

There were four of them, in fact. Five, when he added himself to the forces of good. Alan Jones felt a reassuring surge of power coursing through his veins. They'd show the bastards who was in charge here, now. How could these impertinent sods think they could come breaking into the house of a dead man and get away with it? He gripped his asp firmly and strode towards the house beside his leader.

The two people who had been searching the upstairs rooms realized too late what was happening. Only when the car stopped at the gates did they realize that it was coming here, and by that time they were trapped. Caution was no use to them now. They tumbled rapidly, clumsily, noisily down the stairs and out of the front door they had opened so cautiously twenty minutes earlier.

Straight into the waiting arms of the police. A man and a woman, realizing swiftly that they were outnumbered and that resistance was useless. A confused, scuffling scene, with obscenities flying through the night. They were turned with arms up their backs and their faces against the cold stone of the house and assured in urgent monosyllables that they were nicked.

PC Alan Jones was allowed to issue the formal words of the arrest, to announce to the two heavily breathing miscreants the absurd formalities, that they had no need to say anything but that it might prejudice their defence if they failed to declare things which they might wish to use in court. It was his collar, the sergeant said, so he was duly belligerent as he shouted the words through the night.

The captives said nothing as they were put in the back of the second car when it arrived, their heads assiduously lowered by the police to prevent injury as they entered it.

As the police vehicle began its careful journey to the station and the cells, Jack Dawes and Becky Clegg stared steadily ahead of them into the darkness.

Eighteen

Saturday morning. A still, mild, November day, with a weak sun rising late over a quiet landscape in Gloucestershire.

Maggie Dalrymple hurried her husband through his breakfast and then stood in the bay window of the big house, watching his car disappear down the lane. He often went into the works for a couple of hours on a Saturday morning. It was quiet then, so that he could get on with a few checks on financial matters without the inevitable interruptions of midweek.

Sometimes his wife protested that he worked too hard, that he should be taking things more easily now and enjoying the benefits and privileges of success. Today she was happy to see him go.

She was determined that she would not play the local grande dame with the visitors from CID, sensing that they would be less impressed by her councillor and JP status than most other people whom she met in the course of her busy life. When they came at nine fifteen, she took them into the spectacular dining kitchen and sat them down on the other side of the big rectangular table. If they were surprised to be accommodated here, they gave no sign of it. She felt Chief Superintendent Lambert's grey, observant eyes upon her from the moment he entered the room.

She managed to wring a rather wan smile from Bert Hook, and tried not to think of the very different circumstances in which she had recruited him against his will into the cast of the ill-fated *Hamlet*. That now seemed much more than twelve days earlier. DS Hook said, 'There are one or two things we now need to clear up, Maggie.'

He was still using the form of address she had asked him for, but he looked as if it had cost him an effort.

'I'm ready to help in any way I can, of course,' she said,

finding herself anxious for this preliminary fencing to be over. Maggie Dalrymple was used to tackling issues head on.

Lambert accommodated her in this. 'You concealed the closeness of your relationship with Terry Logan from us. Lied about it, in fact.'

Maggie found herself blushing furiously. She could not remember the last time she had been called a liar. She wished now that she had put on make-up, instead of presenting herself groomed but unadorned to them, in the hope that such defencelessness might imply honesty. She said with all the dignity she could summon, 'I think you mean the closeness of my *former* relationship. That is history. It is a mere distraction. In terms of Terry's death, I thought you would be only concerned with events in the immediate past.'

Lambert ignored that. 'You had an intense relationship with a murder victim, which ended with great bitterness on your side. You are too intelligent a woman to think that such an affair is irrelevant to our investigation.'

She set her lips in a firm line for a second or two before she spoke. 'There was nothing between Terry and me at the time of his death.'

'Your husband was plainly doubtful about that.'

She wondered exactly how much Andrew had revealed to these observant men when he spoke to them yesterday. More than he had been aware of, no doubt: he was very easy to read, was Andrew, she thought with a flash of irritation.

'Perhaps he was doubtful, as you say. If so, he was wrong.'

'Was it not natural for him to be suspicious, when you not only joined Logan's cast for *Hamlet* but went round recruiting people like Sergeant Hook to take part? You were acting as Mr Logan's assistant. That implies a close relationship between the two of you.'

Maggie took her time and allowed herself a knowing, slightly patronizing smile. 'You have obviously not been involved in amateur dramatics, Mr Lambert. Terry was an excellent director: I'm sure other people have already told you that. Much more than that, he was offering me the chance to play the Queen in *Hamlet*. I'd have killed for that!' She gave a nervous little giggle as she realized what she had said. 'Well, not literally, of course – that is just a piece of stage exaggeration. But this was almost surely my last chance to play

Shakespeare; certainly my last chance to play a plum part like
Queen Gertrude. I'd have given a great deal for that. Certainly
the fact that I had a past with Terry Logan wasn't going to
stop me. The only really important fact was that I had confidence in him to produce something good from his cast. Possibly
something exceptional.'

For a moment, she was lost in the thought of the possible
triumph which this death had denied her. Lambert was irritated by what seemed to him a ridiculous distortion of values,
but he believed that this production had been as important to
her as she said. Nevertheless, it was still possible, he told
himself, that a passionate hatred of the man who had treated
her badly had overridden this enthusiasm for what was after
all a hobby. Joining the production had been her best opportunity to get close to the man who had ended their affair so
brutally. He said, 'I understand that there was great acrimony
when your affair with Mr Logan ended.'

She threw him a fleeting look of pure hatred before she
recovered herself. 'No doubt Andrew has given you his account
of that. My husband is very protective of me. Terry and I had
enjoyed what I considered a tender relationship for about a
year. He dismissed me as if I was little more than a tart.'

'To set himself up with a man.'

'A young man, in fact. A man less than half my age at the
time, as Terry pointed out to me. The break-up showed me
his very worst side. I have been glad of that in the years since
then. It has made it easier to see what a fool I was to get
involved with him.'

'And the young man in question was Michael Carey.'

'It was. A very attractive young man, as Terry Logan was
at pains to tell me.'

'A man who was also to appear in this production. Wasn't
that yet another thing which should have kept you away from
it?'

She smiled again at his naïvety about the fascination of
drama. 'Michael Carey is the most gifted actor I have seen
outside the professional theatre. I have no doubt that he would
have made a striking and exciting Hamlet – indeed, he probably still will at some time in the future, in a professional
context. It would have been a privilege to appear alongside
him in the play.'

'Even though he had replaced you in Logan's bed?'

She was not thrown by the directness of the phrase. 'Michael Carey was discarded himself in due course. No doubt as abruptly and cruelly as I had been. We might even have exchanged bitchy remarks about our director when we had got closer to each other, after a month or so of rehearsals. Michael Carey's acting capacity was far more important to me than his history. And I'm sure that in turn he was far more interested in me as his mother in the play than as a former bedmate of the director.'

Lambert nodded slowly, then said quite casually, 'Your husband wasn't in the house when you got home from the rehearsal on Wednesday night, was he?'

Maggie felt her head spin. She even lost sight of the calm, relentless face in front of her for a moment, as her senses reeled in the face of this sudden, unexpected challenge. Again she found herself wondering how much Andrew had told them. How much had he revealed of himself and her to them, when he had thought he was being cautious? How much had they already found from other sources as their team went about finding out the truth of Terry Logan's death? She'd already lied to them once, about her affair with Terry, and they'd come back and humiliated her about that. She couldn't afford to lie again. She said like one in a dream, 'No. Andrew wasn't here when I got in.'

Maggie Dalrymple looked round the big, modern kitchen, with its immaculately clean sink, its rows of cupboards, its food mixer and its array of stainless steel pans. This room which had seemed so innocent before their arrival now seemed threatening. She was beset with the absurd idea of being involved in some grotesque animated cartoon. For a moment she had the feeling that these shining kitchen implements were about to leap forward to denounce her, if she did not tell the truth, the whole truth and nothing but the truth.

It seemed to her a long time before Lambert asked, 'Where was he at that time?'

'I don't know.'

'Where do you think he was?'

'I've no idea.' She wanted to muster some of the spirit and indignation which the normal Mrs Dalrymple would have shown on the phrase, but it would not come. She waited for

Lambert to go on, but just when for the first time she wanted words from him, he did not speak. He watched her with his head just slightly tilted, through those grey eyes which never seemed to blink.

Maggie felt compelled to speak, to fill the silence which seemed to be gathering about her like a tangible thing as she sat at the big deal table. 'This removes Andrew's alibi for the time of the death, doesn't it?'

'It does, yes.' He sighed, then gave her the standard bromide phrases. 'Until we find conclusive proof that he was elsewhere when Mr Logan died, we cannot eliminate him from our inquiries.'

'Andrew didn't kill Terry.'

Lambert didn't react to that. Instead, with a small, mirthless smile, he said, 'The fact that your husband was not here when you returned means also that we have no witness to your own whereabouts at the time of this murder, Mrs Dalrymple.'

Michael Carey had been up since seven. At nine, he took the tray into the bedroom, smiled at the face which emerged reluctantly from beneath the bedclothes, and said brightly, 'Breakfast is served, Tom.' He was only two years older than the twenty-two-year-old in the bed, but he decided to enjoy the role of middle-aged mentor to the young reprobate.

The young man in the bed levered himself up and ran a hand through his tightly curled black hair. 'Do you have to be so damned cheerful at this hour?' he grumbled, surveying the cereals and toast without any obvious enthusiasm.

'It's a sunny autumn morning and you're wasting it,' said Michael. 'I've already been for a brisk run. The autumn colour in the woods around here is something else! I can see why they call this part of the country the Heart of England.'

Tom Baldwin groaned at such animation and enthusiasm. Michael was only two years older than him, but there were times when he seemed to be much more than that. Tom poured the milk on to his cereal and took a first spoonful, as a healthy appetite asserted itself. He munched milk and muesli with full concentration for a moment, then mustered his first grin of the day. 'I don't know how you have the energy to run about the countryside like that after last night,' he said, stretching his limbs luxuriantly beneath the sheets at the memory.

'Personally, I'm still recharging my batteries for the rest of the weekend.'

Michael frowned for a moment. Time for a switch of roles to the concerned but regretful lover. 'There's a snag with that, I'm afraid. I'll have to leave by lunchtime.'

Tom's face clouded. His lips set into the sullen pout of the frustrated child. 'But we agreed we'd have the full weekend together. I've cancelled other things to be with you.'

'Something's come up,' said Michael. 'And no, it's not that, you dirty young sod. Not this time. I've had a phone call from the CID, back in Oldford.' He tried not to sound too important; this must surely make him a more intriguing figure to the man in bed, who had led such a sheltered life himself.

'I thought you'd given them everything they wanted.'

He certainly hadn't done that. But there was no reason to take Tom fully into his confidence. Some day perhaps, if things worked out and this was all over . . . But in his heart, he knew that he would meet other and more exciting people at drama school and in the theatre. He felt with that knowledge a sudden, overwhelming tenderness towards the slim young figure in the bed, who was now preparing to tackle the toast and marmalade.

He tried to sound unconcerned as he said, 'It's this murder they're investigating. The death of the man who was directing me as the Prince in *Hamlet*. They say they want to ask me some further questions, in the light of what they've now learned from other people.'

Tom tried to pretend he cared less than he did about this departure. He said as lightly as he could, 'They'll have you under lock and key if you're not careful.'

Michael Carey sat down on the bed and laughed aloud at such a preposterous idea. 'I expect the plods would like to have the opinion of a man like me on the crime. They offered to come to Warwick, said they'd drive up here to talk to me here, but I thought I'd rather deal with them on my own patch.'

'It's not that far, as they say. You could come back again, after you've spoken with the police.' Tom tried not to sound too desperate.

'I might just do that, if I can get them out of the way quickly enough.' Michael knew even as he spoke that he wouldn't.

'You should have let them come here, then.'

'I'd rather deal with this down there. I don't want your place to have any connection with the sordid business of murder.'

He had improvised the argument to pacify Tom, who didn't know anything about how close he had once been to the murder victim. But as he drove the old Fiesta out of the car park by the flats and waved cheerfully at the wan face beneath Tom's black curls, he realized that it was true.

Michael Carey didn't want what had happened in Gloucestershire to soil the delights of his liaison with Tom Baldwin in Warwick.

'We'll see them together, I think,' said Lambert. 'We can always take up any issues with them separately later, if we should think it necessary.'

Becky Clegg and Jack Dawes were brought up from the separate cells where they had spent most of the night and the entire Saturday morning. Once they were arrested, they had had no opportunity to confer about tactics. They looked shyly at each other in the soulless little cube of the interview room, almost as if they were strangers. Each of them was wondering how much the other had already been questioned about the previous night's fiasco.

Becky was hoping that Bert Hook, whom she now regarded as something of a father-figure, would be questioning them. Instead, she was confronted by Chief Superintendent Lambert and a younger, good-looking, very intense man, who was announced to the cassette tape recorder as Inspector Rushton.

Lambert surveyed the two youngsters impassively for a moment whilst they waited expectantly. Then he gave a world-weary shrug of his shoulders and said, 'We can charge you with breaking and entering, of course. Attempting to steal the property of a dead man: opportunism of the most cynical kind. I can see the magistrates taking a dim view of that. As you've both got criminal records, you might well get custodial sentences.'

It was part of the softening-up process, a preparation for the questions he really wanted to ask them. Perhaps Jack Dawes divined something of that. He said sullenly, 'We didn't do much damage. It was a big oak front door with only a Yale lock. The security system wasn't operating.' He made it sound as if that was unfair, as if the forces of law hadn't been playing by their own rules.

The system hadn't been set because no one knew the code for it; that secret had died with Logan. 'There was a police presence in the house,' Chris Rushton said. 'Less stupid people than you would have expected that.'

Jack Dawes considered the notion that they had walked into a police trap which had been deliberately set for them. He didn't like the idea that he had been both predictable and foolish; the young are thinner-skinned about these things than more practised criminals.

'We didn't steal anything from the house.'

'No. You were surprised before you got to the items you wanted.'

'Or perhaps the items we wanted weren't there.'

Lambert was on to that very quickly. 'What were you looking for in a murder victim's house, Mr Dawes?'

'Papers, that's all. Nothing of value. There was good stuff in there, but we weren't even going to touch it.' He glanced sideways at the white-faced Becky Clegg, who gave an eager confirmatory nod, as if grateful for even this minor acknowledgement of her presence beside him.

'So, what were you after? What was it that was so important to you that you landed yourselves in this mess?'

'Logan kept records. We wanted to get those. To destroy them.' Dawes stared hard at the small square table and the recording machine bearing a cassette which was turning slowly and silently.

'What sort of records, Jack?'

He glanced up sharply at Lambert with this first and unexpected use of his forename. 'Records of what he'd done in the past. Dates and that sort of thing. Logan kept all kinds of details. He had a filing cabinet.'

'And why do you think Mr Logan did that?'

'It gave him a hold over people, didn't it? All kinds of people.'

'You're saying he used it to blackmail people?'

'No. Not for money, anyway. It gave him a hold over people.' He glanced sideways at Becky again and seemed to be reassured by her quick nod of approval. 'He didn't need money, he had plenty of that. But he loved having power. He could make you do what he wanted you to, because he knew things that you wouldn't want revealed.'

'But you didn't find what you were looking for last night?'

'No. We hadn't even found the filing cabinet when your lot sprang the trap on us.'

Chris Rushton couldn't resist an intervention. 'You wouldn't have found it if you'd had the whole night, Mr Dawes. We had already removed that cabinet. It has been in the CID section for the last two days. We are still analysing and documenting its contents.'

This time Jack Dawes and Becky Clegg looked each other fully in the face. Becky had told him that it would be so, but she wasn't going to remind him of that now. She turned back to the two observant men opposite them and said quietly, 'You know what we were trying to conceal, then.'

Chris Rushton repeated stiffly, 'We have recovered a mass of material from Mr Logan's house. We are still processing and recording it.'

'Logan kept all kinds of stuff. He said you never knew when it might come in useful.' She tried to imitate the threatening, derisive tone in which the dead man had used the phrase, but in this soulless place she could not summon it up.

'You are telling us that Mr Logan was a blackmailer then.' Rushton sounded as sceptical as he intended.

'No. Not if you mean he used these things for money. Jack told you, he didn't need money, Terry Logan.'

Jack Dawes heard the bitterness in her voice and came in to support her. 'He kept records of the things he had done himself and the people he had slept with. He was obsessive about it. Like Becky said, he used to say you never knew when these things might come in useful.'

He caught Logan's taunting inflection on the phrase, as Becky had not been able to do. It fell as an eerie echo of the dead man into the quiet, claustrophobic setting of the interview room. There was a little pause before Lambert continued. 'He couldn't use this stuff against you when he was dead. So why risk breaking into his house to steal it?'

Becky glanced quickly at the face of Dawes. 'He liked having power over people, did Logan. Knowledge is power, he used to say, as if that were some sort of joke. He kept stuff from when we were at school. Stuff we didn't even know he had, until he told us about it after we'd left. He also kept tabs on us years later. He knew – well, he knew all about who I was with and what I'd been doing. He knew more than you lot do about me and the people I was with. He knew I'd cut a girl with a blade. He said he could put me behind bars if he wanted to. That was one of his favourite expressions.'

She stopped abruptly on that. She could see the exact look on Terry Logan's face, his quiet smile turning slowly into a leer, as he mouthed the phrase. She wished again that Bert Hook was here; he would surely have understood her pain at being at Logan's mercy, as these two unsympathetic pigs would never do. She said unwillingly, as if it were a confession of weakness rather than something in her favour. 'I've just got myself a decent job. I want to keep it, to go on from here. I didn't want what Logan had in his files destroying all that.'

Jack Dawes glanced sideways at her, then decided to make his own admission of weakness. He said abruptly, 'He had things about my mother in his files. Things I didn't want anyone to see.'

Lambert hadn't yet had a chance to see the papers the team had recovered from the dead man's house. 'You were trying to take away stuff he had recorded about your mother?' he said wonderingly.

Dawes bristled with anger. 'You pigs think my ma's just a slag, don't you? Well, she's better than that. She doesn't deserve the kind of things a bastard like Logan would write about her.'

'The two of them had an association?'

He nodded. 'When I was in the school play. Mum was quite a looker then. Logan pretended to be interested in me to get close to her – said that I had talent, that he could help me with my career. It was all rubbish, as we found out later, but it helped him to get my mum into bed. She got a lot of men excited in those days. Logan wasn't the only one who wanted to get inside her knickers, I can tell you!' It was patently important to Dawes to convince them of his mother's voluptuous charms in her youth, as if he was acutely conscious of her present rapidly fading attributes. He made a curiously touching figure in his distress.

Lambert said with unexpected gentleness, 'So you wanted

to remove whatever he might have recorded about your mother.'

'I didn't want her to have to face whatever he'd written about her. She was quite taken with him at the time, thought it was going to be a long-term thing. He laughed at her when he'd finished with her, asked her how she could ever have thought that a man like him would consider anything serious with a cheap tart like her. I could guess the kinds of things he would have put on paper about her. I didn't want to see things like that coming out in public and Mum having to face it.' He stared fixedly at the small square table, as if he were detailing some vice instead of a praiseworthy desire to protect his mother.

Becky Clegg understood better than anyone in the room how a young tough like Jack Dawes, with a reputation to keep up among his set, would see this as a weakness in himself. By way of additional explanation, she added, 'Terry Logan told us he had things about both of us on file. Things about how we'd broken the law. Taking an interest in his former pupils, he called it. He knew things about Jack and drugs, as well as a couple of rucks he'd been in. I don't know how he found out about some of the stuff, but he did. We didn't want you lot to get hold of any of that.'

DI Rushton stared at the young pair with distaste. Both of them had criminal records, which in his book meant you didn't take anything they said at face value. 'If Mr Logan was such a monster, why on earth did you get involved with him in this production of *Hamlet*?'

Becky Clegg glanced sideways at Jack again, and found him still staring down at the table. She said, 'He was a good director. The best.'

That again. They all said that. To Chris Rushton, with no experience of amateur dramatics, it was both tiresome and irrelevant. He said impatiently, 'Good enough for you to tangle with him again, in spite of what you thought of him?' He sounded his disbelief in every syllable.

Becky heard it and sighed. She disliked this eager young copper even more than the old bloke. 'I was trying to make a new start in life. I'd been good at drama at school. Good at school generally in those days, though you probably wouldn't believe it now.' She spoke like a weary fifty-year-old, rather than a young woman who was only twenty-one. 'Taking a part in a play, with the different set of people who would be involved, was part of my resolution to change my ways, if you must know.' She glanced up into Rushton's clean-cut, sceptical face. 'Detective Sergeant Hook understood that. I think it was the same for Jack as well. We were both trying to make a break with the recent past, the way you pigs are always telling us to do.'

Becky thought Jack Dawes would never admit to this, might even spring forward with a denial of anything so preposterous and wimpish. Instead, still staring at the table, he said, 'Drama was something we knew about, something which was supposed to be respectable. Something we'd been good at and felt we could do again.' He looked up for the first time in minutes, stared round the confines of the small, square, green-walled room and said unexpectedly, 'Where's Bert Hook? He was going to be good in *Hamlet*. He'd understand what Becky's trying to tell you.'

Lambert said gruffly, 'Perhaps as a fellow thespian he felt too much involved with you to be objective. If he was here, he'd have been listening to you giving us a clear account of a murder motive. He'd have heard you detailing the reasons why you hated the man who died on Wednesday night.'

Becky Clegg flashed a look of hatred at the lined face which was within two feet of her own. 'He'd have heard us trying to be honest.' She glanced from one to the other of the two very different but equally impassive faces opposite her. 'You lot are always telling us to "mend our ways" and "be decent citizens", but when we try, what help do we get from you?'

Rushton looked hard into the animated, attractive features. 'Your last act, the one which brought the pair of you into the cells here, was breaking and entering at the home of a murder victim. You're hardly in a position to ask for the benefit of the doubt, Ms Clegg.'

Lambert looked at Jack Dawes, wondering inconsequentially that this thin, striking young face could still contain the wariness that he had seen in the features of many an old lag. He said softly, inconsequentially, 'What time did you really get in on Wednesday night, Mr Dawes?'

Jack's brain had been racing with the effort of trying to convince the most senior fuzz he had ever dealt with that he was trying to mend his ways, as Becky had told them he was.

He was completely unprepared for this sudden and dangerous switch of ground. Had the police talked again to his mother, whilst he was here in the cells? He knew they'd have been round to see her, to let her know where he was and why. There was no knowing what she would have said, especially if they'd got to her when she'd had a few drinks. He couldn't get his brain to work as well or as fast as he wanted to. He said limply, 'It was later than I said.'

'How much later, Jack?'

The first name again: the come-on; the assurance that we were all on the same side, that what you said here was safe enough whatever it was because you were talking to friends. Did the old bugger think he was a fool?

After a restless night in the cells and this grilling here, he hadn't the resources to put up a proper resistance. He'd make mistakes if he tried to lie; he might make the case they already had against him even stronger. 'Much later. It was almost midnight, I think.' He was dimly aware that his mother had been too befuddled on Wednesday night to know what time it had been, that even if she had thought she was being honest, she might have told them a different time. He added rather desperately, 'Becky can confirm that!' and felt her nodding vigorously beside him.

'So what made you lie when you spoke to us on Thursday?'

'Obvious, innit? You'd have one of us in the frame for Logan's murder, as soon as look at us, if we gave you the chance.' It was a return to his normal truculence with the police, but he couldn't give it his usual energy or confidence.

'So you lied about it and put yourself in even deeper. Not very clever, I'd say, Jack. What were you doing until that time?'

'I was still in the village hall for quite a long time after the rehearsal was over. I was talking to bloody Logan, wasn't I? Telling him to lay off my mum, telling him not to use the stuff he said he had against me.'

'And what did he say to that?'

'He laughed at me. Said we'd see how the play went. Said he needed to know all about the private lives of his cast, if he was to bring everything they could offer out of them.'

'So you waited until he came out and slit his throat.'

'No! It . . . it took me a few minutes to find Becky when I came out.'

He glanced speculatively sideways, and his companion came in eagerly to support him. 'I'd got tired of waiting for Jack. It was cold out there in that car park. I wandered off towards the centre of the village, where I could see lights. I was trying to keep warm by stamping my feet and moving about. I knew it was going to be cold on the way home, on the back of Jack's bike.'

Jack grinned, for the first time since they had come into the room. 'I shouted for Becky from the edge of the car park. She was back with me pretty quickly and we shot straight off on the Yahama. I dropped Becky at her place and was home before twelve.'

Becky thought about the three minutes of breathless, excited, confused kissing in the darkness outside her shabby flat, which she thought had taken both of them by surprise. Jack had certainly been excited by something: at the time she had taken it to be the ride through the night on his powerful motorbike. Well, there was certainly no need to tell these two about that: some things were best left to the admittedly limited police imagination. She said, 'Terry Logan was still inside the place with the lights on when we left.'

Rushton glanced at his chief. 'We shall decide in the next hour or two whether to charge you with breaking and entering,' he said stiffly. 'We shall have to make a decision in due course on whether to charge you with much more serious offences.'

Becky Clegg wondered as she and Jack Dawes were taken back to their separate cells just how much of what they had said would be believed.

Nineteen

Chris Rushton had feared all week that the weather would break on Sunday. It would be just his luck, he thought, if there was steady rain and the golf had to be abandoned.

He need not have feared. The morning of Sunday, November the nineteenth, saw a bright sun climbing bravely above the splendid autumn colours of the trees of the Forest of Dean, and the forecast assured him that the weather was set fair for the day. Perhaps his luck was changing.

The presence of Anne Jackson at his breakfast table reinforced that thought. She looked very young and very pretty in his blue silk dressing gown, with a pink knee peeping alluringly from its folds as she munched her cereal like a dutiful schoolgirl. Chris had to remind himself once again that Anne, with her hair dropping so appealingly over her left eye, was less than ten years younger than him, that he shouldn't be worried about the Lolita syndrome because this was a mature young woman who knew exactly what she was doing.

It was the first time she'd stayed with him overnight. Both of them had been a little surprised when she agreed to do so. Breakfast together was another new experience. Anne refused to have anything cooked. She looked round the small, neat modern kitchen and voiced the thought she had never meant to declare to him. 'I expect you've done a lot of this sort of thing. I haven't, so I don't know what you're supposed to say on the morning afterwards.' She smiled up at his intensely serious face. 'Thank you for having me, I expect.'

Chris grinned, but kept his attention upon the steaming pan and his scrambled eggs; men weren't supposed to be good at multitasking. He heard himself saying, 'I haven't done much of it either. Not much at all. We both need more experience of these things in my view.' That was very daring for him. He rather spoiled it by adding hurriedly, 'With each other, of course!'

She felt very tender towards him. But she said briskly, 'What time's the golf?'

'One o'clock. They said we might just get eighteen in, before the light goes, if it's a clear afternoon.'

'I must be on my way soon. I've got to collect my clubs and change into my golf gear. Are these friends of yours good players?'

'Quite good, I think. John Lambert's played for a long time, but Bert Hook's almost as new to the game as I am. Bert's about eighteen handicap, but John's a single figure man.'

'Nothing too fearsome, then.' Anne Jackson stretched her legs luxuriously, exposing a tantalizing glimpse of thigh, and decapitated her egg with a decisive blow from her knife.

Chris Rushton was more impressed than he could ever tell her by this casual dismissal of his chief's golfing prowess.

He smiled an exquisite, anticipatory smile.

An hour later, Michael Carey opened the door of his flat to the two senior CID men he had met two days earlier. 'Chief Superintendent Lambert, isn't it?' he said cordially, pleased with himself for remembering the full title of this local detective legend. 'And you again, Bert, whom I remember from our brief hour of glory upon the boards. It had better be DS Hook, in this context, I suppose!' He gave them his most dazzling smile and led them into the long, low-ceilinged room with the Beardsley prints and the portraits of Kean and Irving. He had given them his gauche young juvenile lead last time they were here; he wondered what he should do for them on this sunny autumn morning.

As they sat down on the red velvet Victorian sofa where he had positioned them, Lambert studied this exotic creature shamelessly – and found that the man was not at all embarrassed by his attention. Michael Carey was almost too handsome, he decided, though there was probably an element of envy in that. His clean-cut, regular features looked only more elegant under his light, unlined skin. His fair hair looked only more attractive for being just a little out of place. His fawn sweater and light grey trousers hung perfectly upon his slim limbs, without any suggestion of tailoring. His suede loafers sat as comfortably as slippers upon his neat feet. You catch me in an informal

moment, Michael Carey's whole appearance declared, I do not
fear you, and the world has patently nothing to fear from me.

Lambert was anxious to trap this exotic butterfly. He said
tersely, 'You lied to us last time we were here, Mr Carey.'

Michael looked concerned. His role was decided for him,
then. He must play the penitent young man, whose inexperi-
ence of life had betrayed him on that previous occasion. He
looked suitably apologetic as he said, 'If I deceived you in
any way, it must have been an unwitting deception, I'm sure.'

'And I'm equally sure it was not, so let's cut out the frip-
peries. You lied to us about your relationship with a murder
victim.'

'Terry Logan and I—'

'We asked how well you had known Terry Logan and DS
Hook took notes of your reply. You said, "Not well at all. We
had a mutual love of the theatre and enjoyed chatting about
any production we'd both seen. We hadn't much else in
common." We now know that this is quite untrue.'

Michael took his time. He had always known in his heart
that it would come to this. You shouldn't underestimate the
police machine; they had obviously talked to other people,
found out the reality of things. But he wasn't nervous: on the
contrary, he found that he had that heightened awareness of
what he was doing and the effect it would have on others,
which usually only came to him on stage. 'I'm sorry. I
shouldn't have kept things back. It was foolish of me.'

'It was more than foolish, Mr Carey. We have to ask
ourselves why you did such a thing.'

'I'm gay, Mr Lambert. Perhaps you knew that. I've found
it pays me to conceal that, in some contexts. I've no great
experience of dealing with the police. Some of my friends tell
me that there is a high incidence of homophobia among male
police officers.'

'You're out of date, Mr Carey. You're also intelligent. You
must have realized that lying during a murder investigation
could only bring suspicion on you. I'm forced to conclude
that you had a greater reason for your dishonesty. Whatever
it was, you're now a murder suspect.'

'I was always that. You made that clear enough to me on
Friday. I was unable to provide you with an alibi then, because
I live alone here. You questioned me about my actions on the

night when Terry Logan was killed and I had no one to back
up my story that I came back here and stayed here from about
nine thirty onwards. I panicked a little and kept my mouth
shut about how well I knew Terry. It may not be praiseworthy
in me, but it is surely understandable.'

Lambert tried not to be nettled by the young man's cool-
ness under fire. 'You didn't merely keep your mouth shut.
You deliberately lied to us, Mr Carey. You'd better give us
the full details of your dealings with Mr Logan.'

'I lived with him for almost a year when I was twenty.'
After his previous evasions, the directness of this was dramatic,
as he had intended it to be. He could never resist extracting
the maximum impact from a situation. He acknowledged that
to himself now with a wry smile. 'That should be honest
enough for you, Chief Superintendent, if a little belated.'

'You lived with him in the house he was occupying at the
time of his death?' Lambert felt as if he had finally netted
this exotic butterfly. Now he had to pin him down.

'I did. We were fairly discreet about it, but I did. He said
at the time that discretion was necessary because of his teaching
job at the comprehensive. I later came to the conclusion that
the secrecy was because he wanted to indulge in other, more
random and casual, liaisons.' Michael was proud of the even,
balanced way he delivered that, without any evidence of the
pain which this dawning knowledge had brought to him at
the time.

'How did this affair end?'

'It wasn't an affair, Mr Lambert. We were both of us free
agents, conducting a partnership. Or so I thought at the time.'
He looked at the faces in front of him, then at his perfectly
groomed nails, as if to emphasize the calmness he was acting
out. 'It ended in the way I suppose most of these things do;
with mutual recriminations and much bitterness, on my side
at least. When I look at Terry Logan more dispassionately
now, I'm not sure that he was capable of deep feelings or real
passion, so perhaps he wasn't as bitter as I was.'

'And yet, despite this admitted bitterness, you were anxious
to get together with this man again. It doesn't make sense,
does it?'

Michael allowed himself a small, rueful smile: he mustn't
allow himself any real mirth or it would detract from his role

as the penitent. 'It does, actually, if you understand the theatre.
Terry Logan was the best director I've ever worked with. He
was also offering me the chance to play the lead in *Hamlet*.
That was a combination which stronger characters than mine
would have found it difficult to resist.'

John Lambert frowned. It was preposterous reasoning, he
told himself: if you hated a man, you didn't agree to work with
him again in some tinpot amateur Shakespeare production. But
even as he told himself this, it was his own argument which
sounded ridiculous, and Carey's which sounded convincing.
The handsome young man sat there with that self-deprecating,
slightly apologetic air, and convinced them that he would have
made almost any concession for the chance of playing the
gloomy Dane. Perhaps his argument rang true simply because
he so obviously believed it himself.

'The more obvious explanation is that you took the opportunity of getting near to Terry Logan to give yourself the chance
of revenge,' Lambert said sourly. 'A theatrical enterprise was
obviously your best and perhaps your only opportunity of
achieving that.'

Michael gave a slow, puzzled smile, then nodded, minimally
and slowly, as if accepting a line of reasoning he had never
considered before. He brought it off very well, he thought. He
told himself not to overplay, not to enjoy what he was doing
too much. He might be playing a game with these two much
older men, but it was a deadly serious game. 'I can see the
logic of that, now that you put it to me. The trouble is that I
don't think like a policeman, you see. I might not have got
myself into this situation if I had managed to do that.'

Bert Hook had seen how brilliant the young man was on
stage. He had missed no dramatic opportunity in his lines or
his movements, even in that first rehearsal, where others had
been stumbling. It struck him now that good actors were oppor-
tunists, that this might be an opportunist's murder.

Bert said bluntly, 'I can't see how you would get a better
chance of revenge than by taking part in a play which Terry
Logan was directing.'

'And *Hamlet* is a revenge play, isn't it?' Here was the occasion to show a little of his knowledge about drama to these
lumpen policemen. 'It's a classic example of Shakespeare
taking a crude formula and using it to produce something

much more than that.' Michael seemed to be genuinely excited by the coincidence.

Bert watched him brush his hand through his mass of fair hair as the animation of the parallel took him over, and tried not to be swayed by the brilliance of the performance. He said calmly, sticking resolutely to his point, 'And no doubt a young man like you would subscribe also to the notion that "Revenge is a kind of wild justice".'

Michael grinned: a genuine, winning grin this time. 'A policeman who quotes the Bard. I shall spread this abroad.'

'It's Francis Bacon actually, not Shakespeare.' Bert Hook tried not to sound smug – and failed. That thought about revenge was dredged up from the old Barnardo's days, not the Open University. They'd been strong on moralist essays, in the home and the school he'd attended. 'I think you'll find that Bacon goes on to say that the law must be supreme and must control such urges in men. That's where policemen come in. I was with you until around nine o'clock on Wednesday evening. Tell us again what you did after you left me and the others in Mettlesham Village Hall.'

'I told you that on Friday.'

'And on Friday you also denied any previous close connections with the dead man. You've now totally revised that section of your story and told us that you lived with Mr Logan for almost a year. I'm giving you the opportunity to revise your account of your movements on the evening of his death.'

Michael looked at Bert Hook more in sorrow than in anger, the way the ghost looked at Hamlet in the play. He was trying to convey the thought that he would have expected more consideration from a fellow acting enthusiast. 'I drove back here in my faithful old black Fiesta.' He liked to mention the car whenever he could: it showed that even a man with his exotic intellect had no pretensions to flashy material things. 'I remained here alone for the rest of the evening. I have no witness to that. I am sorry for my sake and for yours that it should be so – more for mine than for yours, needless to say – but I cannot make it otherwise.' He gave them an apologetic but reasonable smile.

Bert resisted the impulse to answer with a smile of his own: this was altogether too winning a young man. 'So who do you think killed this man whom you have confessed to hating?'

Michael pursed his lips and frowned, as if wondering whether to contest this notion of hate before he answered the question. He carefully avoided any suggestion of insolence as he said apologetically, 'I've really no idea. I've thought about it a lot since Wednesday night, of course, as is only natural. One of the cast, I should think, wouldn't you?'

Lambert stood up and looked at the draft of an advertising poster which Carey was working on at the far end of the room. It had been placed on the desk there almost like a stage prop, as if to demonstrate that this man had other skills as well as the stage ones which everyone recognized. Lambert wanted to say that hands as meticulous and skilful as this could easily have been the ones which slit Logan's throat so precisely. Instead, he said acerbically, 'Mr Casey, you've radically altered your story, as DS Hook has just pointed out. If there are any further changes or any further thoughts on who killed the man you hated, no doubt you will get in touch with us immediately.'

'Of course I will, Chief Superintendent Lambert. And apologies once again for my foolish attempts at deception.' Michael Carey gave them the modest smile of the penitent as he held open the door for them.

Lambert and Hook were unusually well-dressed for golf.

New sweaters had come out. Trousers were freshly laundered and had creases: they had lost that distinctive soiling around the turn-ups which comes from muddy autumn golf. Lambert had even chosen the occasion to launch his new waterproof winter golf shoes, which were of a white so dazzling and uncharacteristic that friends of his pretended to shield their eyes in the changing room. Hook was resplendent in the expensive woollen sweater which had been given him for his last birthday, which he had hitherto designated as far too good for golf.

Playing with a young woman was a new experience for them.

Chris Rushton was his usual smart self. Rushton was an example, Hook thought darkly, of life's inherent unfairness. With his slim, lithe frame and chiselled features, Chris was a man upon whom clothes invariably chose to sit well, whereas on him even expensive garments soon looked untidy, as if they took exception to the burly figure allotted to them for their display.

Anne Jackson had youth upon her side. Her light blue sweater and navy trousers sat pleasingly upon her trim figure. Rushton, who had noticed appreciative male appraisals as he signed in his visitor in the pro's shop, glanced aggressively towards the car park, whence he thought he caught envious moans of suppressed desire from men depositing their clubs in car boots after their morning round. He was confronted by an impressive display of raised boot lids.

'I expect everyone is taking shots from me as usual!' sighed John Lambert, with mock dismay at his stature in the game. 'I'm playing off eight at the moment. It's a hard life.'

'You'll have the luxury of shots from me today, John,' said Anne Jackson, extracting a golf glove from the pocket of her bag and slipping it on to her small left hand. 'I'm five, I'm afraid. And pretty rusty to boot, I fear, because of my studies in college, so I hope you'll put up with me.'

They looked at Rushton, who gave them the briefest of nods, trying hard to suppress a smile as he saw the amazement which even these practised faces could not suppress. Lambert glanced at Hook in a stunned silence as Anne Jackson stooped to select a ball from her bag. The five handicap was not a joke, then.

They courteously invited Anne to play first, but she explained patiently that it was usual for the men to lead the way on the grounds of safety, their tees being a few yards behind the spots allotted to the weaker sex. Bert Hook found himself unusually nervous for some reason. He was pleased to get his drive away, low but running, and only just off the fairway on the right. Lambert hit one of his best, his usual fade bringing the ball back from the left into the very middle of the fairway. 'He doesn't miss many fairways, the chief!' said Bert Hook loyally to the young woman waiting patiently beside them.

Rushton, who was very anxious to do well in front of Anne on this first golfing outing together, endured the usual result of such ambition in this ridiculous game. His slow, deliberate back swing reversed itself into a desperate lunge in the downswing, and his scuffed ball travelled directly along the ground and no more than thirty yards from the tee.

'Bad luck!' muttered his opponents automatically, though all four of them knew that it was nothing of the sort: it was simply a dreadful shot, that common first-tee phenomenon.

The first hole at Ross-on-Wye Golf Club is a shortish par four. Anne Jackson eyed the distant green and selected a 3-wood rather than a driver. Lambert raised his eyebrows, then nodded sagely. 'Better safe than sorry. This is a tight driving hole. Making sure you're at least on the fairway is good thinking here.'

Anne stood behind her ball for a second, eyeing the line she had chosen. Then, without even a practice swing, she swung the club back and through the ball, smoothly and without any great apparent effort. The ball pitched ten yards beyond Lambert's drive and ran another twenty.

There was a collective gasp before the ritual 'Good shot!' from the three men. None of them, and least of all Chris Rushton, succeeded in keeping the astonishment out of their voices. Anne turned away from them and allowed herself a private smile as she returned the club to her bag. This was a male reaction to which she had become accustomed over the last few years.

Rushton and Hook both played ruinous second shots and picked up. Lambert, with much concentration, bounced his second into the centre of the green and smiled his satisfaction. It availed him not. Anne Jackson pulled out her wedge and pitched her ball four feet from the flag with a minimum of fuss. It stopped dead, and after Lambert had completed his four, she rolled in the putt. One up.

The three men all had shots on the second, and Bert Hook, by dint of an eight-foot putt, managed a five and a win. It was their last success of the day.

Lambert had played with some excellent male players in his time, but never with a woman who struck the ball like this. Anne was consistently longer than her opponents and her partner; the two older men found this difficult to cope with, and not just from a purely golfing point of view. Chris Rushton, on the other hand, was delighted. His own erratic beginner's golf mattered not a jot against the background of his partner's excellence; indeed, by using the generous number of shots his fledgling handicap allotted to him, he even managed to win a couple of holes.

Anne made the occasional mistake, which only served to underline the near-perfection of the rest of her play. She had three birdies, which allowed her to play one below her handicap of five, and she and an increasingly complacent Chris Rushton won the match by five and four. They were back in the clubhouse before the early autumn dusk, enjoying the tea and toasted teacakes provided for them by a subdued but impressed John Lambert.

Anne Jackson looked at her watch. 'I must get away, I'm afraid,' she said. 'I've work to prepare for my class tomorrow. Golf is very simple compared with keeping thirty eight-year-olds interested!'

She left rather an awed silence behind her, with Chris Rushton still basking happily in the reflected glow of her glory. A rather dazed Bert Hook said eventually, fairly sure that he was not merely talking about golf, 'You've got a gem there, young Chris. If you've any sense you'll stick with Anne Jackson. That's if she's daft enough to have you.'

Rushton reflected on the fact that, at thirty-two and having reached Inspector rank, he was still 'young Chris' to these two old hands. Perhaps that was a good thing. He said modestly, 'I'll have to improve my golf.'

'It was great to play with her,' said Lambert eventually. He found, slightly to his surprise, that this was true. He'd really enjoyed watching someone play this tantalizing game as it ought to be played. He was shaken but impressed.

Moreover, they'd all three of them had to concentrate for three hours on the matter in hand, in the sunshine of a glorious autumn afternoon. They would surely return to the case with renewed insights on Monday morning. A little shell-shocked, but refreshed.

He tried to sound convincing as he announced the idea to his fellow officers.

Twenty

As the chastened John Lambert and Bert Hook returned from the golf club to their families on that Sunday evening, four other couples were preoccupied with the events of the preceding Wednesday night, when the seemingly universally unlamented Terry Logan had met his end.

Margaret Dalrymple had made one of her best curries, in an attempt to placate her husband for the information she had been forced to divulge to the police. After fillet steak, beef curry was Andrew's favourite dish. She went to some trouble to furnish the table with all the trimmings he liked. You didn't drink claret with curry, he said, so she'd set two cans of lager beside his favourite tankard on the table.

Andrew seemed to be in a good mood. He complimented her on the excellence of the curry and noted how much trouble she had taken with the meal and the table.

Maggie tried hard to relax, to set the tone she needed for this exchange. 'We should do this more often,' she said, gesturing vaguely at the gleaming silver cutlery and the glasses. 'It's too easy to sit in front of the television, when there are only two of you. And I know that I'm out far too much, with my committees and my work on the Bench.' She shook her head over her wifely neglect and added coquettishly, 'You deserve better than a slut like me.'

At forty-nine and with a build which was stately rather than delicate, Margaret was not well equipped to play the coquette. But Andrew Dalrymple did not notice that. 'You could never be a slut, Maggie. But if you want to play the slut for a little while, that's fine with me!'

The forty-nine-year-old Juliet raised her glass of tomato juice and winked over the top of it at her portly, fifty-two-year-old Romeo. To most outside observers, it would have looked ridiculous, but there was a genuine warmth between the two which overrode appearances. They had been through a lot together over the years, survived the crises of infidelity on both sides and emerged as a tighter partnership than ever. *With that bugger Logan out of the way, we can move on serenely from here,* thought Andrew,

She read most of that in his face as she studied him across their table. Because of her affair with Logan five years ago, she normally made no mention of her former lover: it was like walking on broken glass to mention him to Andrew. But now she said daringly, 'I'm glad Terry is out of the way. Glad he's dead. He wasn't a good man, was he?'

'He was a bastard, as far as I'm concerned. But you'd hardly expect me to be objective, after I found he'd been slipping a length to my wife, would you?'

All his old hate and bitterness came out in the coarse phrase. For a moment she cursed herself for mentioning the name of the dead man. She reached across and put her hand on top of his. 'I'm sorry, Andrew. I can't say how sorry. But all that was over a long time ago. I can see now that Terry was a danger to almost everyone around him – certainly to anyone who got close to him.'

He nodded, seemingly calmed by her assurances. But he needed more. He ran a hand across his receding hairline. 'You didn't take that part in *Hamlet* because you wanted to get back with him?'

'No. I told you I didn't. I wanted a good part in a Shakespeare play. Wanted you to be proud of me – no, that's not fair. I did want that, but most of all I wanted to play the Queen in *Hamlet*. I knew I'd never get another chance. I just wanted to show off, you see! I told you I was a slut.'

He knew he should leave it at that, but he couldn't manage it. He toyed with the handle of his tankard and, like a man picking at a healing scab, said, 'Everyone says he was a good director.'

'He was. Very good. But that's the only reason why I went anywhere near him.' She looked earnestly at Andrew across the table, willing him to believe her. He gave her a small, uncertain smile and she responded with a much wider one of her own. Then she took the plunge and said, 'I had to tell them that you weren't here when I got in from the rehearsal on Wednesday night.'

'Why? Why did you tell them that, for God's sake?'

His face flared with anger and she thought for an instant that she had misjudged the moment. She said hastily, 'I had no choice, Andrew. They seemed already to know about it. They've a big team on the case and they've been talking to all and sundry. They'd already found out that I'd concealed my affair with Terry from them. I couldn't afford to be caught out in more lies.'

'Why? Why couldn't you support me?' His eyes had that wild, uncontrolled look which filled her with fear: the look she had seen in them four years ago when he had found out about the affair, when she had feared that he was going to strike her.

She said hastily, 'Andrew, they now regard me as a leading suspect for this killing. Can't you see that? They'd found out about my affair with a murder victim, they knew that he was the one who had ended it and that I had been very bitter about that. They thought I was the wronged woman taking revenge. They even put those arguments to me.'

He was breathing heavily, staring at his empty plate, as if he expected some message to appear on it, like biblical words upon Belshazzar's wall. Finally he nodded, reluctantly accepting the logic of what she said. As if the words were torn from him against his will, he said harshly, 'And did you? Kill the bastard, I mean.'

She made herself take a deep breath. It was going to be all right now. 'No. I might have felt like cutting his throat, but I didn't.'

He ran his fingers twice round the edge of his tankard slowly. Then he forced a smile that took a long time to spread across the whole of his features. He looked up at her. 'That's good then. We can move on from here.'

'Yes. Of course we can, and that's what we should do.' She wanted to be out of here and into the kitchen, putting a decisive end to this scene she had feared, spooning out the dessert, releasing her tension in such innocent everyday actions. Instead, she said quietly, 'Where were you on Wednesday night Andrew?'

It could not have been more than a couple of seconds before he replied, but to her it seemed to stretch into minutes. 'I went out to a pub. Maggie, I know it sounds stupid, but I found I couldn't sit quietly on my own in the house whilst you were out there with that man.'

'I was at a rehearsal for a play. With lots of other people. I wouldn't have gone otherwise. The last thing I would have wanted was to be alone with a man who'd treated me as Logan had.'

'I know. But when you're left on your own in the house your mind plays tricks with you. It's like when you lie awake during the night and all your problems seem much bigger than they are.'

She'd experienced that often enough, especially during the months after her affair with Terry Logan had been so brutally terminated. 'Which pub was it, Andrew?'

'One in Gloucester. Don't you believe me?'

'Of course I do. It's just that the police might want to know. It could give you an alibi, couldn't it?'

'I suppose so, if I need one. It wasn't busy: I'm sure the land-lord would remember me. But the police don't think I killed Logan.' His mouth set in a sullen line, as if he could make it so by sheer determination.

Becky Clegg had expected Jack Dawes to live in a better place than this. With his thin, sharp-featured, handsome face, he was a glamorous, dangerous figure in that strange half-life they had led on the edge of the law. Dawes commanded unthinking loyalty from his less intelligent followers. He had always seemed to her to know so much more than she did about their world of violence and petty, unthinking, lucrative crime.

Now she realized that he had pretended, just as she had. Pretended to be harder than he was. Jack had seemed to her invulnerable, a man who knew all about drugs and thieving, knew just how to surround himself with the thugs who could provide him with muscle. She looked round this shabby, stuffy flat, with its peeling paint on the window frames, its wallpaper hanging off the ceiling in one corner of the room, its thin cotton curtains which did not quite meet when he drew them. Becky realized now that there was no more luxury and even less glamour in the place where Jack Dawes slept at nights than there had been in the grotty flat which she herself had recently vacated.

She found this comforting rather than disappointing.

Perhaps he noticed her scrutiny, because he said defensively, 'Mum likes it here. I said we should get somewhere better, but she says it's convenient for the town and the shops. She didn't mention the pubs. That's probably where she is now.'

He stood in the doorway of the kitchen, thinking how pretty

Becky looked as she sat on the stained sofa with its fading orange cover. He tried not to contrast the bright, kittenish beauty beneath her very dark hair with the more bloated round face of his mother who usually sat there.

Conscience stirred within him with that thought. He said, loyally but with a hint of apology, 'She's been good to me, my mum. She's not had an easy life. I . . . I try to look after her, when I can.'

'No need to be defensive. I'm glad that you help her. I wish I knew where my mum is. I'd like to feel I wanted to look after her, but I feel nothing.'

'We can go out if you want.' He was suddenly embarrassed by what he saw as his weakness and was anxious to change the subject.

'No hurry, is there? It's nice to have the place to ourselves. And you've no need to apologize for it: I've been in a lot worse! It's . . . well, it's homely, I suppose.' She brought out clumsily the word which had been a favourite with her aunt in her childhood. A white lie was surely permissible when you were still feeling your way in a relationship.

He grinned at her, delighted with her uncertainty, and went and sat beside her on the sofa. He put his arm round her, drew her to him and kissed her, first gently and then with increasing passion, as he felt her respond. He slid his hand beneath her sweater, felt the firmness of her breasts, the flatness of her stomach. He slid his hands down to her thighs, then upwards with increasing urgency towards her crotch and those areas of delight which were suddenly of supreme importance to him.

'Not yet, randy Jack Dawes!' she whispered into his ear. 'Not whilst your mum might come in at any minute!' He pulled away obediently, and she was glad to see no rancour in his face when she smiled up into it. She enjoyed the feeling of control it gave her, the feeling of steering this relationship along at the pace which suited her. She said with a grin. 'I don't fancy meeting your mum for the first time with my knickers in my hand!'

He grinned at that image. He was pleased that this bright, sharply intelligent girl seemed to want to meet the mother he had concealed from his contemporaries for so long. He kissed her again briefly, then sat upright on the sofa, still with his arm round her shoulders.

Voicing the words against his will, he said, 'Do you think the fuzz believed us at the station?'

Becky wondered how he had come back so surely to the thing which would not leave her own mind. Her teenage reading of romantic fiction told her that this meeting of minds meant they must be compatible. Reality told her that he had simply voiced the most important question in both their lives. She said carefully, 'Who knows? We've both got records as far as they're concerned. I want to go straight, when this is out of the way, but you can't expect the pigs to believe that.'

Jack stared straight ahead of him, noticing for the first time how much dust had accumulated on the screen of the silent television set. 'I want to do that. Go straight, I mean, like you. When bloody Terry Logan is finally out of the way!' It was the first time he had confessed that to anyone. Mum would be pleased, he thought, and then immediately castigated himself for such a wimpish consideration.

Becky squeezed his hand, then said, 'It took you a long time to find me on Wednesday night. I didn't realize that I'd wandered so far away from the hall.'

Jack wondered once again exactly where this restless, attractive girl had been at the moment when Logan had died. But all he said was, 'Yes. There were no street lights and I didn't want to go shouting your name around Mettlesham, at that hour of the night.'

'Did you kill him?'

The simple, shocking question surprised the speaker as well as Jack. Becky had been conscious of no intention to ask it. She added weakly, 'Before you came looking for me, I mean.'

'No.' The monosyllable was barely audible. He stretched his slim right leg out in front of him, watched her smaller foot follow his; any sort of movement was welcome to release their joint tension. 'Did you?'

'No.' A stronger and more determined denial than his had been.

'You could have done, you know. You were carrying a blade.'

She didn't know that he'd been aware of that. She wondered if the shape had shown under her tight jeans or whether he had felt the knife when she pressed herself hard against him on the pillion of the Yamaha. She said limply, 'I didn't use it, though.'

Jack went on as if he hadn't heard her. 'You could simply

have waited there whilst I went off looking for you, and killed him as he came out to his car. It didn't need any great strength. Anyone who took him by surprise from behind could have slit that wanker's throat.'

'I suppose so. I didn't.' She felt nothing at all, as if she was listening to someone else's denial.

Each of them felt the other's limbs relaxing on the shabby, lumpy sofa; each of them wondered in the silence how much they believed the other's denial.

Jack Dawes tried to force conviction into his voice as he said, 'Well, that's all right, then.'

Ian Proudfoot didn't want to talk about the death of Terry Logan, but his mind was drawn back to it constantly. As he washed the dishes at the sink after their evening meal, he felt Angela's presence in the kitchen behind him. He didn't turn round but continued with the methodical, mindless work, as if innocent actions could reflect an innocent mind.

'You changed your story to the police when they came here on Friday.' Her voice was sour, recriminatory. She'd already had a go at him for bringing the squalor of a murder investigation into her innocent house.

He didn't turn round, didn't cease his careful stacking of the plates in the drainage rack. 'I had to change it, Angela. I'd tried to conceal that embarrassing episode when he threw Sophie out of the school play, but they'd found out about that. They've found out a lot of things over the last few days.'

'If you ask me, you should never have been in that damned *Hamlet*. I said so at the time.'

'Yes, you did. Repeatedly. And as it's turned out, you were probably right. Hindsight is a wonderful thing.'

He should have known by now that irony was not the best tactic with Angela. She studied his stooped back at the sink and said waspishly, 'What time did you actually get in on Wednesday night?'

He stopped dead for a moment, watching the white foam slide slowly down the back of his hands. Then he forced himself to resume, to treat this most important thing as a careless trifle, as Kipling had taught him to do in his far-off schooldays. But he was almost at the end of his task, and when he had set the last dish on the drainer, he had to turn and face his truculent wife. As evenly as he could, he said, 'What do you mean, Angela?'

'It's a straightforward enough question, surely. You were stupid enough to lie to nosy coppers in the first place. You tried to conceal the complaints we'd made to the school about his treatment of Sophie in the play and the trouble Logan had given you at the bank by way of reprisal.'

'You were as upset as me about Logan at the time. I just didn't want our dirty linen washed in public. That might have been stupid, but it was understandable.'

Her expression of contempt for him did not change. She went on as if he had never spoken. 'Apparently you told them at your first meeting that you'd been back here at half past nine, and expected me to support you in that lie. On Friday, when they exposed you and produced a witness who'd seen you in the pub at Calford, you then told them that you'd left there at around half past ten and been back here before eleven.'

'That's right.'

'But you weren't back at that time, were you? Perhaps you just lie all the time now and your wife is the last one to notice. They say that that is often the case, don't they?'

'Angela, I don't lie to you. I don't know why you should think that—'

'I'm asking you a simple enough question. What time did you actually get back to this house on Wednesday night?'

'I don't know. I wasn't watching the clock at the time, was I? Probably at about the time I told the police I got here.'

'Oh, no. I'm not having that. I went to bed at eleven o'clock, and there was no sign of you then.' She smiled at him vindictively, as he stood in front of her, a ridiculous figure with his back to the sink, his glasses sliding down his nose, and his sleeves rolled up over his thin, sinewy, pathetic arms. She couldn't see what she had ever seen in him that was desirable. How had she rolled in bed with this balding, apprehensive figure and produced four children? She said spitefully, 'You're not used to having to account for yourself, are you? You don't have to do it at the bank – or when you're posturing about the stage in those plays.'

'Angela, don't.' For a moment, he saw only the petulant hatred of him in her face, and he was beset by a wild temptation to tell her that he was the murderer of Terry Logan, that he would now have to silence her too if she was not going to be more cooperative. He did nothing of the sort, of course. He said quietly, 'Angela, does it have to be like this?'

'I don't know what you mean. I'm simply trying to get an explanation of—'

'I don't know what time I left that pub. There's no reason why I should have checked my watch as I left, is there? If I was a little later back here than I said, there's surely nothing very sinister in that, is there?'

She wanted to tell him that if he was much later than he'd said, he could have killed off the man she knew he hated, that if that was what had happened and he wanted her to lie for him, he should come straight out with it and be done with it. But her tongue, which had previously been so active, was suddenly stilled. She didn't want to voice any more questions, didn't want to hear any more answers.

Angela Proudfoot was the victim of a sudden, startling, frightening tenderness. She said limply, 'You've been very foolish, haven't you, Ian?'

Michael Carey didn't think of himself as dishonest.

He knew more about himself now than he had done a few years ago, but he saw himself as a loner most of the time, a man who liked to watch the world around him and keep his own counsel about what he saw. When you were gay, he felt it paid to be cautious about your private life, even amidst the supposed enlightenment of the twenty-first century. That in turn tended to make him a little ruthless, perhaps rather cavalier about the emotions of those who lived their lives around him.

He knew now that there were times when you had to act and it was best then to act decisively.

Nevertheless, he was not always fair to people, Michael decided, as he drove back to Warwick. It was his conscience that had prompted his return. He hadn't meant to go back there after he had spoken to the fuzz, but the memory of Tom Baldwin's white, vulnerable face, sad as a chastened puppy's, as he drove away, had popped up in his mind's eye for the rest of the day. It wasn't so far to drive back, after all. Moreover, the stirrings of sexual excitement which he had felt after the danger of his interview had disturbed him for the rest of the day. By dusk, he was springing into his car and heading cheerfully north-east, towards Shakespeare country and the comely young man who awaited him in Warwick.

Tom was delighted to see him, as Michael had known he would be: his face lit up as he opened the door of his flat and saw that his lover had returned. It was always delightful to feel genuinely welcome, and Michael set himself out to be accommodating and pleasant. He had no idea how long this latest relationship would last, but you owed a certain amount of honesty to a partner.

For Michael Carey, that was a novel concept.

He moved restlessly about the neat, modern flat which was so different from his own residence, firing off witty, brilliant phrases, watching Tom Baldwin's delight at his fertile vocabulary and his easy dismissal of life's tribulations. Then he realized abruptly that he was doing what he loved to do, what he did for most of his life, often without even realizing that he was doing it.

He was determining a role for himself and acting it out; playing a part rather than being himself. Everyone did it, he knew; everyone needed to conceal a little of his real self from the world around him. But he did it more than most. Perhaps that was because he did it better than most: he tried to prick the bubble of vanity which contained that thought, and failed.

Role-playing might be all right for the world at large, but you owed those who were close to you something of yourself. A lot of yourself, even; certainly more than he had previously been prepared to give to Tom. Michael Carey stopped moving, sat down with uncharacteristic heaviness upon the leather sofa, ran a hand through his hair with sudden weariness and dropped his bitter, brilliant gibes about the police. He said, 'Actually, Tom, it wasn't fun. It was no fun at all.'

Tom Baldwin's smile dropped away as suddenly as Michael's mood had changed. 'But the police surely can't think that you killed this man Logan.'

'Who knows what they think, young Tom? Who knows what anyone thinks, most of the time? I'll tell you one thing, my inexperienced young friend: don't underestimate the CID. I think I did, to be honest.' Not a phrase he used very often, Michael thought in sour self-knowledge.

'But it was all right, wasn't it? You gave them what help you could and left them to it, surely?'

Michael was tempted to go off on one of his dazzling, brittle, philosophical discourses in the face of such naïvety. Tom, he knew, would be a receptive and rewarding audience. He rejected the temptation and said with abrupt simplicity, 'I lived with that man Logan for almost a year.'

'I didn't know that.'

'No. That's why I'm telling you now. And you can wipe that hurt rabbit look off your face, Tom. It had nothing to do with us.'

The wide, hurt, infinitely vulnerable eyes looked into his. 'How can you say that? You kept something from me.'

'It was four years ago. Long before I'd ever met you. In another life. When I was a very different person.' All of that was true: Michael ticked off the phrases to check that he was being honest. 'Terry Logan knew a lot about the theatre. I think I was bowled over by that. When he said he fancied me, he had something going with a woman nearer to his own age – a married woman. He ditched her like a shot and laughed in her face. I should have divined something from that. Logan didn't give a damn for her or for anyone else except himself.'

'You sound very bitter.'

'I am. Or I was at the time.' Michael grinned at himself for this caution where it was not needed. 'There are lots of people around my neck of the woods who hated Terry Logan.'

'But the police think you killed him.'

The high, brittle sound of Michael's laughter rang curiously in the low-ceilinged modern flat. 'I don't know what the fuzz think, Tom. I gave a good account of myself, to judge by the way they reacted. Told them I'd been too embarrassed to talk about living with Logan when they first saw me. Poured it all out in a rush this morning and played the penitent, inexperienced young man for them. Rather successfully, I think, although I say it myself.'

Tom Baldwin waited for what seemed to him a long time to see if Michael would say anything else. Then he said slowly, 'You play a lot of parts, don't you, Michael? Spend a lot of your life acting the roles you decide to play for the people who are with you at the time.'

It was so precisely his own criticism of himself as he had driven here in the car that Michael Carey was shocked. Shocked by the perception of this inexperienced partner as much as by the accusation. It was ironic that it had come just at the time when he had determined to be honest. But life seemed to be increasingly full of ironies. One of the worst ones was that it should have been necessary for Terry Logan to die just when he had offered him the part of the Prince in *Hamlet*. A part to kill for, in the ordinary order of things: another irony there.

Michael said, 'I suppose I do choose to play certain roles at certain times. Everyone does, don't they? But perhaps I do it more than most, because I'm so interested in acting, you see. But I wonder if that might even be something I should indulge in myself, now that I'm going to RADA.' He wrinkled his brow on that thought. Just when he was trying to be honest with innocent Tom Baldwin, he was accused of acting. Just when he honestly accepted the claim, here he was asserting that perhaps it was something he needed to do.

Tom said, as if it were another accusation, 'I don't really know you at all, do I?'

'Which of us knows everything about anyone, Tom? We all have our little secrets, even from those closest to us. Perhaps we need a degree of privacy. I sometimes think that some of us have secrets even from ourselves, in that we do not acknowledge the darker parts of our psyches.'

'Feelings are just a theme for philosophical discussion to you, aren't they, Michael? Not a source of emotional turmoil.'

'Let's leave it, shall we, Tom? I've had quite enough questioning for one day. I don't fancy any more examination, even if it's self-examination.'

They had what on the surface was a relaxed evening, though the conversation between them was sporadic and trivial. At eight o'clock, Michael said, 'I'll stay the night. I can get up early and drive back in not much more than an hour.'

It was the first time that Tom Baldwin had not been delighted by such an offer. At two o'clock in the morning he was still awake. Things kept passing through his brain as if on a looped tape. Tom was reviewing all the little cruelties, enumerating the thoughtless acts of violence, which he had seen in the man who lay soundly asleep beside him.

You could be very intimate with someone, and yet know nothing about the dangerous side of him.

Twenty-One

O ne of the facts which the murder investigation had established beyond all reasonable doubt was that the murder victim had not been an admirable human being. He had been a talented director of theatrical productions, but this was excellence in a congested industry. For the rest, an overcrowded planet might well be better off without the likes of Terence Charles Logan. But the law had to take its course, and the law said that the hunt for Logan's killer should be pursued as vigorously as if he had been a saint.

Two unlikely sufferers from this death emerged in the Bert Hook household. Jack and Luke found it difficult to confront the idea that their father's promising dramatic career might have been nipped in the bud by this untimely death. 'You surely can't give up now, Dad,' said eleven-year-old Luke. 'Not when you're on the verge of stardom.'

'Playing Polonius in an amateur production of *Hamlet* does not represent even a hint of stardom,' said Hook firmly.

'I read the other day that Sir Ian McKellen says he's too old to play Hamlet now, but thinks he could still make a good hand of Polonius.'

'I expect he could, too,' said Bert, rather relishing the idea of the eminent theatrical knight in the role which had escaped him.

'Shows what a triumph you'd have had in the part, that does! You've an enormous amount in common with Sir Ian, haven't you, Dad? Both off and on the stage.' Jack Hook shone a wide, enthusiastic smile towards his father's bewildered face, then studied the back of the cereal packet as if it had acquired a compelling interest for him.

Bert decided that he would not pursue these comparisons. 'My impulse to tread the boards will have to be regretfully abandoned.' He was amazed to find that the regret was genuine:

he had eventually been filled with anticipation as well as trepidation by his minimal involvement in the now aborted *Hamlet*. He thought back to the time when the formidable Mrs Dalrymple had come to the house to persuade him that his participation was necessary for the success of the enterprise, remembered how he had fought hard but ineffectively to resist the tide of her persuasion. It couldn't be much more than two weeks since that contest; it seemed now to belong to a different era.

'You could play a character in a soap, Dad,' said Luke, reluctant to leave this fertile breakfast theme. 'A drunk, perhaps. I could see you being good as a drunk – you've got the build for it. You could even corner the market in drunks, if you got yourself a good agent.'

Eleanor Hook, listening from the next room, decided that she could not enter the kitchen because she would never be able to keep her face straight. Her boys were growing up remarkably fast. That was sad in many ways, but it had its compensations.

Jack Hook now said thoughtfully, 'Mr Williams from school says that our church in the village needs what he calls a "robust baritone". That could be you, Dad. Then you could go on to do musicals. Dance about with all those girls in tights and strike poses.' He threw himself on one knee with arms outstretched and mimed a top-note finish to a show hit.

'You watch too much television,' said Bert severely. 'And if you're not ready for off in two minutes, you can walk to school.'

Twenty minutes later, he watched the boys leap from the car and run eagerly towards their fellows. Bert marvelled as he often did at this point about the contrast between their boisterous joy in youth at home and school and the more muted existence of his own youth, as a boy who went back to the institution at the end of each school day.

He drove steadily on towards Oldford Police Station, reviewing the process of his reluctant involvement in *Hamlet* and the surprising sadness he felt at being deprived of the experience. In retrospect, he decided that it was something which stirred in his subconscious mind at this point which gave him the ultimate clue to the case.

* * *

In Lambert's spacious bungalow, breakfast was a less frantic meal than at the Hooks, because his children were adults. The daughter who was unexpectedly back home with them had provided her own excitements over the last few days, but they were of a different and more complicated nature than those visited upon Hook by his spirited schoolboy sons.

John liked silence best in the mornings, and his wife knew it. Christine slid toast on to the table beside him as he finished his cereal, but was not sure whether his non-committal grunt was thanks to her or derision for the latest politician's non-speak in response to James Naughtie on the Radio Four *Today* programme. He was buttering his toast methodically when the phone shrilled in the hall. He sighed resignedly and went to answer it.

It wasn't for him, as he had expected. His whole body stiffened as the speaker on the other end of the line announced himself. 'I'm not sure whether she is available,' he said coldly. 'If you hold the line, I'll see what I can do.' He put the phone down carefully, stared at it for a second before he turned reluctantly away from it.

Jacky was standing beside him at the door of her room. He had not known that she was there, and he started as he saw her. He glanced back towards the phone, then half-mouthed and half-whispered to her, 'It's Jason.'

She gave a tiny smile at his distress, then said in a normal, even voice, 'It's all right, Dad. I'll take it.'

She listened for what seemed to him a very long time. He realized that Christine had come out of the kitchen and was standing at his shoulder. For some reason, he was reminded absurdly of the wedding photograph just a few yards away from them, when a young and pretty bride had stood unbruised by life at his shoulder and the world had seemed a place of infinite possibilities.

Jacky listened quite calmly to the increasingly uncertain male voice on the other end of the line. Then there was a pause. And then she said very evenly and very clearly, 'Jason, I'm only going to say this once. You can piss off!'

There was another long, increasingly agonized and insistent outburst on the other end of the phone, which became so strident that Jacky held the instrument a little away from her ear.

Then she exercised her female prerogative to contradict what she had said and repeat herself. 'Jason, will you please *piss off*!'

Although she did not look distressed, she was trembling a little in spite of herself as she slammed down the phone and turned to face her parents. Christine said automatically, 'I'm sorry, we shouldn't have been listening. It's just that—'

'I'm glad you were. Glad that you witnessed the final brief, undignified ending of it all. I'm all right, Mum, honestly I am.'

Her mother went forward and took her into her arms. Jacky trembled a little still, but over her mother's shoulder, she gave her father a most unexpected wink.

Chief Superintendent Lambert drove to work in high spirits.

By the time Bert Hook reached Oldford CID section, the idea had emerged from his subconscious and crystallized into something much more definite. He could scarcely believe it; he told himself that it was slim evidence on which to base an accusation of murder; yet he found himself increasingly convinced that he was right.

Meanwhile, Detective Inspector Rushton was collecting a much more tangible item of evidence from a charity shop in Gloucester. He should have sent a junior constable to collect it for him, but Chris could not bear to send a minion to collect what might in due course become a key exhibit in court. An item, he told himself immodestly, which derived wholly from his initiative.

After several high-profile cases, John Lambert by now had a national reputation to complement the local one he had enjoyed for many years. That reputation had secured him a Home Office extension to his service a little while ago. Chief Superintendent Lambert had always paid generous tributes to the large teams involved in the solutions of serious crimes, but there was no doubt that his individual insights and attention to detail had been crucial on many occasions.

This time, it was the two people who worked most closely with him who provided the crucial thinking, as well as the evidence which would send a murderer to jail. Lambert would pay handsome and specific tribute to his subordinates in due course, but the press, who love their police heroes to be individual and uncomplicated, would pay little attention to his words.

The latest forensic evidence was interesting but not conclusive. Various hairs and clothing fibres which did not belong to the dead man had been found on his corpse. Wherever DNA was possible, it had been taken and retained, ready for future matching with that of whoever was eventually accused of this killing. 'We've got a DNA match with the two youngsters, Jack Dawes and Becky Clegg,' said Chris Rushton, 'because we already have DNA profiles from them on file, as a result of their previous crimes.'

Bert Hook shook his head slowly. 'I told you before that I doubt whether you'll be able to use DNA matches from anyone who took part in the rehearsal on the night when Logan died. He was moving among us during the first court scene, pushing us into exactly the spots he wanted us to adopt on stage. It was important for him to position people exactly, because there were a lot of people involved in that scene and the stage in the village hall is quite a small one. He must have brushed against most of us.'

Rushton nodded impatiently. Normally, his inclination would have been to push the case against the two youngest suspects, who already had criminal records. But he knew that he had a more weighty and significant piece of evidence and a bigger fish to fry, when he judged that the moment was right.

He continued his summary of the newly arrived forensic findings. 'As we already knew, Terence Logan died from a single efficiently administered cut to the throat. The weapon was a single-edged knife which has not been found – indeed, probably never will be found.' He frowned in distaste at this uncharacteristic departure from the facts into speculation of his own. 'Logan was almost certainly killed from behind and taken by surprise. This means that no great strength was involved, so that his assailant could have been either male or female. There were spots of blood upon the deceased's clothes, and so almost certainly upon those of his killer. Although we must bear in mind that at the key moment his attacker was behind Logan, forensic think it likely that there would be blood on at least the sleeves of the murderer's clothing.'

'Which he or she has probably now disposed of or destroyed,' said Lambert, gloomily thinking aloud.

Rushton continued without comment. This list of the laboratory's findings from what had been gathered at the scene of the crime was after all just a prologue for his own sensational coup. 'There was blood on the dead man's shoes and on the gravel nearby. It has now been analysed, but as we expected, all samples came from the dead man and none from his assailant.'

Three faces nodded glumly at this expected blank. There had always been a chance that the victim had tried to defend himself and had diverted the knife to cause a cut on the murderer's hand or arm. But none of them had expected such assistance on this occasion. Lambert noted the eagerness which Rushton was trying ineffectively to conceal. He said quietly, 'Have you anything else to report, Chris, apart from the forensic findings?'

'We've had uniform out to check on the whereabouts of people on Wednesday night. Ian Proudfoot was in the Crown Inn at Calford, as he told us he was. The landlord remembers a man answering his description; he says Proudfoot seemed very preoccupied with something at the time. No one in the pub can remember seeing him there after about ten o'clock, so he could have left at any time after that and still had ample time to wait for Logan to emerge from Mettlesham Village Hall.'

Lambert nodded. 'But at least his story checks out. He was where he says he was, for at least part of the time between when he left the rehearsal at nine and the moment when Logan was killed, at some time between eleven and twelve.'

DI Rushton tried and failed to keep exactly the same non-committal tone for his next item. 'On Friday, I took it upon myself to circulate the charity shops throughout Gloucestershire and Herefordshire, asking them to notify us of any shoes which have been donated to them since last Thursday. It was a long shot: we know that anyone with blood or other incriminating matter on shoes or clothing would be well advised to destroy the items, or at least make sure they were binned and dumped. But murderers don't always think as we do. They're some-times not habitual criminals, so they don't dispose of evidence in the way that experienced villains would.'

Lambert tried hard not to smile at this earnest little lecture. He said impatiently, 'I gather that your initiative has paid off, Chris. Let's have the news.'

Chris reached under the desk, produced the plastic bag, and extracted the innocent-looking shoes; he had the air of a conjurer completing a trick. 'They've been cleaned, but forensic may still find blood upon them. There's certainly a little mud and grit on the inside of the heel, which I think will match with samples from the car park at Mettlesham.'

Lambert gazed hard at the unremarkable footwear. 'So we look for a Cinderella whose feet will fit these. Or more properly an ugly sister, as this is murder.'

Bert Hook had been silent for a long time. Now he said slowly, 'I've a good idea who might have worn these.'

Then he surprised them with his theory and the source of it. There was a long pause before Lambert said, 'I think we'd better get round there right away, Bert.'

Twenty-Two

The wheel had come full circle, thought Bert Hook. This strange business had started with Councillor Margaret Dalrymple descending upon his home to persuade him to take part in *Hamlet*.

Now it was ending with John Lambert coming to her much more imposing house, to make an arrest for murder. The detached, double-fronted Edwardian house stood impressively on its gentle rise. The CID duo studied it for a moment after climbing out of the police Mondeo at its gate. The rich dark red of the Virginia creeper had diminished a little since their last visit; dead leaves drifted steadily from it now, even though there was little wind on this calm, mild November day.

They were well into the second half of the month now, but there had still not been an overnight frost. Dahlias still blazed their unseasonal brightness in the borders beside the path to the front door, as if revelling in this reprieve from the winter which was waiting. The pink and red of climbing roses bloomed defiantly against the mellow bricks of the house's high front elevation, as they rang the bell beside the broad oak front door.

It was Andrew Dalrymple who opened it. He said breezily, 'Thank you for coming here rather than to the works. My staff would begin to talk if they saw me entertaining the CID on successive working days.'

They did not respond to his bonhomie.

Nor did Councillor Margaret Dalrymple, JP, who was in the high, dark hall as they entered. She gave them a token smile and led them into the spacious dining room at the front of the house. They sat down beside the huge, antique mahogany dining table and found the Dalrymples positioning themselves formally on the other side of it. They seemed a long way away across that dark gleaming surface; Detective Sergeant Bert

Hook reflected that there could scarcely have been a greater contrast between this quiet, spacious setting, with original oils and watercolours upon the walls, and the claustrophobic box of the standard police station interview room, in which he had conducted so many hundreds of interviews over the years.

Andrew Dalrymple eventually broke the silence he could not endure. 'We're ready to offer any help we can, of course. As each of us has told you individually, we are not going to grieve for Terry Logan. But my wife has some experience of the law, and we both realize that it must be upheld at all times.' He glanced sideways at the white-faced Maggie. 'We both recognize that whoever killed Logan must be brought to justice. Nevertheless, I doubt whether we can add anything useful to what we have already told you.'

He was looking hard at the intense face of Lambert, but it was the less menacing figure beside him who now spoke. Bert Hook said evenly, 'Mr Dalrymple, when we saw you on Friday, you told us that you were glad to see Terence Logan dead.'

Andrew glanced quickly again at the woman beside him, then slid his hand over hers beneath the edge of the table. 'I'm not disputing that. I detested the man. By the time he died, I think both of us hated him.'

'Where were you last Wednesday night, Mr Dalrymple?'

Margaret answered quickly, almost before Hook had delivered the question. 'He was here. We've told you that before. I got in at about half past nine and he was here waiting for me.' She spoke firmly. But curiously, her very vehemence told against her. She sounded as if she was mouthing some sort of ritual, hoping that its very familiarity would give it weight.

It was Andrew Dalrymple who said unexpectedly, 'It's all right, Maggie. They probably know that's not true. I expect I was sighted that night.'

Hook looked at him curiously. He didn't have his usual notebook at the ready to record things today: events had moved beyond that point. He recognized the form of the ritual and played out his part in it. 'You'd better give us the details of where you were.'

'I was in the Lamb and Flag pub in Gloucester.'

'And no doubt you have witnesses to that.'

Dalrymple looked at him curiously, sensing an oddness in the man's tone, knowing that something had gone seriously wrong, but unable to pin down exactly what it was. 'I expect you could turn up people who would confirm that I was there, yes. I chatted to the landlord for a little while. The place wasn't as busy as it usually is.'

Maggie felt the tightening of Andrew's hand on hers. She said in her most masterful manner, 'So he couldn't have been out murdering Terry Logan, could he? I suggest you go and talk to the landlord of that pub and his clientele, and confirm that my husband was nowhere near the scene of this crime.'

Hook looked at her. The wheel had indeed come full circle: he felt a curious sympathy now for this woman who had so intimidated him at the outset of these events. 'I'm sure that we shall find people who will confirm that you were in the Lamb and Flag last Wednesday night, Mr Dalrymple. No doubt they will also inform us that you left with ample time to get to the village hall at Mettlesham before the murder victim left it.'

'Possibly. That doesn't make me a murderer.' Andrew felt that the blood was draining from his normally rather florid face. He wondered if that was visible to the enemy, wondered if they could see the paling which he felt in his cheeks.

'You admitted to us on Friday that you hated Terence Logan because of the affair he had conducted with your wife and the way he had treated her at the end of that affair.'

Andrew glanced automatically at Maggie, looking for a reaction in the way he had done when anyone mentioned Logan's name in company over the last four years. This time she was as still as marble. He strove for a little of his normal aggression. 'That is correct, yes. I hated him, and so did Maggie. This is merely repeating what I told you on Friday.'

'Who was it who financed this ambitious theatrical enterprise?'

It was Maggie who answered. 'We hadn't got as far as that. Costumes and publicity for *Hamlet* would have been expensive, it's true, but—'

Hook did not even glance at her, but kept his eyes steadily on the face of his quarry. 'Who paid for the hire of the village hall in Mettlesham, for two nights a week for the entire rehearsal period?'

Dalrymple's voice dropped a full octave. 'You obviously know the answer to that. I did.'

'You were anxious that your wife should never meet this

man again. And yet you set up the opportunity for her to meet
him repeatedly over a three-month period. Maggie told me that
at the outset, when she came to my house to recruit me for the
play. I should have recalled that fact much earlier than today.'

Maggie Dalrymple remembered that. Remembered how her
tongue had run away with her as she pressed hard for the
Polonius she wanted to play alongside her. But she'd had no
thought then that Andrew was planning this, that the hatred
she had seen in him would lead to this awful climax. 'My
husband knows how interested I am in the theatre,' she said
desperately. 'He knows that I have yearned for years for the
chance to appear in Shakespeare. He was an indulgent husband,
and nothing more than that.'

She looked at Andrew, tried to give him a loving and affectionate smile of gratitude. But the unthinkable suspicion which
had haunted her since last Wednesday night was becoming reality,
and she could not do it. She turned back to this rubicund, comfortable detective sergeant, who would have made such a good
Polonius, who was now transformed into such an intractable
foe. 'Terry Logan was a very good director, you see.'

The leitmotiv of this investigation, the theme which each
of the principals involved had in turn delivered to them. For
the first time it rang hollow. Hook addressed himself to Andrew
Dalrymple. 'You would never have put your wife in close
contact with Logan again. Not without some other motive.
You were setting up the opportunity to dispose of him.'

Andrew Dalrymple felt Maggie's hand slide away from
beneath his. He said dully, 'I was in the Lamb and Flag in
Gloucester. They'll tell you that – the staff there, the landlord.'

'I expect they will. I expect you took good care to establish the fact that you were in there on that night. What time
did you leave? Ten o'clock? Ten thirty? I'm sure we won't
find anyone who saw you late on in the evening.'

There was nothing conclusive about that, Andrew told
himself. They couldn't make anything stick in court without
more evidence than that. He fought against the overwhelming
sense of hopelessness which had fallen upon him with this
accusation about him financing the enterprise. He heard his
wife say what he should have said himself. 'You need more
than this. You can't say that Andrew killed Logan just because
he left the pub at a certain time.'

It was now that Lambert spoke at last. 'You took some arti-
cles into the charity shop on Eastgate in Gloucester on Saturday
morning, Mrs Dalrymple. The lady there remembers you.'

'She would. I do the rotas for the volunteers who staff that
shop. I collect clothes and other items like china locally. I
take lots of things in there.' She could not see quite where
this was going, but she had a feeling of impending disaster.
She had told that too-observant Bert Hook that it was Andrew
who had set up their *Hamlet*. Now no doubt she had provided
the enemy with some damning piece of evidence against him.
If only Andrew had told her what he had done, she could have
protected him, could have organized things to save him. She
had always been good at organization.

Those steely grey eyes of John Lambert seemed to her to
see everything she was thinking. He now said inexorably, 'The
items you deposited at the shop included a pair of your
husband's shoes. These contain minimal traces of blood and
gravel. I have no doubt forensic examination will confirm that
the blood is that of Terence Logan and the gravel that of the
car park behind Mettlesham Village Hall. I believe that these
are the shoes Andrew was wearing when he slit the throat of
Terence Logan.'

She started, then glanced suddenly and accusingly at
Andrew. Why had he done this dreadful thing? And why hadn't
he told her he'd done it, so that she could have arranged things
differently?

He did not look at her. Instead, he said dully, as if speaking
to someone other than the three in the room, 'My mother would
never tolerate waste. She said it was a sin to waste anything.
She was a teenager during the war, you see. The knife is at
the bottom of the Severn. I should have sent the shoes after
it. But they were too good to throw away.'

Maggie said sadly, accusingly, pathetically, 'You said you
weren't going to use those shoes again. You didn't tell me
why. I took them in to the charity shop with some dresses of
mine.'

Lambert felt the searing pathos of her helplessness, of her
retreat into small, useless things. He said calmly, 'I expect
our forensic laboratory will find traces of Logan's blood upon
them. There will certainly be something we can match with
the surface of the car park in Mettlesham.'

But all four of them in the room knew that this was an irrelevance now, that Andrew Dalrymple was not going to deny the crime.

'Why, Andrew?' his wife asked in a hollow voice. 'Terry Logan was no threat to you any more. I hated him.'

Her hands were on top of the gleaming polished mahogany now, and Andrew took the right one into his left, as hesitantly as an inexperienced lover making a first move. 'You kept photographs, Maggie. Pictures of you and him together. In your drawer in the dressing table.'

She did not know what to say. She could have said that the pictures meant nothing, but she wasn't even sure if that was true. And whatever she said could have no meaning now, in the face of this overwhelming thing which he had done. She said hopelessly, 'It was just a bit of my life which I didn't want to throw away. It had nothing to do with us.'

It was Hook who stood up and came round the big table to utter the formal words of arrest. Polonius rising from the dead, she thought, with a searing recollection of that Queen in *Hamlet* which she would never play.

They didn't handcuff him to take him out to the car. There was no need for that final indignity, for Andrew Dalrymple had no energy left with which to resist them.

He stopped in the doorway, looked down at his wife, who was still staring hopelessly at the dark surface of the table. 'Maggie has always been a pillar of the law. She knew nothing of this. She has no connection at all with this death.'

It was the last thing he was able to offer to the woman he loved.